Gramsci's Fall

THE GERMAN LIST

Gramsci's Fall

NORA BOSSONG

Translated by Alexander Booth

LONDON NEW YORK CALCUTTA

This publication was supported by a grant from the Goethe-Institut, India.

Seagull Books, 2020

Originally published in German as 36,9°

© Carl Hanser Verlag, Munich, 2015

First published in English translation by Seagull Books, 2020

English translation © Alexander Booth, 2020

ISBN 978 0 8574 2 691 8

British Library Cataloguing-in-Publication Data

A catalogue record for this book is available from the British Library.

Typeset by Seagull Books, Calcutta, India

Printed and bound by WordsWorth India, New Delhi, India

For my father

And it is true that we will do certain mean things to those we love.

Antonio Gramsci to Giulia Schucht

I. A PONCHO   The old man opened the door to me in his robe. Feet stuck into a pair of slippers with pompous tassels, a scarlet red scarf across his shoulders like a stole, his smile was elegant and shy and mad.

'The *dottore* from Germany! *Piacere piacere piacere—*'

In prayer-like fashion, Professor Brevi repeated how happy he was to meet me and then, with majestic slowness, shuffled down a long hall leading to various rooms all full of antiques and knick-knacks. The flat made a stately impression, if of a stateliness at least a hundred years old, and smelt of naphthalene and lavender. A shadow flitted behind one of the glass doors. The old man stopped and said, '*Il Dottor Stöver è venuto, cara!*' Then, turning to me, he explained: 'My housekeeper Gabriella.' He smiled and blushed slightly. The door opened, and I saw a tiny old woman wrapped in a red evening dress. Though the dress might have fit, say twenty, thirty years ago, now it was too big and hung heavily over her raisin-like body.

'Oh, we have company?' the woman asked with a Sardinian inflection, looking at Brevi for help. 'But Pippo, I haven't even done my hair yet.'

And with that she disappeared behind her glass door and we could hear her moving nervously back and forth. The old man nodded thoughtfully, then said, 'We must move on!' as if we were setting off on an expedition for a distant land.

On the walls hung a tapestry with a faded floral pattern and various pieces of junk lay scattered in place of furnishing. I heard two women's voices arguing and something clatter against the floor. The buildings here had been built so that the clacking of your neighbours' shoes and their various noises would travel from flat to flat, from building to building and over the courtyards to turn into a horrible, sleep-defying hum.

The old man glanced around to see if he could show me something, point out a piece of furniture, brag about some rarity or other. But he didn't find a thing.

'Are you pleased with the room?' he finally asked.

'Absolutely!' I declared.

Brevi happily rocked his head back and forth. 'Now then. From here you can reach the Istituto Gramsci in just a few minutes.'

He closed the door, leaving me alone in the half dark. Light fell meagrely through the slats of the shutters. A coil groaned as I sat on the bed which stank of mildew and rust. I stood back up, padded across the cold floor. I stubbed my toes against the desk chair and swore. The shutters opened with a bit of force. Down below, a man was driving in circles on a Vespa, a bottle shattered on the sidewalk, someone cursed. For a moment I longed to be back in Göttingen, back in our renovated flat in the half-timbered house. I missed the silent streets, the clean city centre with its Gänseliesel fountain and Lichtenberg college, health food and home decor shops, the students on the wooden benches in front of Thanner's.

To describe the palazzo as cosy would've been an exaggeration. A crooked building that had limped on through the centuries, leaking and crumbling everywhere. It became clear to me that achievements like isolated windows and cold-foam mattresses were relatively recent phenomena.

In my suitcase I looked for a white shirt that had managed to make the journey without getting wrinkled. Once I had it on, I felt a little better. More ordered. In front of the mirror, which teetered more than hung on the wall, I tied my tie, looked at my face, the crow's feet at the corners of my eyes, the little cracked veins at the edge of my nose, and registered a movement in the bottom left corner. As I pulled the end of the tie through the loop, he crept closer, reared up, was there. Gramsci. Standing right next to me, not even five feet tall, looking through his round glasses onto the spotted mirror as if through a windowpane. He saw neither himself nor me, but I did, I could see the two of us standing next to each other, almost like brothers. I was taller, but only by a bit, maybe the length of a hand. A large hand perhaps, but only a hand.

In all the years we'd been working together, or, rather, all the years I'd been working to a much greater degree on him, we'd moved on to addressing each other informally, or, to be more precise, I'd insisted and he hadn't been able to say no. Gramsci, full name Antonio Gramsci, had been dead for more than seventy years.

You need to picture him as a bit stocky, though not big. That stated, great thoughts don't come from the heights but from the depths, or, let's say, a certain girth and that he had in full. An incredible girth that didn't begin at his hips, spill out over his belt or waistband and then swell around his navel. No, this one grew below his neck, between his shoulder blades and beneath his sternum. Perhaps a fall was to blame. The housemaid denied it, denied it, vehemently denied it, but then, in the end, admitted she'd let him fall, the three-year-old Gramsci, and the way he grew afterwards violated every rule. By the time those around him were shooting upwards, some more, some less, he'd already given up and set his interests on more distant shores. In his thoughts too he began to take detours, and, up through the end, never turned back. The little guy. Nino.

If you're short, and especially if you're a man, if you're so small that others think you're stunted, or even a dwarf, then at a certain point it's probably best you say goodbye—and the sooner the better, for it'll be less painful—to the sensual life and build yourself a house of thoughts instead, or let one grow around you, like a snail, and withdraw inside it.

That's one option.

Or you can train yourself to have such an abundance of sensuality that everyone around you will be perplexed, will no longer remember anything else about you, will never say a thing about who you were or how tall. Your body has to remain under constant pressure. A fluorescence of the nerves. An infectious trembling. An exaggerated warmth which flows from this body to that, infecting others like a fire springing from one house to another until the whole city lies in a pile of smoke and ash.

That summer I'd turned forty-six, and the closer I got to fifty, the more I saw my counterparts beginning to buckle. Portly or completely worn-out, brittle or overconfident, their bodies going to seed under poorly cut jackets and their hands growing sweaty in mid-air on the way to touch a young woman's arm. So, forty-six, and two years ago already Hedda had begun to notice my skin becoming softer, my arms beginning to sag in a strange way when she grabbed them. I didn't really believe it. On the contrary I suspected that Hedda thought she could recognize something in me that was happening to her own body, because I could feel it, I could feel it from her shoulders downwards, I could feel it around her waist, her stomach which she'd attempted to torment with deep muscle exercises, it didn't have to do with the fat that Hedda had never had much of, *it's just ageing, Hedda*, it's that simple.

Up till that point my body had defied the years, and I thought I knew why. It was extremely important for me to remain flexible, for if I suddenly grew old, I'd once again be as tall as I'd been as a kid, would shrink back into being that pre-teen the other guys pushed around in the schoolyard and the girls didn't bother to even laugh at. Not even that! Now, after a whole lifetime of keeping up with Gramsci, of being overshadowed, stepped on, forced into the

4

smaller frame, it was his turn to once, just once, stand next to me. Behind me were weeks and months chock full of accusations and rejections, insanity and noise—oh what am I talking about, *years*—and my ears were ringing. I had to come to my senses, and getting there, that much I knew, would be impossible alone.

In the end, the Istituto Gramsci was on Via Sebino, just a few streets away from Brevi's flat, but already in front of the Casino Nobile on the grounds of the Villa Torlonia my steps grew slower and soon I found myself tiredly closing my eyes. Around me I could hear a warm buzz of voices, and I thought of the institute's librarian, that last example of Soviet Russian folk art who wouldn't let you out of his sight the moment you held one of his beloved books in your hand.

Coming past a lilac bush, I ducked into a side street. A building was growing out over the street, here some roots were coming across a wall and behind me the traffic circle was full of cars chasing after each other as if possessed. Cracks split the facades surrounding the square and water stains had been thrown on top. The institute stood between the branches of various banks and a perfume store, and seemed more like a military installation. A camera coldly returned my gaze and on the doorbell panel only the word *fondazione* could be read, as if the real institution needed to be kept a secret.

Staring at the bell I felt completely run down, I just wanted to stretch out in front of the metal door and go to sleep until someone opened up. That or lie there defiantly until the next day or until the police scooped me up as a vagrant and threw me into a cell with all those other apathetic criminals who couldn't be bothered to run away from state authority any more. The sunlight glowed on the wall, the metal door burned. I looked around for a place in the shade, a bench, a section of wall, a Piero Sraffa to bring me a parasol, and cursed underneath the awning of a greengrocer.

A bus stopped and then went on its way. People elbowed past me, it all seemed unreal, as if I'd fallen out of the scenery that surrounded me.

I couldn't say whether she'd come from the institute, a doorway or simply down the street. She was wearing a poncho, *a poncho in this heat*, and had crossed the road. Her frizzy, chin-length hair bobbing up and down to the rhythm of her steps. She didn't move quickly, but in a remarkably feisty way. Not at all lazy. Not at all self-conscious. In her hand was a bag: *Punto, il suo supermercato*. The poncho was milk-white and had a brown pattern along the seam.

Someone honked their horn. I turned and saw the woman disappear between two parked cars. The automobile rounded the corner. The street was empty. Just the woman, me and the monotonous thud of a rubber ball against the side of a building. I carefully took a step into the street, then a second and then a third, like trying to cross a stream on slippery, wobbly stones, foot-over-foot. Her poncho flamed in the sun.

When she came to a stop on Via Nomentana, I saw her profile for the first time. The contours were soft and dark, her nose straight, but not perfect, her mouth full but not trashy. Her fringe touched her eyebrows, in a moment she'd blow at it, I thought, but then she turned and began to walk again.

We crossed the Via Nomentana, she in front of me, and drifted off to the left. Then, on the other side of the road, she rushed back to the right as if she'd caught scent of her pursuer and wanted to shake him off or at the very least confuse him. A bus bucked along below its overhead cables, cars made their way on towards the tunnel past Porta Pia.

That poncho, that fringe, this woman, it all was crazy. Of course, I liked women, or some of them anyway, and under the present circumstances some a bit more, but I never let myself be enticed by them on the street. By a kind of haircut. By folkloristic South American clothing.

The poncho stopped in front of a rubbish bin. A hand emerged from under the alpaca wool, small, sun-tanned fingers which would lighten to a dull olive in winter. What did her winter have to do with me? She wedged in an empty cigarette pack. At the latest this is where I should've turned around. The carelessness of her movement, and then the brand: Marlboro.

She ambled on with me behind her, turning into the bends around the Villa Paganini. Soon a men's clothing store and a restaurant with a three-wheeled delivery truck idling out in front appeared between the apartment buildings. The tomatoes shone smoothly on their palettes, two had fallen to the ground and split apart. Their ripped-open skin and splayed flesh marked with the imprint of her shoes. Suddenly the chirping of a mobile startled me. She pulled it out and looked at the display for a moment before taking the call.

'Hello?'

A bit throaty, but with a young woman's bright tone beneath it, the dark tinge simply due to a passing cold perhaps.

'But I told you!'

She ran a hand through her hair, gave the air a small kick.

'But that wasn't what we'd agreed.'

She turned her face towards me. Dark, small eyes crowned by the cynical arc of her brows. She broke into pliant contrition, 'No, you tell me.'

My hands in my pockets, I mimicked those unfamiliar passers-by, took a few steps back, and looked at another doorbell panel, peered at her arm which shot back and forth as if shaking the ghost she was speaking to by the neck.

'And what's that got to do with me?'

Binotti, Franceschini, Martelli. I heard her steps behind me, hard, swift drops on stone. Brescoli, Fratoni—now only a trickle— Gentile Nannetti.

By the time I turned around, she'd disappeared. I slowly made my way up the street. One building had been split in two by the front of a discount supermarket, another by the shaky flag of Canada. I continued to roam through the little street which curved in the shape of a half-moon, then stretched back out, forked and came back together, before finally giving her up as lost.

II. QUISISANA CLINIC   On Wednesday, 25 April 1937, Tatiana, full name Tatiana Schucht, is handed the document for the release of Antonio Gramsci. For more than ten years he has been a prisoner of the fascist regime. On 8 November 1926, at half past ten in the evening, he was taken prisoner by a number of *squadristi* at his flat in Rome. He was put into solitary confinement at the Roman prison of Regina Coeli and then, following stints in jails in Milan and Bari, banned to the island of Ustica. Throughout the years of incarceration he played cards with his fellow prisoners, and, once, a flower made its way up through the tiles of his cell. He survived harassment and underwent new ones, was awoken in the middle of the night, put into solitary. He received threats, grew shorter and more frail, practised gymnastic exercises in his cage so that he wouldn't completely lose what remained of his body, scaled his thoughts and gasped for air at the small window above, and wrote—quickly, nervously, feverishly—in order to keep from going insane.

Tatiana holds the document close to her body as she leaves the bureau of the supervising judge of the Roman court and, as every day, makes her way to the Quisisana Clinic where the critically ill Gramsci is being treated. She had fought to get this paper, ceaselessly, had got hold of the doctor who had checked on Gramsci's physical condition, had sought out another doctor who in his assessment was a little less beholden to the Duce, had carried the certificates back and forth, had pleaded, had tried to convince people throughout the various ministries of Rome, with the Party in Moscow, at the prison in Milan, had pleaded with Gramsci who was against any preferential treatment, against any form of pity: 'But Nino, this is your health we're talking about, not a privilege, they cannot send you back to prison.'

Now the release form is there, and even if it's only paper, even if it's only a pledge, it's an official one, stamped and signed. At half past five, she enters the clinic with the papers; Gramsci is waiting. He plays it cool when she lays her hand on the blanket.

'Don't you want to see the papers?'

'That can wait until tomorrow.'

He is too tired, too exhausted, and he doesn't know what awaits him outside, whether it will be the same, which is to say, a form of prison, albeit with a differently constructed cell. He slowly pulls his hand from under the blanket, places it on Tania's, and in his face a longstanding tension dissolves, one which during his time in prison has been necessary for survival. His body long ago reached a level of decline closer to that of a dead man than one of the living, and perhaps that is why he has been granted release: the fascists don't need a martyr. They want him out of their jails before he dies.

Up until dinner, Gramsci and Tania talk about the latest papal encyclical in which Pious XI has condemned communism as destructive, spiteful and godless (and that at its very heart). Indeed, Christian charity alone was what counted, and they go silent when the nurse brings in the dinner tray. She puts it down on the table, sizes the two of them up with a strict glance and, straightening her cap, leaves the room without a word.

'Shall I show you what Christian charity is?' Gramsci hisses and points to the tray. 'Here it is.' Broth, cooked fruit, a little dried piece of cake.

Tania cuts up the cake for him, adjusts the tablet resting on the blanket and opens her Larousse.

'Put that away,' Gramsci chides her. 'Or is that why you came? Did you intend to do your homework here?'

'Sorry,' she whispers and mechanically takes the cloth from the nightstand, wipes it across his brow. His skin feels like heated wax. He pushes the food away and, with difficulty, stands up to go to the toilet.

While Tania waits for him, she goes back to browsing through her French dictionary, but it's taking a long time and she begins to grow nervous. She stands up, goes to the door to check on him, sees three men swaying towards her carrying a chair and in the chair the figure of Gramsci. Tania staggers backwards, stunned. The three men place him down in front of her like a piece of furniture. Gramsci's gaze is broken, the left half of his body is hanging down, a clump, a feeble thing.

I feel fine, Gramsci says. She shouldn't act like she's been confronted with a vision of Mary.

'He fell down in the toilet,' one of the men says, 'thank God not on his head, he managed to pull himself to the door and call out, another patient heard him and got help.'

Tania is standing close to Gramsci as Dr Marino takes his pulse and listens to his breath. In any event, Gramsci is conscious. His left side is paralysed. The doctor takes a look beneath his eyelids, taps his frail body with various instruments.

'A shot,' Gramsci says with a dull voice, 'double the regular dosage,' and means the shot they've given him there a few times already. The doctor shakes his head and pulls Tania out into the hall. 'Brain haemorrhage,' he explains, 'it's shaken up everything in there.'

A cold-pack on his forehead, a hot-water bottle on his feet and a salt enema. A little while later, Gramsci is lying there as if a temperature gradient might heal him. He wants them to perform a phlebotomy, they let him wait, he vomits, then vomits again, Tania wipes the smell of stomach acid from the corners of his mouth with a washcloth. His nose is blocked with leftovers.

At ten o'clock, they finally let his blood.

During the night, the doctors call a priest.

Half-asleep, half-awake, Tania sits at his bedside; she's been there all along. The light in the room slowly grows brighter, her eyes hurt and she doesn't particularly want to see what she does. Gramsci's fleshless lips in his wilted face, long ago uraemia had cost him all his teeth but now his muscles seem to have given up as well. Sweat covers his brow, a yellow shadow shines up from deep below his skin. Tania bends over him, feels his hand, his forehead, hopes to see some glimmer of his getting better or at least the final fall.

When a doctor comes by to check up on him at mid-morning, Tania pulls him to her and in a whisper asks how he is, 'and please be honest.'

'I cannot tell you.'

'Something. You have to be able to tell me something.'

'An architect has nothing more to say about a building which has collapsed either.'

The doctors place leeches on Gramsci's temples and have injections drip into his veins, he is being made into an evermore grotesque creature that simply dozes off, hallucinates, sleeps, wakes once more. Through the drawn curtains the light falls into his room in thin strips, it could be noon or even afternoon already, perhaps it's evening, during his delirium time has dissolved, in any event, it will no longer play any role for him at all but simply remain a flickering until everything stops. From the garden he hears a rustling and grinding, boughs are probably being cut from the treetops. He thinks of Giulia, of walking down Tverskaya Street, shoulders lightly touching, he thinks of his sons, they emerge before his eyes as flat as photographs, and he thinks of the show trials where they took everything away, in the end even his own truth.

Gramsci calls out into the room, demands to be allowed a long-distance call to London. All at once he is completely lucid, his mind, his thoughts belong to him once again. The rummaging in the corner grows louder, someone comes closer. He would like, no, no, he *must* speak with his friend Piero Sraffa. Were they listening to him? Did they understand? The nurse next to his bed controls the injection dosage and pays no attention. He insists; she wants him to see a priest. What would he do with a priest? He doesn't need a rosary but his friend Sraffa.

Sraffa had always helped him. In all his years in prison, he had sent him books from Sperling & Kupfer in Milan, had written him letters and would not allow Gramsci to give up, he had kept in contact with the Party, for Sraffa was not only a friend of Gramsci's but Palmiro Togliatti's too, the head of the Italian Communist Party, and not only Togliatti but the philosopher Ludwig Wittgenstein and the economist John Maynard Keynes. 'You must always discuss things with your cleverest opponent,' he'd once told Gramsci. 'Only when you are able to convince him will you be able to convince at all.'

That is precisely why he needed Sraffa, and needed him right now. Gramsci has too many opponents and he'll have even more if his notebooks fall into the wrong hands after his death. But he isn't thinking about death, he doesn't have the strength.

The nurse clacks out of the room with her wooden shoes. Tania wipes the sweat from Gramsci's forehead. Over the next few hours, his condition will vary between clarity and derangement. Tania doesn't know who she's looking at any more. When he's feverish, his eyes are so empty it seems like he'd taken leave long ago. When he's awake, again and again he demands that he be allowed the telephone call. 'Tania,' he whispers, 'it could be the most important discussion of my life.'

In the evening, they finally accompany him to the phone. A buzzing in the line. Perhaps England is too far away, Cambridge, where Sraffa lives and teaches, unable to be reached by an Italian telephone. Or Sraffa isn't at home, he's gone for a walk with his friend and colleague Keynes in order to enjoy winter's mild and rainy end and to discuss a lecture on financial policy. The nurse watches Gramsci as he pushes the handset closer to his ear.

A clearing of the throat. Let it not be his imagination, let it indeed be Sraffa, but whether it is or not Gramsci has no choice, he has to believe it. With a broken voice he whispers into the mouthpiece, he speaks quickly, swallows syllables, Sraffa has to ask him to repeat himself a number of times, Gramsci is struggling with his lips, his tongue, for a moment his words become clearer before his voice again drops, once more Sraffa has to ask: 'And no one from the Party is to know?' Gramsci repeats it another time. At last they seem to agree.

During the night there's another crisis. Tania holds his hand, wipes his brow. Every time he closes his eyes, she thinks: it's over. Her left hand clutches the blanket, she doesn't know if she should scream or take a breath. She stays at the side of his bed, only goes for a quick nap, comes back, she can hardly feel her body any more, every moment it threatens to sink away together with consciousness, but she must stay awake, she at the least.

It is three in the morning when his breath suddenly stops. Tania notices, bends over him, presses her lips to his, blows her breath into his mouth, listens, blows breath into him again. With her ear to his lips, she can hear how weakly and intermittently the air streams out of his mouth. Then stillness once more. Stillness. She should call a doctor but she cannot leave him here alone, bends over him, blows breath into him. And again. She presses, she breathes, she swallows, her chest hurts and her lungs too, she listens, breathes, the lips she touches already feel cold. On the morning of 27 April 1937, at ten minutes past four, she gives up.

That same morning Tania carries a stack of notebooks out of the clinic, a bundle of notes that will become famous as the *Prison Notebooks* of Antonio Gramsci, the man who just a few hours earlier died of exhaustion, an advanced brain haemorrhage, terrible prison food, the jailers who kept him from sleep all those years, who'd continuously wake him up throughout the night, the man who died due to a lack of letters from Giulia, due to paranoia, Stalin's leadership, Mussolini's Italy, his own self. There is little of any of that in the doctor's protocol.

Tania had been accompanied into the storeroom, but managed to tangle the young man up in conversation for so long that he was sufficiently distracted and she could stuff the notebooks in- between Gramsci's worthless possessions. Once more, all is due to her skill alone: she is the one carrying out with her the writings of that man the fascist regime had wanted to silence. Later, twenty-nine notebooks of essays and four notebooks of translations will be recorded, each consisting of two hundred pages. Tania labels them; on some of the notebooks the handwriting clearly differs from that of the others. There are numerous labels on top of one another, under the number XXIX in black, hectic script, a red XXXII shimmers through. Marbled notepads made by GIUS. LATERZA E FIGLI in Bari, one of the notebooks is green and decorated with columns, two have been decorated with colourful motifs: a sliver of the pyramids and a hotel in Cairo with three camels standing out front.

3 May 1937

To the People's Commissariat for Foreign Affairs
To Comrade V. P. Potemkin, Vice People's Commissar
From Giu. A. Schucht-Gramsci

In my name and that of my sons Delio and Giuliano, I beg the People's Commissariat for Foreign Affairs to retrieve the personal items, letters and writings that remain following the death of my husband, Antonio Gramsci.

Giu. Schucht-Gramsci

III. LASSE   Hardly twenty-four hours ago Hedda had been standing on the platform with Lasse at her side, who waved at the mirrored glass, and as the train began to pull away she'd seemed relieved, or maybe I was wrong.

For twelve years I'd crawled from one fixed-term contract to another at the University of Göttingen, published articles that no one read, gave teaching my all but saw the students simply fall asleep or look out the window, offered reading circles that no one attended. Two years ago I'd finally been pushed onto the academic siding. My career was over, and when I thought about the university all I saw was a stony, bitter-faced audience looking down onto me in an orchestra pit.

Naturally, I hadn't been released from my life. It continued to turn up surlily but insistently. For one and a half years I wrote for the local paper which paid worse than I let on to Hedda. We lived in a posh flat on Düstere-Eichen-Weg. The rent was pitched at an established professor, not someone scribbling for their daily wage, and so I wrote about all the nonsense I could that went on in that backwater, performances at the Deutsche Theater and inaugural celebrations at the university, student fraternities and bathing lakes, about dead scientists and resurgent restaurants, I wrote and I wrote and over and over again had to travel to Bremen to give my mother a picture of my disastrous financial situation, which would always be followed by her walking across the Persian rug to her bureau and filling out a yellowed, but nonetheless usable, bank-transfer slip.

We had a yard and four rooms, one of which was my office, and I can still hear Hedda laughing, 'What do you need a study for?' One room was a children's room filled with lobster-red cars that would slide across the floor and under your feet as soon as you walked in, a bedroom (which would be better for me not to think about) and a sizeable, 50-square-metre living room that Hedda had decorated, all white and glass and light, every piece of furniture edged in chrome. Around us Hedda had erected a terrarium, and once a week she'd lead visitors through the rooms to have a look at that dying breed, the Stövers.

And those evenings we Stövers were deceptively lively as we made our way round the preserve, Hedda offering guests puff pastries before we all moved on to more solid fare like rolled roast. Hedda had learnt how to cook for me, and not by choice. Back when she'd got to know me, or, rather, my mother, an activist with the Bremen chapter of the Communist League of West Germany (a group which, at that point, she'd wanted to write her dissertation on), she was a true phenomenon of emancipation who rejected everything that could possibly have been seen as bourgeois, be it cooking, ironing or wedding rings.

In the end, however, an art-history professor had saved her by dragging her over to his discipline, explaining that one should never turn one's passions into scientific themes and so she'd written on peasant violence in Peter Brueghel instead, and now even prepared rolled roast. The smell had already penetrated the living room by the time Hedda came back from the kitchen, gave the roast another ten minutes and, with a perfect smile, poured us all Prosecco. She fit the whole scene so well—that constantly luminous appearance, the white skin, blonde hair, she was almost diaphanous—as she walked with the bottle from guest to guest, Kalkreuther, as always alone, a hopeless case, the Schweigerts, and Hedda as the dancing hostess flitting among white and glass and light and a sofa I'd been sleeping on for fourteen months.

'It has to do with a notebook, Herr Stöver, and I believe that notebook still exists,' Brevi had said to me on the phone three weeks earlier, a light little dance in his syllables. For years we'd been exchanging editing questions about the *Prison Notebooks*, though we'd never personally met, and that was the first time I'd even heard his voice.

'Listen,' he explained, 'one could easily produce another anthology of Gramsci's writings, a book about his relationship with Stalin or an essay on the line-ruling of the *Prison Notebooks*. That's a given. But if what I assume is correct, it would put Gramsci back on his feet for us. If—'

He paused and cleared his throat a number of times. Brevi could clearly allow as much silence as he wanted. He'd always been more comfortable in the quiet, he'd never shown up at any conventions or conferences and didn't have to either. Brevi was an eminent authority in the world of Gramsci research, his essays were considered among the most astute, going so deeply into Gramsci's thoughts it was as if Brevi lived in them, or they in Brevi.

'If what?' I asked carefully.

'I have expressed my suspicion in the relevant circles that one of Gramsci's notebooks is lost, and you know what "lost" in this context means. Not simply lost due to someone's recognizing it to be of historical importance too late, nor because it disappeared into a prison's rubbish. Not because time is rather scatter-brained and a lot gets misplaced over the years. No, Anton, lost because the archivists in Moscow wanted it to be. And so lost that it was never even recorded there. But I believe that this notebook still exists, somewhere here in Rome, I am positive that it never made it to Moscow.'

Brevi paused, I could no longer even hear him breathing. Thinking the connection had been lost, I went to the window in the absurd assumption that reception might get better.

'That would interest you too, wouldn't it, Tonio? And that would allow you back into the archives once more.'

'Hmmm, yeah . . .' I murmured while watching a young woman leaning back on a handrail across the street.

'Gramsci will become someone else!' Brevi cried. 'And communism too.'

'But, Signor Brevi, communism—'

'Communism,' he confirmed. The woman opened her jacket to reveal a white, slightly transparent top, turned her head and squinted up towards me, and it would've been so easy to forget for a moment that, outside of Brevi and myself, no one at all was really interested in Gramsci any more.

'Communism is a tad too large for us,' I demurred.

'Oh, Tonio, you mustn't go so far. One has to look where something is to be had. The secret of good research is to look where no one suspects the subject to be,' he said and began to talk about the numbering of the notebooks, about the Communist Party in Moscow, about Stalin's show trials, about Gramsci's sister-in-law. As I bent forward in order to better see the woman on the other side of the street, she pushed herself off the railing, ran up the steps and disappeared.

'When can I expect you in Rome?'

'Excuse me?' I asked.

'I would like you to help me look for the notebook.'

For a moment I thought about Lasse and Hedda's mood when she came back home in the evenings, and the sofa I slept or, rather, laid awake on, I thought about my boss Nordhoff and the view from the window of the newspaper's office.

'In four . . . in three weeks,' I said hesitatingly.

'That's good,' he repeated. 'I'll await you at the end of the month here in Rome.'

As soon as I hung up I lay my forehead against the window-pane and looked down onto the flagstones. Two schoolgirls were walking past, their satchels swaying behind them, a woman walked out of the bakery with a poppy-seed twist. To stay here, to reject Brevi's proposal, simply become as invisible as a book that's been put back in the wrong place and from then on can't be found. But I couldn't handle the silence between us any longer, between Hedda and me. Rome would be good for me, the noise, the liveliness, working at Brevi's side even though I had no idea what exactly I intended to save with such research: my career, my marriage, Gramsci or myself.

'It just wasn't a good fit,' I told Hedda during the last dinner we shared. By then we hadn't eaten together in our flat for a long time thanks to the mutual, if unspoken, feeling that it was just too intimate. Hedda would prepare something, eat with Lasse, and later I would warm up some leftovers for myself, that or simply not eat at all. Now and then Hedda and I would seek out a neutral space, a restaurant or cafe where we could sit across from each other, hidden from our own place like two people that have just got together and aren't comfortable enough with each other yet. That day, however, Hedda had demanded to have dinner at home. Lasse had already been enrolled for the upcoming school year that past summer, it only took a few sentences before the subject turned to us, as if there was anything left to say. Months earlier we'd agreed to no longer have any relationship and to only stay together for Lasse. Hedda had been the first to say it even though I'd thought of it before she had, and I'd already made the decision for both of us long before that.

'It just wasn't a good fit.' That evening I said it again very quietly, unemotionally. Hedda didn't say a word, she just continued to look for carrots in the pantry, *no, no green beans with the meat*. Only when I was no longer thinking about my observation did she let loose with all of her cold disappointment.

'Fit! A suit fits or it doesn't. But ten years? It just didn't fit? A relationship is not a piece of clothing.'

'How lovely to see you know so much about fashion.'

'You can spare me the cynicism.'

'Cynicism?' I responded fiercely. 'Hold on, if you really want hear it like it is, then I'll count it out for you, year for year, month for month. Out of ten years, Hedda, listen, three and a half fit, and of those three and a half years, fourteen months were good, if not really good. Then there were four years where we thought it would get better, and two of those we only thought so because we'd had a son together and you have to. The last two and a half years we just held on, one and a half for Lasse and one because we were too tired to go.'

'I left a long time ago.'

'And yet you're standing in front of me,' I said and my face once more took on that, as Hedda put it, cage-like look. She moved her hand in front of her eyes as if she could no longer stand it. The look, I mean. She'd told me so numerous times: small, but intentional stabs that might have hurt if they'd been a little less obvious. Nevertheless, I knew, I'd seen it myself, when I was angry my face would tighten and every last bit of tenderness that remained around my cheeks would disappear. My expression became as hard as chitin.

'Standing in front of you!' Hedda yelled, throwing the hand towel onto the table. 'And where is that? Take a look around. What kind of place is this? We both would love to have another five rooms each so we could avoid each other even better. Our neighbours are closer to me than you are.'

'But we still have sex with each other,' I objected.

Hedda laughed coolly. She was great at that, being cool, but I hated how afterwards she'd always break down about something so that it was impossible for me to treat her with any respect. We still had sex with each other, but of course I knew it was only because I also had sex with other women. Hedda talked about betrayal, I didn't understand what she meant. I didn't deny it, I would've even been willing to give her details, but she wasn't interested. Be that as it may.

'Your needs are only an escape,' Hedda said as she continued to peel the celery. 'You only want what you can't have.'

'I've always got the women I wanted,' I countered and pushed her hand onto the cutting board. 'And could you leave the celery alone for a moment?'

'That hasn't escaped me,' Hedda said, looked up briefly and squinted, something she thought looked threatening but which really, not that she knew of course, just made me think of our neighbours' Labrador.

In the meantime Hedda suspected an affair hiding around every corner. I had desires, true, but I couldn't desire everything. Even if Hedda wanted me to so that she could finally tell me to go to hell. Hell had caught up with us, of course, just not around the corner. It had come at a moment that overwhelmed us both, one that could not be repeated, and that moment I experienced with you, Hedda, and that was the reason at some point I married you. Not because of Lasse, not because of all of this ridiculous reasoning: if something happens to him, or to me, and then you have to come to the hospital—

'You could've just left it alone,' Hedda said and, together with the celery, pulled her hands from my grip. 'You could've simply pulled yourself together a bit.'

'Sorry, what are you talking about?' I asked.

'You know what I'm talking about,' Hedda said and pushed the cut celery into a glass bowl. 'You know better than I do. After all, you were there.'

'At least one of us was there!' I answered. 'You've completely removed yourself from life.'

'Your greed just exhausts me,' Hedda said. 'That's the only thing you still relate to. Ever faster, ever closer, like some crazy planet that keeps on spinning around the sun. That's not appetite any more, that's obsession.'

I reached for the corkscrew I bought for two euros and forty-nine cents the last time I'd gone to the supermarket. Lasse had exchanged our previous one—one that salvaged the cork out of the neck of the bottle like a kind of drilling station—with a friend for a plastic machinegun. Was loving kids even reasonable? At such moments, not loving them seemed all too sensible. As I tried to drive the two-forty-nine opener down into the cork, my hand kept slipping off.

'You're not interested in politics,' Hedda said, criticising me. 'Not in society, not in art. Just in yourself and your needs.'

'I'm interested in Gramsci.'

'That's what I said. In yourself.'

Accusations didn't really suit Hedda. Her face was too pretty, and when she laughed, when she wasn't thinking about anything in particular, it shone with ease.

'Well, you should know, you know a whole lot about passion, as painstakingly as you avoid it.' I clutched the bottle between my shoes, pulled and wrenched and knew that I looked like Rumpelstiltskin but so what, Hedda wasn't looking at me anyway.

'And where were you the whole time?' I asked. 'You hid away, you weren't there for me any more. What was I supposed to do? I need closeness every so often, and I don't get it from you.'

'I was busy taking care of our son,' she said, cutting into the board with the knife. Now the onions, I thought, *Hedda, take the onions*. Show me how much you can cry.

'Taking care of our son! That's what you call "taking care of",' I replied. 'He can barely think straight the way you've babied him!'

Hedda didn't say a word. Naturally, she hadn't grabbed the onions, she didn't do me any favours any more, though, for all intents and purposes, she hadn't ever really done me any favours. She quartered a pepper, took out the core, what was she even preparing? Were either of us even still hungry? Lasse for his part didn't like vegetables, kids never like vegetables, everybody knew that.

'Someone had to pay attention to him,' she said. Her voice was calm. Hedda knew the game, she was a master of the high art of fighting. That's not one of the reasons I'd got together with her. Well, it was one of the reasons. She could look perfect while hurting you. Precisely at that moment.

'If I hadn't taken care of him, who would have? You were more interested in yourself. In your damn needs. A little child, Toni, doesn't survive on its own.'

'Maybe it wasn't a good idea to have a child,' I said and felt the cork finally give way.

'Not a good idea? This doesn't have to do with an article in the paper, Toni, you're talking about a child, you're talking about your son. A human being, for Christ's sake.'

The cork split, and again my hand slipped off.

'What kind of wine did you buy, Hedda? A six-euro deal at the supermarket? Why are you so stingy?'

Hedda dropped the rest of the pepper into the bin. 'Your needs, Toni. Always your needs. Could you please turn on some music?'

'You don't want to hear any music right now,' I countered.

'Yes, I do. I can stand your talking even less than your being quiet.'

Her barb had missed the target and she noticed. I pulled at the rest of the cork still stuck in the neck. Hedda expected something of me that only a dead man could give her. The rest of us had to live with needs. Life wasn't made up of right and wrong, but major and minor. Did she want to live with someone who'd retreat to his hobby room when he no longer knew what to say in the living room or what to do in the bedroom and for everyone to see it about her? *Hedda, did you want that dull kind of abstinence?* With me, it was never dull. Too loud perhaps, too stressful, yes, but dull it was not.

'Could you please put on some music, Anton?'

I placed the corked wine on the kitchen counter and walked into the living room. I could hear Lasse's soft, anti-slip-socked steps on the stairs. Maybe he was hungry, maybe he was bored, maybe he'd ruined this marriage. Today I'd only accuse him of having traded the drilling station for a machine gun though. That'd be enough for starters.

IV. SILVER WOOD SANITORIUM   A birch forest a few kilometres outside Moscow. A man in a white coat and a grave expression is walking across the paths of the institution. The patients are standing in front of a row of hedges, shiny in their bright gowns. They have just come outside to have a walk in the fresh air. In two hours a gong will call them back for lunch, then the wide-bottomed nurses will take them back into custody, seesawing their way down the corridors.

It is the summer of 1922 and, inside, head doctor Reverend is checking his patients' hearts and kidneys and, above all, their souls. The armada of physicians, nurses and onlookers nods in synch and scampers behind him as he makes his rounds. The hallway is long, endlessly long, much longer than one would think at first, and every few metres a new sensation awaits. Silver Wood houses catatonics and hospitalists, neurotics and rheumatics, the depressed and those who only want to escape—from the Revolution and what came in its wake. There is a man of overwhelming Russian Orthodox stamp who from the moment he rises to the moment he goes to sleep just nods his head, and in bed too, *tock tock tock* against the wall. There is a woman who talks about her childhood in Novosibirsk although, according to the files, in her whole life she has never travelled further than the outskirts of Moscow. There are rooms which have remained as bare as when they were first acquired, a field bed pushed up against the wall, a scratchy blanket and a patient cowering in the corner as if hoping to be overlooked by Reverend and the rest of the world. There are rooms which have been so over-decorated with floral arrangements—a bucket of Narcissus here, a bundle of box-tree branches and rowan there, bouquet after bouquet around the bed, a wreath at the window—one would be forgiven for thinking they were at a funeral. And then there is that tiny savage from Sardinia who has been living in the ward on the left side for a few days now and frightening the other patients with his fits. At times he begins to tremble spasmodically, at others he is gripped by bouts of colic and hisses like an angry cat.

The name of Comrade Patient is Antonio Gramsci and there are rumours that the Comintern itself sent this odd Sardinian here. At the table and during afternoon free-time, people speculate on where he might have led the Revolution. Odessa? Tiflis? As far as people here know, the Revolution has not taken place in Italy. In Moscow, in any event, they haven't heard of him.

But Moscow! Let's not talk about it. Isn't that city to blame for bringing everyone here? The traces of the Revolution are still to be found in the streets, can be seen in the people's eyes, at first seemingly haughty but then quickly sinking to the ground. A few Muscovites have begun to stutter while others boom unceasingly as if having to compete with the thunder of cannons. Great numbers of people just stare confusedly and defiantly into the emptiness, and there are countless streets where passers-by just scurry past, their shoulders hunched as if being chased. This time, however, society won't tip back into its old habits, it will remain turned on its head and the revolutionaries will string up any doubters by their feet. The war and its subsequent upheaval have worn on people's nerves for far too long. The city is plagued by tics.

A young woman, tender in appearance, sullen in her weariness, is one of the most splendid carriers of this pain here in Silver Wood. Eugenia Schucht by name, she is the daughter of an antitsarist and as a child already had learnt to understand words like 'deportation' and 'exile' while growing up in four countries and three languages and fighting in the Civil War for the Revolution. Eugenia is lying in bed and can no longer walk. Supposedly Lenin himself had vouched for her integrity at her entrance into the CPSU, but now no one feels responsible for her legs, and she doesn't either.

'It's no wonder she can no longer walk,' Reverend says, 'she's walked enough, now she's on strike.'

The first time she tries to walk, Eugenia stays close to the fence. She doesn't trust the long-rotten wood hidden beneath the white lacquer, but by now who or what does she trust? She knows she's stubborn but, outside of Vladimir Ilyich Lenin, nothing really holds up. Well, maybe her father, but that remains to be confirmed. In her family, she is the one the others rely upon to make decisions and to direct and to rule, she is the leader of the little foursome of sisters, one of whom, Tania, has now gone missing in Rome. But Eugenia isn't sorry. It's one less mouth to keep quiet.

Apropos Rome. Hadn't she just overheard a few words in Italian? She nestles into her simple little cotton jacket and has a look around.

The strange Sardinian is standing there speaking with a man whose face is shadowed by a flat cap. Enough with the cap, enough with the man, she wants to get a closer look at this Sardinian and at best alone, she's already heard a bit about him, people had, in fact, related some rather handsome anecdotes about him.

Eugenia moves a few steps closer and greets him from across the fence. 'Come è bello il tempo oggi,' she says and the Italian smiles, how much and how well his language is spoken here in the outskirts of Moscow, he says, and from all sides too. *Oh Italy, it's really not that far away.*

They fall into a relaxed exchange about the prescribed diet and the comfort of the beds, Eugenia intentionally ignoring the man in the cap. The Sardinian seems as a mild as a guenon, the diet seems to be having an effect. How were things going in Silver

Wood? he asks. Strictly serenely, she replies. What did one usually do here? Wait. And for what? For waiting to continue.

The cap disappears with a curt farewell. At last Eugenia can dig a little deeper. Her hands slide along the fence, with her unsure steps she leads Gramsci away from the sanatorium building a little, there where every corner and exit has ears. Ahh, he's from Turin. He'd run the communist newspaper *Ordine Nuovo* there. Now, that's something. And he'd played a role in the Soviet movement. Respect. He'd been at the founding of the Italian Communist Party last year, and had enjoyed so much success in Italy that his name had made its way to Moscow. The important figures in the Party are happy with the opinions he published in *Ordine Nuovo*. A great deal.

Gramsci is thirty-one years old that summer of 1922, he's arrived here in Moscow as the Italian representative of the executive committee of the Comintern, at the beginning of June he took part in the second conference, once again he'd worked until he was completely exhausted. Eugenia compassionately rocks her head. It's clear that, as weak as he is, he cannot sit with the Comintern. No, no, you shouldn't do that, Eugenia agrees and she thinks of Lenin who back in May had suffered his first stroke, he will only take over official functions again at the end of autumn. And Lenin was a full-grown man. She looks at Gramsci, that little, twisted heap with the mild, quite handsome, quite calm face which *oh!* is shattered by a twitch. For a moment a completely different person was standing in front of her.

He had never been master of his own body, Gramsci admits, but now he was losing complete control over it, had been driven to a point where his political work was being affected.

How is it he has already begun to open up to the thin little person in front of him he has just met? This is not his way, it is not normal for him at all. Eugenia listens, she carefully takes down everything inside herself while he goes on talking about living in a cold student's room for years, about a shabby suit thanks to which he no longer dared to go out onto the street. Since the founding of the Italian Communist Party and separation from the socialists, he has been working more than ever, slaving away for the Party like a man possessed, she learns, and inside her it rattles and tickers and an endless tape of information gets wound up within that moon-pale head, she can see that he is exhausted and worn down and *Really! You've never been in love in your life?*

V. ERCOLI   The philosophy department was housed in a yellow building surrounded by a small park. Saint Francis of Assisi bent over a little bird by a pond, above the two of them the palm leaves swayed back and forth with eternal indifference. Brevi was the chair of Moral Philosophy at Sapienza University and ruled over his department with the equanimity of God the Father, which meant that he only put in an appearance every few years and that students waited mostly in vain outside his office door.

'All men are intellectuals, but not all men have in society the function of intellectuals,' Brevi quoted Gramsci as we made our way through a small side hallway up to the top floor. Behind a door, a series of metal steps led even higher and suddenly we were standing outside. Brevi ignored the handrail and evenly walked on ahead as I followed behind him teetering and doing my best not to look down.

'I haven't been here for ages. To be honest, all total, I've only been here three times. My goodness, Anton, the climb is a real challenge, don't you think?'

I nodded, still making an effort to steady my breath. The space seemed as if it had been left in a hurry. Used coffee cups, a few exams weighed down by library books that must have been overdue for years by now.

'At least we'll be left alone here. Gramsci's notebook, the notebook we're looking for, number thirty-four, cannot have any confidants,' he explained.

I let myself sink onto one of the desk chairs and looked at the pictures on the wall. On a world map the battles of the Russian

31

Civil War had been marked with pins, next to it was an engraving of Pico della Mirandola.

'Another one with a rather poor nose,' Brevi remarked. He was standing in the middle of the room with sagging shoulders. I wasn't sure how old he really was, at breakfast I'd thought he could barely be over sixty, and yet, upon my arrival in Rome, he seemed like the most antiquated professor I'd ever met, an eminence who exuded dignity due to his birthdate alone. Brevi shimmered. Brevi flickered.

'Look here. I just recently got hold of this. What do you think?'

He handed me two typewriter-punched pieces of paper whose edges had been scribbled with notes in pencil: *It is inadvisable to give photocopies to the family.*

'Dear Comrade Dimitrov!' I read in German.

The family would like a complete set of the photocopies to stay with you. I am against such a decision and the Commission has also taken a position against this. My arguments are as follows:

(a) In principal, it is not right for two archives of Gramsci material to be created in just such a form; (b) Gramsci's notebooks, almost all of which I have studied very closely, contain, in part, material which will only be able to be taken advantage of after precise preparation. Without such preparation, the material cannot be used and, in fact, were some parts to be used in their current form, they would be of no use to the Party. I therefore believe that it is necessary for the material to remain in our archive and to be edited here as well. I have complete trust in the wife of Comrade Gramsci; however, that everything be taken advantage of to the degree advisable and necessary is not a question of personal trust, but organizational

safety (for today and, in particular, for the distant future)—
I ask you to please give an opinion on this matter.

/Ercoli/

25 April 1941'

'You know who Ercoli is?'

'Palmiro Togliatti,' I answered.

'And what, my dear Tonio, did the head of the PCI hope to achieve with this letter?'

'He wanted to have the Schuchts out of the way.'

'And why?'

'In order to have control over the estate. The Party always wanted control.'

'Could it not be,' Brevi asked, 'that he did not want any witnesses? That he, if witnesses there had to be, desired no witnesses with evidence? That the editing of the materials, as he so beautifully calls it, signifies an abridgement? Perhaps the editing away of an entire notebook? That it did not have to do with what could be of use to the Party, but much more to do with what could be of harm?'

'It would really have to do with what Gramsci might have written in the notebook.'

'Please, he either railed against Stalin or praised him to the skies. In the former case, then Tania, Piero Sraffa and Togliatti too would have to have feared that this thinker would be completely erased from the communistic canon. And they'd have to fear for themselves as well and for Giulia and the children. The latter case already allows a bit more license. What did Sraffa think of Stalin? And Tatiana? Now, look here, there is also a third possibility. There is the possibility that Gramsci began to distance himself from communism, or let me put it this way: he laid it out in such a way that not only the Stalinists would have felt uncomfortable.'

'Too liberal?'

'Liberal! *Libertine!* Precisely what wouldn't suit the communists!'

'Did you ever believe in it? In communism?' I asked.

'My dear Tonio, I am a scientist. I do not take positions, I only call them into question. Be that as it may, this project will be my last. If it is unsuccessful ... But it won't be. Why should it?' A thin, tall glass was pressed into my hand. Brevi pulled out a bottle of *limoncello* from his desk and poured one for each of us. 'We have an enormous advantage. There isn't any money, there isn't any money anywhere, least of all at Italian universities. How can all these overly expensive restaurants, boutiques and jewellery stores keep going? Who lives in all the luxury flats in the city centre and who are all these people walking down Via Condotti in their bespoke clothes? In any event, this state has no money, this university even less, it is impossible for us to do any research, my colleagues spend their time hunting conferences abroad, but do you know what? That is an enormous advantage for us. We have no competition we have to take seriously. Do you like the *limoncello?*' Brevi asked and had already refilled my glass.

'I would like to find this notebook,' he said after refilling his own and then downing the liquor in one go. 'And, Anton, we are going to find it.'

And even if it was only the resolute way he opened his eyes up wide, what I now saw did indeed scare me. Brevi's face usually did not show the least emotion, and I suspected that more than just the rest of his thin future hung on this notebook, more than those few years with emeritus honours and high-official invitations to pointless events. And similarly, if it went wrong—that much was obvious—it would break him.

'But if that notebook never really existed?' I replied. 'Or if it got burnt decades ago in an ashtray somewhere on Via Sebino?'

'If it is not to be found, Tonio,' Brevi said, grabbing after my hands with his paws and holding them tight, 'then we shall find it anyway. Do you understand?'

I pulled my hands back. I didn't understand, to be honest, and didn't want to understand. Brevi looked at me sleepily through his glasses, an absolute authority. Only those who were truly somebodies and not simply anybodies could afford that kind of drowsiness. I thought about Hedda and Lasse and the flat to which I'd return once I said goodbye to Brevi's project. And I thought about what I really wanted: to destroy holy Gramsci once and for all.

'Of course I understand,' I said. Brevi pushed his glasses back up his nose and observed me curiously.

'Maybe Gramsci was a Stalinist,' I said, 'or wanted to wring the Stalinists' necks. But maybe, Brevi, maybe there's something completely different in the notebook that we will find. And we're going to find it, I know that as well as you do.'

'Of course you know that. And I knew that, with you, I had made the right choice. Go to the Istituto Gramsci, Anton, do me the favour. Find something and tell me about it this evening. Soon we will expand our radius. We will look through Tatiana's flat and the Quisisana clinic. We are going to find something, Anton. That we will.'

He led me to the door of his bureau and smiled shyly before closing it behind me. I listened for his steps, their steady, almost soothing back-and-forth. Then I climbed back over the roof to the main building. Students were sitting on the floor, laptops on their knees. A female lecturer rushed past me with a stack of papers. For a moment I was overcome by a feeling of melancholy there where I was neither authorized to be nor enrolled. Then I was back in the park, the sunlight falling through the tops of the palms. The Istituto Gramsci was no more than fifteen minutes away.

She was sitting at one of the tables near the window, a toasted *panino* in front of her she eyed more sceptically than eagerly. Incapable of moving or turning my eyes away, I stared at her fingers. The noises around me died down and once again I saw it all in front of me: her shoving an empty pack of cigarettes (Marlboro) into a rubbish bin.

She'd traded the poncho for a washed-out men's shirt with rolled-up sleeves. Her head was sunk over the *panino* and her lips were chapped, which gave the beauty of her face a slightly vulgar touch. People bumped past me. From far away I heard her warm, effervescent voice and saw her mouth, her shirt, too large, it fell to her knees and the material seemed to grow transparent, her body to shiver slightly.

I pushed open the door, soon she would have to turn her face towards me, but then a fat kid waddled in between us, clumsily pulling his tunnel-like jeans up over his arse. The waiter wiped a cloth across the counter. As he began to work on the espresso machine, he shot me a glance. He snapped on a switch, concentrated on a new batch of ground beans, looked back at me once more and made a sign. Come all the way in or get lost.

I hesitated, let the door shut behind me, she didn't notice. I stood there indecisively between a number of umbrella stands and slot machines. I stuck a few coins into the mouth of one of the latter and pushed the buttons. The machine twisted its apple- and cherry-filled eyes and then stopped at a hopeless point. Though it was July and Rome and the now-useless air-conditioning hung *fuori funzione* on the ceiling, I was freezing. She took a bite of her sandwich. I pushed in more coins.

'*Ma dai!*' the fat kid yelled, pulling at the arm of my shirt and pointing to the display. In four of the five fields there were

cherries, the last still spinning, then growing slower, tipping forward, tipping back. The lights sprang like mad across the front of
the machine, money rattled into a metal tray and from the inside
of the machine came a fanfare that was so loud it filled the whole
room. There was a draught from the door. By the time I turned
around, she was gone.

VI. SUNDAY   When Gramsci wakes up on Sunday, he thinks he can hear bells in the distance. But that's impossible. Both bells and belief have been abolished in Silver Wood, and the seventh day of the week is no longer the day of the Lord. The world was not created in seven days. That was just a legend invented by economists. In the silence of Silver Wood, one can see a few things more clearly, and here, Eugenia had explained to him, Sunday is a day of anxiety, of arrival.

In other words, Sundays are for visitors. They come from Moscow, from those avenues where the buildings will grow ragged and dirty until all middle-class life has been stamped out, ten people to a parlour, cooking, washing, sleeping, falling ill together. They come from the outskirts and the smaller villages where, during the Civil War, even the sorriest of shacks were plundered, then rebuilt, then destroyed again, and whose inhabitants now sit grimly and apathetically in front of their wooden hovels, no longer knowing whether walls or rubble are behind them. They come from Podolsk and Selenograd and Balashikha and even from Ivanovo, the upper echelons of post-tsarist Russia, the well-deserved workers and farmers and engineers and teachers and intellectuals leave the chaos and plunge straight into the kind-heartedness of the hospital. All those who truly shared Lenin's thoughts but whose relatives got sick all the same.

A savvy anti-tsarist from Ivanovo—a city of textiles with one hundred thousand inhabitants, an Egyptian mummy, and a music academy which in the years of famine had remained open—tumbles into the glory of the sanatorium, far from socialistic inhospitality. He has already experienced exile on account of his convictions, back when people with healthy senses still believed that no revolution of the proletariat could ever break out in Russia, seeing as that the country hadn't even entered the industrial age.

The anti-tsarist is named Apollo, an important name, an important man, he comes from a wealthy family and has worked his way up through the military before marrying the Jewish woman Julca, née Grigorevna. He spent a few years in exile in France, Switzerland and Italy before making his way back to Russia to experience the October Revolution in Moscow, and then moved to Ivanovo, a hundred kilometres away from the red Moloch. And the Revolution? For the time being, it had taken place in the villages where they stood it on its head and it stuck out its violet tongue in return.

Apollo's convictions, in any event, seem to have gone straight into the growth of his beard—he looks just like Karl Marx. He has a son in Moscow, and five daughters. First, there is Eugenia, learning to walk again in the sanatorium; then Anna, about whom there's not much to say; then Nadina, who didn't come back from the Civil War; Tania, still living in Italy; and Giulia, come to the sanatorium with him in order to visit her sister.

Gramsci, unsuspecting in his good-natured way, is on his way to see Eugenia. Since their first meeting at the picket fence, he has often been on his way to see her, there are things to talk about, things are brewing in Italy, Italy could be the next country the Revolution pulls to its meagre breast, but there it will come from the wrong side and he has to ask Eugenia how seriously people here take Mussolini. The question goes round and round his head, he is intensely agitated, extremely uneasy when he thinks about the former socialist whose *fasci* will drive the communists to the side and play the Revolution by their own rules and there—

there—

the sentences break off. He looks at the woman leaning at the window in Eugenia's room, one hand carelessly dangling, the other on the frame, and now she looks at him. She is tall. She has an oval face, haunting eyes, shoulder-length blonde hair. But that's only half the truth. He can no longer remember whether he slid the door open against the protestations of the rug or whether he closed it. He cannot remember what he wanted to speak to Eugenia about either. He doesn't see Eugenia or her father at all, though with his massive beard Apollo is almost impossible to miss.

The blonde woman at the window is similar to Eugenia, a milder version of the intense little flame of the Revolution, and he thinks that she must be Eugenia's sister. What she is saying comes to him with a delay: for the moment, he only hears words, then a meaning finally comes together. She looks at him and talks about Nadina, the oldest of the Schucht sisters, missing since the confusion of the pre-Revolution. Then she stops for a moment: 'I'm Giulia, and you must be the famous Antonio. My sister's told me about you.'

Slowly his other senses return. The cold of the hallway. The tepid, body-like temperature of the room. The rattle of a trolley against the stairs.

So, Eugenia had told her about him. They'd already spoken about him and now here he was, now she can see him in his full inadequacy, locked into his body, into that bug-like shell. She might have been able to find pleasure in a phantom, but as he is she'll only be able to meet him with pity or disgust.

The front hump presses on his chest while the one on his back weighs down his shoulders. He starts to shiver. Her hand tugs at her collar. A strip of sunlight streams across her cheek.

Neither his legs nor his head obey him, he wants to disappear, go back to the ceiling beam he'd been suspended from as a six-year-old, pulled up by his brother in order to let him hang out his growths in a specially built wire casing. His face twitches. Giulia's hand shrinks from her collar.

'Come over here, Antonio,' says Eugenia.

Like a servant at the tsar's court, he hobbles into the room but cannot speak a single word. Usually, he can make others laugh with just two or three sentences. Today, Eugenia speaks in a different way, and her cheeks, often pale and sunken despite the bright July light, look fresh. Listening to her he trembles and does not know why.

At first, he doesn't dare to look at Giulia.

'Yesterday I had a book of Nadina's in my hand,' Giulia says to her sister. 'I finally took the bookmark out. She had thirty more pages to read.'

'Oh, she read Sorel a few years ago already. She put it aside because she can't bring anything to a close.'

'You just can't miss her.'

'What are you saying, Giulia? She read it years ago.' Eugenia pushes out her chest, turns from her sister and looks towards the window, running a hand along her severe part. The painfully drawn hair gives her face a touch of something mad. Nothing can be disordered. Everything must be dominated. 'Look at these birch trees!' she exclaims. 'They're everywhere. The whole facility is surrounded by them. Tell me, Antonio, have you ever been able to bear Russia? The Russian landscape?'

'Today's Russia is for all of us . . .'

'Give today's Russia a break! Forget politics. Do you see these birches? Don't you have any opinion of them?' Eugenia's finger taps the windowpane. 'I hate these trees. Their white trunks.'

'Do not be so harsh, dearest Eugenia,' says Gramsci.

Eugenia sparkles at him. 'Birches,' she says. 'Birches everywhere. And the Revolution wasn't won with tenderness.'

By the time Gramsci looks to the window, everything has become blurry, the birches are only white shadows, the paths

41

winding confusedly and tremulously like bright eels. In his head, he hears the noise of meetings, the park and the woods disappear behind rows of stools, comrades' backs, red banners. And there, he'd wanted to avoid it, he sees Giulia's face mirrored in the glass. The fine lines of her chin. The glazed stare. They look at each other, look at each other a little longer, then a little longer and a little longer still. He cannot stay here. He is an imposition on what this woman must have presumed about him. That's how it is. He knows it. And there, what is that, what does that mean? She smiles at him.

Run as fast as you can. Something utterly disinterested in rules is pushing back against power, something that refuses to obey anyone or anything, how could it not end in chaos and terror and distress? Flight is the only thing that can help, flight back to his room. So that was Giulia. Comrade Giulia. That was the shock about what you had not understood for so long, about what, in truth, it is all about.

Gramsci is lying face down on his bed. He is racked by shudders more than ever before. A roaring breaks loose in his head and sweat runs down his back. His body is in dull pain, it closes around him tightly, leaving no room for his consciousness.

In thirty-one years he has never experienced this kind of shock. Not when his father was taken away by the police and led from the house, through the yard, down the streets of Ghilarza because he'd hidden a few lire from the land-registry office and in return received five years, eight months and twenty-two days in jail. Not when his brother tied him into a corset and hoisted him up to the ceiling beam to hang like a salami left out to dry, looking down on his family, a distant event made up of whorls of hair, parts at the back of a head. Right now, this is greater than all of that. This here he will not be able to master. He must stay away from Giulia. That much is obvious. It's awful. He hadn't known how the world could be—how huge and terrifying and beyond all reason.

Apparently, true love was real. There was Manzoni and Shakespeare and Dante, *yes, yes, of course*, in one's imagination there was Heaven and Hell and death and the Lord God too. But let us remain in the world. There were sighs like *oh*, that expression of rapt longing, yearning desire, *oh, oh, oh*, but it just did not want any connection to his name. *Oh Antonio*. It didn't sound right to his ears, and even if there were five or five hundred other ways to whisper Antonio, none would ever refer to him. At best, 'Oh, Nino!' would just be a furious shout after doing something wrong.

He cannot explain to himself how to get close to a woman, how to get close to another human being. He is convinced, and has been for years, that it is absolutely impossible for him to be loved and that this has been dictated by fate. He has made himself so at home in the world of thoughts that it has become bearable, overwinterable. Thirty-one years long, and he could have held out another thirty-one, or at least that's what he has believed. It was clear to him that nothing came after winter. He does not need to ask himself why hold out at all, because, for him, such categories—'for me'—do not exist.

He can barely move. The blanket seems too heavy, his body is tired, he can only turn his head. He looks towards the window and there, behind the curtains, hanging in tatters in front of the paths, something is moving. A face appears, her face, and he tries to remember: Petrarch, Manzoni, Flaubert, this kind of face had to have appeared somewhere just like this. Dante, Goethe. What would Ibsen's characters have done at this very moment? They would have failed, but how?

He closes his eyes and sees his mother hunched over a sewing table, trying to repair what has long been irreparable: socks, an apron, Teresina's jacket with the spots on the back. He sees his father under arrest, walking down the street flanked by two policemen, being taken away from the family and what's going to happen now? His sister bent over a schoolbook. She looks up, her dark, serious face turned towards him, a soft tuft of hair on her upper lip through which the light falls. The taste of old bread pushed back and forth through his mouth with a numb tongue. The smell of bitter spring meadows. And then everything drifts away, he doesn't feel his body, the years break away, branches from cold undergrowth.

VII. ILSA   In the autumn of 1967, my mother was a heavily pregnant intellectual diva on a Biedermeier sofa, reading Gramsci's *Prison Notebooks*, one eye trained on Ustica, Bari, Regina Coeli—all of those leprous places with a jail pulsing at their secret core and where Gramsci had written his pieces—while her fellow students' theoretical flights of fancy never made it beyond Frankfurt. I know, or at least I was told, that within left-wing student groups she was held in a certain regard. But I have no idea whether they liked her, no one talked about that, or not to me anyway, the son of that grand dame of the Revolution otherwise known as Ilsa. She set a tone that, though milder than Lenin's, remained autocratic enough to scare my father off through the house and out with the left-wingers of Bremen to distribute flyers in front of the gates of the Klöckner plant, participate in marches and sit through panel discussions. Here I must add that she enjoyed a not-undeserved reputation. Gramsci had been her holy pillar long before he became one for thousands of others in the '70s. Of course, by that point, she'd already gone back to Bakunin and Kropotkin.

In November 1967, after a few complications, her son—I, in other words—came into the world. Thanks to an extremely young midwife and a bad-tempered doctor, she'd almost died in the delivery room because of me, or, rather, my stubborn refusal to arrive, thereby becoming the first in a long succession of women to survive me by only a hair's breadth. While that delicate creature was being lashed by contractions, I simply lay diagonally in her belly and refused to budge.

My father walked up and down the linoleum halls with a bouquet of flowers which steadily grew more feeble as time went on, at first concerned about the delay, then not knowing what to do, then simply done. Chucking the bouquet into a blue plastic-covered bin, he called a taxi to carry him off. However, as soon as his stricken conscience began to go haywire, he had it cart him back to the hospital. I caused my mother to not only almost lose her mind but also her life—and all that even before my existence had been officially registered. She's told me that every single year on my birthday, up till today, before wishing me well, which, as a result, has always come out a bit weak, and she still doesn't know whether she wants me to thank her or if she regrets withstanding that urge to simply drift off, to never wake up, to turn the child between her thighs into an offender while releasing him into a life of endless guilt.

Whether due to a feeling of revenge or a sudden eruption of motherly love, Ilsa did not hesitate, once the worst had been weathered, to name me after Antonio Gramsci. At least my father forbade her from naming me Tonio. 'Tonio Stöver! Please! You might as well just call him Thomas Mann at the same time.' She'd never allowed him to say much to her, but, in the end, he prevailed and thus I became Anton. Anton Stöver.

Stepping across her Persian rugs and gradually integrating my father into a bourgeois-Marxist household, for the most part I was ignored by Ilsa. Now and then she gave me a bottle, changed my nappies when she felt like it, smoked one self-rolled cigarette after the other and simply shrugged her shoulders when her mother would throw up her hands and, grabbing a bar of soap, try to scrub her grandchild clean of all that communistic mess. But what could Ilsa do? Her interests were directed less at that little piece of humanity lying on the changing table than at that great humanity-to-come on her desk. In my parents' house, Revolution was, after all, an awfully common word and nothing changed when it repeatedly failed to take place.

But little Anton Stöver would come into the room every morning with a shrill infant's laugh. And, at night, while the others were handing out flyers in front of the Klöckner plant, this little counterrevolutionary would cry for Ilsa. But she would just send my father who, for his part, really had no idea what he was supposed to do. I yielded, grew quieter, less demanding and older, allowed myself to be palmed off to creches and nursery schools, then thanks to inadequate growth was held back a year, and then, as a reward for finally being enrolled in school, was given my first selection of Gramsci's writings (selected by Palmiro Togliatti) in Italian, although I couldn't understand a word but that didn't bother Ilsa in the slightest. And so I began to lug that ugly paperbound thing around, for though I was only seven, I already understood that it was not simply a book but my destiny that she wanted to push onto me.

While I was still in primary school, Ilsa, starting with Bakunin and Kropotkin and then progressing to Pico della Mirandola and Thomas Aquinas, steadily moved further and further away from the twentieth century. Antonio Gramsci, however, remained and hung like a shadow over my childhood. I pushed him away, the favourite child, but my hands only pushed through air.

I grew older and even a little taller, learnt how to read and, soon, in Italian too; beginning on my tenth birthday, once a week, I'd be packed into a dark, private classroom of bare wood furniture. I learnt *sono sei e siamo siete sano no sono*, and discovered that my Gramsci selection was by no means a complete or even organically fragmented one but a beautifully Stalin-true arrangement that Togliatti had put together. And though up to that point I'd been completely indifferent to the book, that intrusion angered me so much that once again I forgot to grow. At eleven I continued to be teased, at twelve I was almost completely ignored.

When at the start of grammar school I was placed with the girls for gym class, I didn't have any intention of reaching the height of my father, who at six feet seemed entirely unapproachable. But I definitely wanted to outgrow Ilsa by a few inches. At five-foot-six, she had to have given me something, and, in any event, we were related. But names are stronger than genes, and role models—above all, those we don't seek out ourselves—seal our fate, no matter what we do.

My father, however, had never been a role model. For as long as he lived with us, he was simply a silhouette in the study (that is, when Ilsa hadn't driven him out of it), a shadow who at 5 a.m. would be out in front of the Klöckner plant to explain to the workers what a fatherless breakfast meant. Later, once I'd begun to avoid breakfast scenarios myself, I realized that he'd wanted to be out of Ilsa's way and to give space in the communal kitchen to those three, four worshippers she kept but never allowed any closer. Ilsa, the coryphaeus at the coffee machine, was prude and picky and scraped together attention from all sides. In general, she didn't really like men all that much—even I wasn't too high on her list. At the same time, she couldn't do without their adoration. Every now and then she'd toss one of her disciples a crumb of attention, condescend to give a compliment, but only in order to impose a whole catalogue of demands in return.

Later, I hardly wondered when exactly my father left or why. His departure had been too inconspicuous. His yearly existence beforehand had been too inconspicuous. Which is to say, his leaving wasn't anything new for me—my father had been leaving throughout my childhood. Every few weeks he'd whiz through the downstairs hall of our old Bremen row house, grab his hat off the coat hook and angrily promise that this time he was going for good. This time he wouldn't be coming back. 'Are you listening, Ilsa?' He'd give her another two minutes to beg him to stay, to bring him to his senses, two minutes for her to at least show up in the doorway of the living room. But Ilsa never looked up, not even when the front door clicked shut.

I'd sit with her in the living room, sometimes behind the couch, sometimes under the kitchen table, and pretend to be playing but listening instead to the silence of the space, a silence broken only by the sound of Ilsa turning pages. I'd guess which of her devotees would move in with us, for as soon as one man left, another showed up, I'd learnt that from Karsten, he sat two rows ahead of me and during breaks bragged about how his father had taken off.

When the front door opened again, when after an hour (he could never last longer than that out on the Bremen streets) Bernd would come back into Ilsa's home, she'd praise him for his punctuality. Then they wouldn't say another word more about it and his hat would be back on the coat hook just like before.

But even the little respect she had for him was lost in only a few minutes one morning in the late '70s when two federal criminal police agents from the BKA showed up at our front door. A number plate had led them to this visit, many of which were taking place that autumn, a lot of visits, a lot of number plates, the police had nothing else to do but note number plates from Citroën 2CVs and VW buses. Countless times every day, women in fluttering shirts and with half-naked kids in their arms would open the door to them and have no idea what had happened. Paediatricians and health-food-shop workers had to deliver alibis. Fathers began to let people borrow their cars less and less frequently.

Ilsa, on the contrary, knew perfectly well what was happening, and the two officers standing in front of our door that quiet morning probably wished they had never rung; they didn't know if they should take away the whole family at once or never again dare to come here. How could those two poor men help it that, of all people, they had to question Ilsa? Schleyer had been kidnapped, and, as long as Schleyer was away, everyone was deemed suspicious for one reason or another, above all the Stövers, the city's first communist family. Ilsa set much store by that. And had the two officers not rung at our house, she no doubt would have marched to the office of the BKA-president in order to complain about not having received a visit.

The fact that my father opened the door that morning as Ilsa was busy in the study attending to more important matters, was the last mistake in a whole string of evermore fatal mistakes for which Ilsa could never forgive him. A number plate was read out to him like a sentence, he nodded, admitted it was his, eventually offered the two coffee, didn't know why the car had been seen at that time and at that place and under those circumstances.

'Where were you on the evening in question?' one of the officers asked, and my father couldn't say. He counted, Friday, Thursday, 'You're talking about Wednesday?' and still couldn't say.

'Did you drive your car?' the officer asked further.

'Or did you let someone borrow it?' the other asked, offering him a way out.

'In which case,' the first officer said, 'you'll have to tell us to whom and, in addition, provide us with an alibi.'

'At the university!' my father finally remembered. 'At a reading group, from eight to ten o'clock.' He neglected to mention that it had to do with Marx, though it very well might have occurred to the two. Maybe he'd lent his car to an acquaintance, he wasn't sure, he had to think a moment, and then one of the agents saw me sitting on the bottom-most step and cut off my father's rambling with the observation: 'The child surely has a mother.'

My father, hastily and helplessly, acknowledged Ilsa as well as the fact that she hadn't been at the reading group that night, although she usually was.

Ilsa, without any child on her arm and in a severe existentialist jumper, brought the uncomfortable situation to an end in just a few minutes. Did they intend to arrest anyone, Ilsa asked, had they thought it through? Surely the two middle-grade civil servants had no idea what could happen as a result. They were simply following orders which had been decided elsewhere, thinking things through had never hurt anyone and, in the end, they too had to fear for the system's stability, the one in which they lived, and lived well, they indeed loved the monotony around them, did they want it to all come crashing down, their savings accounts, their halves of a duplex, their marriages, just because someone in prison had become a legend?

Ilsa erupted, Ilsa performed, Ilsa quoted and vociferated and embroiled the two in a harsh monologue on the effect of prison writings, painted a picture of how martyrs were made and the power they could, oh, what the hell, *had* to unfold, and wove subordinate clauses of such stupendous length that the poor agents' ears, when not their noses and cheeks too, were glowing, before dismissing them with the dry observation: 'You haven't read a thing, but you're already bona-fide civil servants!'

My father never recovered from that visit. Ilsa for her part appeared determined not to allow herself to tolerate a person at her side any longer who had buckled so miserably when confronted by the state apparatus, and so the days in the shared flat became numbered. I was standing at the top of the stairs when my father, hatless but with two suitcases, finally left. Ilsa surveyed the scene, then looked up at me. 'You didn't even manage to sire a child of normal height. You really were useless, Bernd Stöver!' she yelled after him, but the door was already shut.

VIII. PIA   All of a sudden Pia is there again, the memory of Pia Carena. She has curly hair and is sitting behind a typewriter. She believes in the southern Italian farmers and the power of journalistic style to persuade. She is the editor of *Avanti!* and has been since December 1917. She'd been there a little earlier, but that is of no consequence, for what could she have been? A woman who knew how to type and to edit—in Turin, women who knew how to type and to edit could be found on every street corner, and even smart women, political and determined ones, they could be found too. But something special, that she'll only become in Gramsci's eyes.

He'd had no previous love life to speak of, if what he had allowed himself could even be called life. His suit is so threadbare that for a long time he does not dare to leave his room, and the money for a tailor he's urgently begged his father for over and over again sometimes arrives, sometimes does not. The family has money problems and, so far away from Turin, on the island, in another world, by the time Gramsci's plight arrives to them it is only a faded note. During his studies, he only has 70 lire from a royal scholarship, which, in the end, doesn't feel too royal at all. The little he takes he spends on books, rolls are the only food he permits himself, 50 grams, 10 *centesimi*, and at night he hallucinates from hunger. In Sardinia, the most he could do was look at women. *Don't you dare look at me, not even in my imagination would I allow a cripple to touch me*, one said to him once and laughed. Some women seemed to enjoy insulting him.

In Turin, since the early summer of 1919, he'd received an income as the editor of *Ordine Nuovo*, there were colleagues who believed in Gramsci like devotees, there was the radical movement and there were the *case chiuse*. Sometimes they are long hallways in the back of guesthouses flanked by single, sparsely lit rooms. Sometimes they are basement flats. Sometimes they unashamedly call themselves brothels. The women come from the countryside to seek work in the city but find only derision. They have been abandoned by their men or taken flight themselves, some still share a narrow, run-down flat with them at the city's edge, but the money they earn is rarely enough to pacify them, one can see the mark of leather belts on their backs. With Gramsci they are either affectionate or rough, they allow him to penetrate them without making fun of him or asking for anything more than a few lire. Some of the women send him away immediately, they don't want to know who this man is, they don't want to know about any of them. Some of them talk with him as they clean themselves over a washbowl in the corner. He wants to hear their thoughts about the Turin radicals, the general strikes and the liberation of the worker. 'We should go on strike now and again here too, then you'd all look pretty old,' one of them says.

One day, his lust is greater than what's leftover from his salary. Like a schoolboy he sits on a stool in front of the room, someone's called his friend Leo Galetto to come and cover him. The women streak past. Two stop, size him up from head to toe, then break into clear, high-pitched giggles.

'It's like you haven't eaten in ten years!' Galetto says by the time he's finally standing in front of him.

'Let's take it as a sign of being healthy,' he says, pays the girl, pushes Gramsci down the hall and back outside.

And then, at some point, there is Pia Carena. Attilio, her brother, one of Gramsci's co-workers, introduced the two of them. After an exhausting meeting spent talking about the Brigata Sassari and the possibilities of initiating strikes at the Fiat-Brevetti factories, he'd grabbed hold of Gramsci's arm and taken him home.

A massive solidarity strike against the counter-revolutionary moves of the Entente is planned for July, but how will this starved man, who constantly runs off to meet the radicals at the factory in order to take part in discussions, make it till then? Gramsci has always seemed too skinny to Attilio, his work seems to steal the very marrow from his bones.

Attilio's sister is standing in the kitchen preparing fish with fennel for dinner and browsing through a book, as if she were reading a recipe, by Ugo Foscolo, which is lying on the windowsill. Then, at the table, she laughs a lot watching the new guest picking the bones out of his fish as carefully as he can. Pia is interested in the idea of workers' democracy, in the factory councils that were to take the capitalists' place instead of negotiating with them and in marriage (which she wants to enter into as a virgin). She loves rainy afternoons and perhaps, but here she's not entirely sure, a young Italian man.

'A strike cannot paralyse operations. The workers must be responsible for continuing to produce,' Gramsci explains and lays a bone on the side of his plate with his fork. 'It has to do with self-empowerment. Trade unions keep the workers dependent. Better conditions within dependency, that is all they are fighting for.' Attilio nods and Pia looks at him thoughtfully. When she begins to clear the table, it is already around ten. She presses her arm close to Gramsci's body, a clear move he cannot fail to recognize.

They say goodbye in such a familiar way, it is as if they have known each other for years, and he soon returns to them, to a house with bright stone tiles which seem to be warmer than the tiles in the other houses in Turin. After two weeks, he begins to visit Attilio, Pia and their books on the windowsill regularly. Here he relaxes from all the spiders on his ceiling, from hunger and from his ascetic student years, his self-imposed confinement. At one point he places *The Kreutzer Sonata* on the sill, which by his next visit already seems to have been read; yet another time he ties her apron for her, his fingers gliding across her waist. She feels different from the women in the closed houses, warmer, fuller, as if she were truly filled with life and not simply liveliness.

Together with Attilio they found the 'Club of Moral Life', a debate club where young people can meet, talk about workers' self-determination in all production processes, about the radical movement in Turin, which could spread, that *would* spread, about how the Revolution could not begin in a Party office but in the factory, at the place of production. How calmly and yet determinedly Pia speaks in front of everyone. Gramsci leans forward in his chair, observes the curls falling across her cheeks, her straight posture. With a quick movement she draws a line through the air: that's how it is!

Indeed, Gramsci thinks, that's how it is.

When she stops speaking and looks into the faces of the audience, he nods at her. Pia looks at the floor, runs her fingers through her hair and then Gramsci sees that she is smiling. The smile of a child.

'If we are unsuccessful at taking power,' he explains to her later while Attilio says goodbye to their guests at the door, 'then others will. And they will be the dregs of the bourgeoisie. Grimaces only, no more faces.'

'Sometimes you frighten me,' Pia says, who has sat down on the windowsill and is looking into the darkness.

'You believe so strongly in our will, but what is that? Have you ever asked yourself who still has the strength for that? We're tired, Antonio, most of us are tired.'

'But not you, Pia.'

'On the contrary. I am too.'

'You are ten times stronger than I. You are the strongest of us all.'

She gives a start when he caresses her back, and sits up straighter.

'You should go now,' she says quietly.

After that evening, they do not see each other for a while. On 20 July, Gramsci is arrested. Wearing a dark suit, he is sitting in a cell on a plank bed covered with straw, he brushes a bunch of stalks with his fingernails and lets the other prisoners stare.

'You can't be Antonio Gramsci,' one of the men finally lets slip. 'Gramsci is a giant!'

'That's what I always thought too,' Gramsci replies. 'But do you know what? It's not true, I checked.'

Gramsci plays melodies on the clipped reeds for his fellow prisoners to guess, he jokes with the warder who brings them thin soup and a crust of bread, and out of a little piece of dough makes a tiny game of *boule* which entertains them all until evening. The next day Gramsci is the prison's favourite, he speaks Sardinian though he is the only one, he laughs a lot and off the top of his head tells them what they could be if they just refused to hide behind their humiliating roles. Accompanied by a troop of young warders he leaves the prison, they wave after him, they would have loved to have kept him for themselves. By evening, he is standing outside the Carenas'.

'You see the point,' Attilio greets him. 'In order to judge a state, you have to see its prisons from the inside, but in order to understand its power, you have to try the beef tenderloin. For weeks we've only eaten pasta, and hardly do we have a piece of meat in the pan, there's Sig. Gramsci in front of the door.' And he calls back into the hall: 'Pia, guess who's joining us for dinner tonight?'

Pia only casts him a quick glance as he walks into the kitchen, then bends back over the pots. He tries to make her laugh by telling jokes, but she just wrinkles her brow and counts cloves. He sits next to her at the table, but she has forgotten something in the other room; and when she returns, she stays on the other side. Attilio gets worked up about Bordiga's ideas of avoiding the vote.

'What do you think, Antonio?' he asks and plunks the wine glass onto the table. Gramsci murmurs single syllables and cuts his meat. Attilio jokes a little more about the king who no doubt will have his own ballot box placed in the palace but then he too grows quiet and looks at his two silent comrades. In their mouths, the tenderloin grows tougher and tougher.

Attilio excuses himself early, he still has to take care of a few things. 'Wouldn't you like to come, Antonio?' but Gramsci shakes his head. Pia begins the washing up in the kitchen and stares at the soapy water. When Gramsci comes up behind her, she drops the dishrag and rushes into the living room where she says she's forgotten something but doesn't find anything and remains standing indecisively in the middle of the room. Isn't it a bit too sticky in the flat? The two of them should go for a walk. *A bit of fresh air,* she says, *just a bit of fresh air*. She walks close to Gramsci through the Piazza Solferino, past the Alfieri Theatre, they walk past the train station and jump back from a tram bending around a corner. By the time it begins to rain, they are close to Gramsci's room. For a while they stand next to each other in silence beneath the porticoes. Then they rush across the wet cobblestones, dodging the puddles. Only because she doesn't want to catch a cold, really that's the only reason, she says, Pia accompanies him up to his room. They sit down on the bed; there is neither chair nor stool. It is quiet. Above them someone is walking heavily across the room. Outside it continues to rain. Pia crosses her arms over her chest in a protective manner when Gramsci moves closer.

'You know what I think about all this,' she says.

'About what?' Gramsci teases while running his hand over her shoulder.

'I don't want it this way.'

'Oh, right, once again that strange idea of yours about marriage.'

'It's not strange.'

'Of course not! Because everyone thinks the same way. Because everyone should think that way. Because it just makes us more efficient. We'll be able to concentrate in the factory thanks to our stable relationships. And you will fit in to the production process perfectly to the degree you serve your husband as a plaything and bearer of his children. Is that what you want? Nothing more?'

'You don't know what I want, you don't have the faintest idea. And I don't want you to speak to me this way.'

'You are downright exemplary in your self-discipline. You know how to control yourself. You are repressing your desires.'

'And how should it be, thank you very much? Should I cast myself at every man?'

'Why not? Monogamy is an invention of industrialism. They want to conserve the workers' strength, so that they can function at the conveyer belt according to the specified tempo.'

'Do you really think so?' Pia asks.

'And you, do you only think about your precepts?' he replies. 'Or can you still feel something too?'

'It's ridiculous to be keeping score.'

'You think I'm keeping score between us?' Gramsci asks, but Pia doesn't answer. For a while they only listen to the sound of their breath, the longer they remain silent the more intimate, almost obscene, it sounds.

When Pia leaves his room the next morning, the sun is hanging dimly behind the clouds but the pavement is dry and the puddles only hazy spots.

She continues to write to him at his address in Moscow, everything reminds her of him, she writes, nothing is as beautiful as it was just a few weeks ago, and do you know what? The second meeting of our club? She writes to him again and again, steadily grows more timid and more objective. The last issue of *Avanti!* cost her a lot of strength. Was the work on the committee coming along well? One letter manages to reach him in Silver Wood. Gramsci does not even answer with a postcard.

IX. LITERARY ESTATE At nine-thirty the next morning, the Istituto Gramsci slowly opened its metal gate, the archivists pulled the folios straight and checked to see if the ghosts were still there. Because this was where what the PCI had been able to protect from Moscow for years— first from the monster of the USSR, and then from the other monster that had eaten away at the USSR until it finally collapsed—had been stored. It's just that there was a problem. Since that time, Eurocommunism had steadily crumbled away into merely a historical term. And, well, there was another one. There simply was no money from either Moscow or the Italian Party. What up to the splintering of the PCI had been massive and conceited and nothing less than the hope of a communism without dictatorship now had to be conceived of in a much smaller and completely mundane way: it had to do with sorting books as well as staff, and hoping that the next water break would only happen a few years down the line.

I entered the sloping concrete space that led down to the entrance. An old tyre was disintegrating along the wall, a piece of wire stuck out of the ground. Then the glass panes slid open, I walked into the entrance hall and the man at reception scrutinized me over the edge of his glasses. Eyes like damp gravel.

In the reading room, I found myself alone among mummified PhD students. I imagined the poncho sitting at the table, writing another section of her thesis every afternoon, but I didn't hear her steps even once. There was not a single woman in the room.

I was so tired that I had to cross my arms on the table and rest my head. I could barely keep my eyes open. I squinted towards the window. Out in the courtyard, red plastic cordon tape had been unrolled and a bunch of temporary fences carelessly thrown on top of one another. They'll tear us down, I thought. If I fall asleep and miss closing time, they'll cart me off with the dismantled shelves and pulled-out walls and dump me in the outskirts in-between the grey, dreamless blocks of flats where the rubbish heaps blow their insouciant breath towards the river.

At the end of April 1937, Tania sends a telegraph to her sister from the embassy of the USSR. She should not be concerned about the notebooks, Tania had collected everything. By the time the telegram reaches Moscow, however, its content has been lost. Tania doesn't learn what exactly Giulia Schucht gathers about the retention of the notebooks, whether she knows anything at all or is just confused. Tania only understands that everything between Moscow and Rome has been misunderstood, and, when she learns of her plea to the People's Commissariat to concern themselves with her husband's belongings, that her sister is having troubles. No less than Potemkin himself was to take care of Gramsci's possessions: a pair of pyjamas, a watch, some dress shirts. Notebooks and letters. Stuff.

Her husband! A fairly despicable, legalistic formulation. Years ago, Gramsci had been lost to Giulia as a lover: as a friend, as a confidant, he'd continued to write her letters, but how can two people be intimate when the one doesn't understand a thing about the other's life? Tania is uninterested in gathering the remains of a love affair that for a long time had passed into a dialogue of the deaf in two different handwritings. In the photographs, there is no trace of longing in Giulia's face. There is nothing at all. Just an empty smile that's been pasted on for the photographer. At best, her sister's will, the Party's. There is the concern over a few thoughts discussed in the notebooks, always with an eye on more time, more concentration, a life beyond the jail cell. But life had never brought more time, more concentration or better health.

The people at the Soviet embassy would certainly be able to send a message to the wife of Italy's most important communist to inform her of the status of the notebooks. But they don't. They don't want to. They leave Giulia alone with her ignorance about the status of the notebooks. Eventually Tania writes her sister a letter at the beginning of May but without getting the diplomatic watchdogs involved.

'You don't have to worry about his manuscripts, everything's been taken care of, but I will not be sending you any of his work or letters just yet.'

Gramsci's notebooks must be brought out of Italy and to Moscow as soon as possible. They are not safe in Rome, no matter what hiding place Tania finds for them, whether she sews them into her mattress, gives them to the embassy or buries them beneath a loose plank in a faraway house. They must be taken out of Rome, and as quickly as possible.

The notebooks cannot be sent by regular mail, that much is clear. Before making it through the post office they'd have lost their addressees and only a few hours later ended up on a desk in the Ministry of Popular Culture.

There are three possibilities.

They can be sent to Moscow in a diplomatic pouch, protected by the last rules of etiquette still valid between the two ideologies. That stated, of course, they will reach their goal by landing in the hands of a Party cadre and Giulia will have to beg to be allowed even a glance.

Tania or a trusted friend of Tania's can smuggle them across the border, through Poland and the Ural, wrapped up in a pair of women's underwear in her luggage. How many hands will rifle through those discreet white undergarments lying in the suitcase as unattractive as potholders or handkerchiefs?

Three: meet the director of Banca Commerciale, who just happens to be an acquaintance of Piero Sraffa's, Gramsci's last friend, and let the notebooks sit in a safe for months until, with a few bills and derivatives, they make it to Russia, most likely with a detour through London where the bank keeps a branch up until 1940 and where Piero Sraffa is living.

Naturally, Tania knows that it's only a tired attempt to protect the notebooks from the Communist Party. Russia is the CPSU, the CPSU is Russia: like a heavy rain, it has softened everything and seeped deep into the earth. There is no difference between the state and civil society any more. The Party is everything.

But even if Giulia grasped what Tania wanted to tell her and how urgent it was—*Giulia, do you hear me? The notebooks cannot go straight to the CPSU, keep them to yourself at first*—it's pointless. Where Giulia is, there is Togliatti, and wherever Togliatti is, there is the Party too. He's set himself up under the wings of the power apparatus in Moscow, he quickly learnt how to be in line at first with Lenin, then with Stalin. But what was he supposed to do? There is no other way to survive in Moscow these days.

I heard her enter the room. Her steps sounded brighter, more determined, more bound to the earth in a pure way than the mummies' shuffling gait. For a while I remained seated and just enjoyed knowing she was behind me, enjoyed the intimacy that rose up between the two of us (one which no one else noticed, naturally) and existed for the two of us alone.

'The microfiche they gave me is blank,' she whispered, close behind me. 'Have a look.'

I turned. A man was standing next to her, a library employee who usually spent his time prancing back and forth in the hall to the archive like a circus horse on a lead. He bent awkwardly over the strip of film that Tatiana held out to him.

'Ah! Indeed. Then we'll have to make a request for permission to research. I'll bring you a form.'

'I don't want a form,' she explained. 'I'd like you to explain to me where the right film is.'

'That is the right film.'

'The film is blank,' she repeated.

'But, look here, the label shows the right year.'

'Then perhaps you can explain why, all the same, you can't see a thing.'

The employee moved closer. I got up and stepped over.

'Good to see you, Tatiana.'

She looked at me and for a moment her breath stopped. She glowed. Then she went completely limp, as if she'd just let go of an age-old resistance.

'That's why we need to make a request for permission to research,' the clerk explained, failing to see how he had just become superfluous.

The film shook. Tatiana opened her mouth but did not say a word. I looked at the cream-white edges of her teeth, at the spittle glistening in her mouth. I'd only have to have put my hand on her cheek and pull her head towards mine, that's how easy it would be to kiss her.

'Oh come on, then, give me your goddamn form.'

The clerk pranced in place, shaking his head.

'Didn't you hear what the woman just said?' I asked. 'Leave her alone. With or without the form.'

She placed the film back in the drawer and stumbled into the hall to the archive. Martinelli, I read on the order form. Tatiana Martinelli, I repeated to myself and stuck the piece of paper in my jacket pocket. Moving to follow her, the clerk stepped in my way.

'Excuse me, but you require special authorization to enter the archive. You have to fill out a request form. Processing it, however, will take a few days.'

'Leave me alone with your form!' I said angrily, tried to push past him, but he held me back. I returned to my seat and looked out at the palms. I waited and lost myself in a warm, justifiable fury. Tatiana stayed in the archive. The clerk came back and laid his form, which I refused to touch, on the table. What was he up to? I looked towards the hall where Tatiana had disappeared and listened to the photocopier's hum, the mummies clearing their throats and the various cracklings and scrapings grow softer over time. The clerk came back to me.

'You really are obsessed with your forms,' I hissed. 'But you know what? I'm not going to fill it out. I'm simply not going to fill it out!'

'I just wanted to inform you that the library is closing.'

I looked around. The room had emptied, only a lanky little man was twisting himself into a jacket arm.

'But there are still people in the archive,' I said.

'No, there's no one left.'

'But Tatiana's still there!'

'There's no one left. If you would please leave now, we're closing.'

Confused, I grabbed my jacket and tumbled towards the exit.

X. FIELD BEDS   Gramsci's skin is as pale as ash, his teeth are loose, his stomach revolts against everything they offer him. His convalescence, which had been going so well in Silver Wood, has come to a halt, Reverend has to admit. After a short-lived improvement—how hopeful they were!—it has now gone in the other direction. The doctor demands Gramsci's diet be checked again, a nurse hurries through the halls in order to rap the female cooks' fingers but when she comes back it is clear that, as far as Silver Wood's kitchen is concerned, no mistakes have been made. According to the current state of science, it should be going better; if anything, however, science is just another bourgeois relic and those who trust in it are fools.

Gramsci complains of memory loss. He has barely finished reading about the fall of Milan when he has to start over. Milan falls again. Gramsci's tics have become so strong that new entries to Silver Wood take off in fright. For the last few days, he has been suffering panic attacks in the middle of the day. In Italy, the black shirts are marching on Rome, fifty thousand men have come to topple the government and make their vision of a dictatorial one-party state a reality, they are camping out on overflowing fields. Mussolini travels with the night train from Milan and is named prime minister by the king.

Eugenia had said it so casually, as if she were telling him that Reverend would show up an hour later the next day: if Giulia is in Moscow on the weekend, and she most likely will be, she'll come for a visit. Sunday. If she's in Moscow. But who said she was coming to Moscow? There are so many reasons to postpone a trip. On every street corner the Revolution continues to crumble and has to be secured by faithful comrades.

Gramsci is lying in bed, exhausted, looking out the window onto the pale green paths disappearing into the distance. An old couple, chronic gastritis sufferers, walk by arm-in-arm. Earlier he'd been talking with Eugenia about Trotsky, about how heavy the palm fronds in the Villa Torlonia will be when summer pulls at the trees with all its weight, but now Rome has disappeared and Trotsky is gone. It's Monday already. He waits for the knock at his door. Listens to the silence. Perhaps she did not come after all, perhaps she wasn't interested in going to Moscow on the weekend. But he knows that if he leaves his room, that's the very moment she'll knock. If he goes for even a thirty-minute walk through the park, they'll miss each other. And so he doesn't risk it. When the knock finally comes, it is only Reverend.

Gramsci doesn't dare go to bed at night, sleep evades him for a long time, and, when at some point it does arrive, only a thin, twilit dream envelops him, one in which all the day's anxieties repeat themselves. He should concentrate on his dietary mealtimes, make them the temporary centre of his life, Reverend orders him. 'And less reading of the newspaper!'

'Didn't I tell them?' Gramsci whispers to the retinue from his sickbed. 'Didn't I always tell the comrades that the fascists were no normal bourgeois party? That the tyrant did not have one face and three names—Turati, Don Sturzo, Mussolini—but one name only, Mussolini, and, in any event, two godfathers?'

'Could be,' Reverend says calmly, 'but here and now we're concerned with recuperating and not the goings-on of the Comintern's session hall. You concentrate on your mealtimes, Comrade Gramsci.'

He wants to reply but Reverend declares the visit over.

'Mealtimes, Comrade, mealtimes.'

Should they go through the letters the patient receives from Italy and withhold the worst ones? the head physician asks his assistant in a whisper.

'That would be like attempting to constrain the Revolution of the Proletariat just because of a few idiots!'

'Most of the time there are a great number of idiots. That aside, I would indeed be happy if our Revolution spared us from them,' he replies and directs his team out. Gramsci hears the entourage tramp down the hall, chitchat and chirping out in the corridor, a door opening, then quiet. He moves over to the small table they've allowed him to work.

'Did you come to Moscow on Sunday, as you had announced?' he writes. 'You weren't in Moscow at all, no? Otherwise, you certainly would have visited me, at least for a moment. Will you be coming soon? Will I see you again?'

He quickly folds the piece of paper. Quickly, before he reconsiders. Folds it a second time before he begins to feel ashamed of his, what? *Lack of discipline.* It must be a lack of discipline, for it is something with which he is unfamiliar. Of course Giulia won't answer him, how could he believe otherwise? There's no reason for her to, and even if she wanted to, he'd just be a curious insect she'd paste into her revolutionary herbarium and label with an informative note. You study beetles, you don't touch them. You deal with beetles carefully.

He sticks the letter into an envelope, but knows it could always not arrive. The Revolution hasn't made the post any more reliable. In fact, somewhere between here and Ivanovo, the letter could easily fall prey to the whims of a postman suddenly asking himself what this all had to do with him: this country, this time, this recently ended war. Russia was big enough to get by without him—a postman in a suburb of Moscow—and he lets the mail pouch fall into a ditch at the side of the road, right where four years ago he saw a young boy fall, his forehead burst open, as stone-cold dead as those love letters now lying there that will never arrive anywhere and thanks to which perhaps some relationships will come to an end, but the postman doesn't care any more, he walks away, and who could blame him?

That's how it will go, Gramsci thinks as he seals the envelope. Who really believed in a quickly concluded revolution? The Revolution is continual, and the disorder and chaos in people's heads will remain a constant too. One could consider the loss of a few love letters good luck.

And then she's simply out in front of his door. Gramsci is bent over his daily correspondence. A statement to Zinoviev, a letter from Bordiga, reports about the situation in Rome: comrades are being hauled out of their offices and assaulted in the middle of the street. The knocking continues and he only raises his head belatedly, neither yells *Come in!* or makes his arduous way across the room to open up himself. The door opens. And there she is. And he's here. Trapped.

To leave the room he'd have to squeeze past her. *Just stay calm.* He can feel that he's about to start trembling, something will twitch, his face, his hand, he tries at least to quiet his mind, he thinks about Sorel's historical bloc which he imagines to be like the connection between skin and bone, but even if one doesn't fall in love with a woman because of the shape of her skeleton, it still contributes to the harmony of her appearance. The way her skin is draped over it. To sexual excitement.

He stares at her and doesn't even know if she's received his letter. And if she has read it, what she thinks about it. Whether she's comfortable with him writing, perhaps she just wants to tell him that he can refrain from doing so. Then she should say so, so that it's out, this leaden moment finally done and over with.

Although he hasn't invited her in, she walks across the room as if it were normal. Not a word about the letter. Her soft gait. At the same time she doesn't have any reason to be in his room; she walks here, then there. Gramsci is beside himself, he wants to throw her out. *What are you thinking, Comrade, don't you have anything better to do than keep the executive committee from working?*

And then she finally sits on a stool which is right up against the window—and how much closer he is now to her legs, her thighs—then gets back up, stays standing close to him.

'They've raided the newspapers,' he says flatly.

'What newspapers? What are you talking about?'

'In Italy. The democratic newspapers. Mussolini's *squadristi* have barged into the editorial offices and smashed everything to bits. And they are beginning to detain communists. They have nothing on our comrades, but they are arresting them and dragging them off the streets.'

'They won't manage to do that.'

'The fascists are going to win. In Italy, they're going to win,' Gramsci says.

'Don't speak like that.'

'But I'm just telling you how it is.'

'Then it'd be better you not speak at all.'

Her hand seems to brush his shoulder in passing, but what does 'in passing' mean at moments like these? The tiniest gesture can hurl the whole story in another direction. Prudence. He cannot handle it here any more. He jumps up too quickly; Giulia observes him in astonishment.

'We're going for a walk.'

'If you say so, Comrade.'

And she trails behind him at an appropriate distance.

Outside, they can already smell the coming fog. Every day is cooler now, autumn is approaching, soon the dried leaves will be rattling in the treetops, will turn brown and fall.

'You wrote me,' Giulia remarks in her withdrawn voice.

'I did not mean to inconvenience you.'

'It made me happy.'

'I did not mean to inconvenience you,' Gramsci repeats.

'You are odd,' Giulia says and laughs. 'But look at the birches. You can never be sure if the leaves are green or white, a quick gust and everything changes, that's what I like so much.'

'Your sister cannot stand birch trees.'

'And you believe her? My sister is not afraid of the white birch, but the brigades of the White Army. Haven't you noticed?'

Gramsci tears off a branch, extends it to Giulia—a timid attempt to tease her perhaps? She waggles a finger at him, 'Please, now is not the time.'

'Do you always listen to what your sister has to say?'

'How so? What did I do?'

'You turned towards her whenever you spoke. As if she had to nod her head in approval.'

'You just imagined that.'

'I simply observed you closely.'

'No, it's just that . . . Sometimes I simply don't understand what's happening around us any longer. Here . . . in Europe . . . naturally, the Revolution will be victorious, but then again . . .'

'You should not confuse historical development with a law of nature,' Gramsci responds with a laugh.

'But isn't it so? Isn't this crisis inevitable?'

'I do not believe in the inevitable,' he replies, 'and I don't want to. It would mean that we are superfluous.'

'Do you believe that women should wage war?'

'Do you believe that any one should wage war? Or would you rather be on the side of the pacifists?'

'There aren't any pacifists any more. The pacifists had the wrong opinion in this country, and that will not be tolerated.'

Giulia takes the branch out of Gramsci's hand. 'Eugenia doesn't talk about the Civil War. But the two bearded men upstairs on the second floor, they talk about the White Army dead and those nights when every sound can mean an attack. If I really think about it,' Giulia says, tilting back her head, 'my sister's right. The white trunks are horrific, and the green leaves turning over every second too, suddenly white, the whole fickle populace, and in the end they'll stab us in the back as well.'

'Indeed, we have to win the minds of the people. If you simply tell them how to live, they'll turn against us.'

A root which neither of them see causes Giulia to stumble, Gramsci rushes forward, grabs her arm, their first vigorous, if unplanned, contact—but who wants planned contact? It has to be sudden, and this contact would have been even more vigorous had Giulia not quickly regained her balance. They look at each other bemusedly, Gramsci's hand still on her forearm. They are standing close to each other, a silence has come between them and it's growing longer and more embarrassing and more urgent. How do you get out of this? Under normal circumstances by now—but everything speaks against normal circumstances: the place, the time, those involved, so enough with those normal circumstances which would potentially lead to a kiss introduced by a casual movement, but then all of a sudden, with hidden determination, their lips meet.

Just don't lose control! This is Comrade Antonio Gramsci, a man in a weak state, in body as well as mind. And next to him stands Giulia Schucht, no less fragile. In order to recover from this shock, they have to calm down in an arbour, in that dubious corner of the premises where the bushes smell like musty fruit because that is where the gardener dumps whatever is inedible. Giulia sits far enough from Gramsci so that, if someone comes by, they can move further away from each other. They make their way back to Tolstoy, to Lenin and the necessary united front, they have to team up with the socialists in order to make headway against the fascists, anything else would be an illusion, and Giulia speaks about the festering and bubbling in Italy, about King Vittorio Emmanuele III and how he's had himself photographed next to the socialists. 'Have you seen the photos?'

Giulia glows when she speaks; for him, it's as if it's the first time anyone has spoken to him, not only with him, and he knows that he must be careful even if he no longer wants to be careful. The stomachs of people who have long been hungry grow smaller and then engulfed by the superfluous acids. When they wolf down anything they can get their hands on, it is easy for the stomach wall to tear, and then, right as the first feeling of being full has set in, they begin to bleed. Their last feeling will still be hunger.

The two say goodbye to each other in the corridor, in the dark, at this hour the lights have been turned off. Behind one of the doors Patient Genovyev is snoring, a short while ago he shaved off his moustache but that did not help against his saw-like sleep. Giulia's fingers are cold as she gives Gramsci her hand in farewell. Her chin briefly at his cheek. Then her tripping along through Genovyev's sleep.

Gramsci's bed: 90 x 180 centimetres. Sheet cold as a washcloth. He thinks about how, back in her room, Giulia must be undoing the lacing of her skirt, thinks about her loosening the last loop of the labyrinth of lace and simply sliding down her sleeve, how she lets her shoulder free, the obscure movement below her collarbone.

Gramsci hears a dripping sound from one of the corners of his room; perhaps it's the little heating stove. He begins to get undressed, lays his jacket over the stool, undoes his shirt collar and lays it on top. Somehow one will get to sleep. Will get up tomorrow. Alone. The dripping grows louder, it's no longer coming from the heater in the corner where all of a sudden it's eerily still but from the hall. His first thought is to go over to the stove and check if everything is fine. He opens the door instead.

A strip of light is falling across Giulia's throat, she is standing in the hall before his door, her face in shadow; for anyone but Gramsci she'd be unrecognizable.

'They've put in field beds,' she says.

'Field beds,' Gramsci repeats and holds his unbuttoned shirt together. Beneath his hand he can feel the mound of his chest, the hill of gristle.

'Three of them and they're already asleep,' Giulia says. 'On my bed too. I cannot wake them, it's much too late.'

Down below, near his navel, the fabric is wide open.

Giulia looks past him, casts a glance at his bed and then quickly lowers her eyes. Ninety centimetres for two, movement impossible, sleep precluded and just don't think about touch. What if he has another one of his fits? How easy it was to talk with him about Tolstoy and syndicalism. And now—she has already taken a step into his room.

'I don't have a second blanket,' it occurs to him.

'It's too warm for me as it is,' she replies, but of course she's lying, of course he'll have to give her the blanket. She comes even closer. That's her skin, that's her smell, that's her hair, cool to the touch like the bark of a sycamore tree. She makes him feel shy, standing here in front of him as she is, in the middle of the night.

'You can't even keep your bed free?' he asks. He only wants her to go. He has no idea what to do with her. He has no idea how he is supposed to act.

'I did . . .' she says and stops, doesn't move, stares at the floor. If only it was Terracini in front of him. Gramsci has to go to sleep or in the morning he'll be tired when he sits down at his desk, he'll be shaky and unfocused, a foggy monster. That he cannot allow, he cannot allow any of this.

'Let's go and lie down,' she says quietly.

'This is ludicrous!' he cries, his final attempt to chase her out. To once more have the upper hand in the empty room. 'You're just a spoilt little daughter of the bourgeoisie.' Now he is growing loud, his neighbours no doubt awake. 'Oh, the poor elite that can't do without a single night's sleep.'

'Let's just go and lie down,' she repeats.

They do not get undressed in front of each other, they just slip off their shoes, and even to do that they turn away from one another. Ninety centimetres, austerely divided in two. Which yields less than 40 centimetres, for neither of them dares to take the centre. For six hours, their breathing is shallow and flat.

XI. ORANGES She was standing under the awning of the grocery store, a cigarette between her fingers, her lips slightly pointed, thin streams of smoke slipping from her mouth. She had a pack of Gauloises reds, which puzzled me, for all the smokers I knew obsessively stayed faithful to one brand. She didn't seem picky, and if she was, then her choice clearly depended on her mood. I didn't know if that made me sceptical or if it excited me or if it didn't matter at all. In the end, cigarettes taste of smoke. I observed her delicate, somewhat too small thumbs brush the filter. A birthmark, as big as the head of a pin, spotted the back of her hand. She didn't look over towards me, but had to have felt my proximity. A bus went past. She moved to toss her cigarette onto the pavement, paused and then took one last drag. The bus closed its doors.

How soft her face was, exhausted and soft, I'd only need to stretch out my hand and in a single movement I'd pull her to me. Behind her a mountain of oranges smouldered in the sun, plump, almost ruddy little balls that if just one were stolen would all spill out across the pavement. Here in the sun the severity that had echoed in her gait as she hurried out of the library had disappeared. Then she turned towards the oranges and observed them with an almost tender curiosity.

'Excuse me, but you missed something.' I was standing so close to her that had she felt me, she would have jerked. But she just slowly looked up and raised her eyebrows.

'If I miss something, then it's unimportant to me.'

I smiled, composedly boyish. Five seconds to allow it to work. Ten and it would be transparent.

'We met over there,' I said and pointed towards the cafeteria.

'I didn't meet anyone.'

'It's my fault you ran off so quickly.'

'Your fault? Who do you think you are?' She flicked her cigarette away and picked up an orange, weighed it in her hand, put it back on the slope of the mountain.

'Who do you think I am?' I took another step closer, felt the vibration in her skin, soft, like a trembling of water when the waves cannot yet be seen.

'Do you have anything like a sense of shame? If you do, I'd like to ask you to use it. You're standing on my foot.'

I liked her rebelliousness. It flared once again, fiercely, and I knew what such fierceness could feel like if it found the right channels.

'Let's go have a coffee,' I suggested.

'Absolutely not.' She pulled out her pack of cigarettes again, she was clearly nervous, whereby we were on the right path.

'Think about it.'

'Thanks, I already have.'

I pulled a piece of paper out of my jacket pocket and wrote down Brevi's number. 'Once you've thought about it, give me a call, Tatiana. Any time.'

'Why are you calling me Tatiana?'

'I think that's your name.'

'Don't think too much. You don't know a thing about me.' She stamped out her half-finished cigarette, turned away from me without taking the piece of paper and took off down the street, a barely noticeable swing to her hips. A bus stopped next to me, the doors opened. I grabbed an orange off the mountain and sprang inside, settling between a number of old people dressed in black and beating the air with plastic fans and tourists smelling on onions. Standing at the light, Tatiana briefly looked up as the bus rattled past.

Naturally, she wouldn't forget me. Even those women who tried to avoid me sooner or later came running after me, they had no choice, and, had they been able to accept that, things would've gone better for them, you can't feel guilty about the inevitable. A lot of the women I've met made their lives unnecessarily difficult, there was nothing they could do about it, or, rather, there was nothing they could do to organize themselves against it. I simply attracted women, the pretty and less pretty, those I sought out and those I would've preferred to have avoided. Hedda never understood that, or didn't want to understand. She thought you could just brush them off, like dust off a coat.

'At the very least, you could pull yourself together in front of Lasse,' Hedda said to me later that evening after Lasse's birthday party. I was at the kitchen counter, exhausted, the noise from the children's party still in my head, the last guest, packed into their parent's arms, had disappeared fifteen minutes before and I just wanted some peace and quiet, a glass of wine and to forget the boisterous voices.

'Do you even know what kind of reputation you have in the elephant group?' she asked.

'Elephant group! I had no idea I was a member of an elephant group.'

'Haven't you noticed how everything goes silent when you come into the cloakroom?'

Of course I'd noticed. I'd stand in front of the twenty-two animal motifs, below them the coat hooks, the little jackets, the children's hustle and bustle, make my way through the room and grab Lasse's jacket off a chubby-faced male mouse. The mothers would watch every one of my movements; the fathers would roughly pack their children into their parkas.

'Elephant group!' I called out once more.

'It's a kindergarten, Anton. How else do you want them to name their groups? The post-revolutionary syndicate?'

'I'd prefer it. I don't constantly want to dumb myself down to the level of six-year-olds.'

'But you should. Don't you see how, in the end, everything comes back to Lasse? Robert's parents no longer take Lasse with them and Caroline is uncomfortable with the way you constantly size her up.'

'Uncomfortable? Maybe she's just jealous of you.'

'Jealous, of course.' Hedda laughed drily. 'And who else? Do you think I haven't noticed how early you've been heading off for kindergarten recently?'

Hedda always delivered her accusations at exactly the right time, right when I was too exhausted to defend myself and would just shrug my shoulders, something she naturally took for an admission. At that moment I was completely worn out by the whole Robert-Maria-Esther-Hannes-Wiebke-noise. Maria had tripped, Hannes had begged for more cake, Esther had wanted to go home and didn't trust us Stövers an inch. Naturally, Hedda again overlooked my presence in the children's room. It was only in the late afternoon when I helped Wiebke's mother out of her coat a tad too warmly that I became visible again, and now she scented a dirty story in its arms.

'Hedda, nothing's going on there, and even if there was, you don't have to lecture me any more.'

'I'm not lecturing you about anything. Just please, not in our flat too!'

'This isn't our flat any more, it's only a substitute.'

'But we're living here.'

'If you call this living.'

'Don't talk like that in front of Lasse.'

He was standing in the door, slamming two newly received Matchbox cars (which, he thought, were also speaking with him) into each other. Her property entirely, Hedda ran a hand through his hair and took the cars out of his hand. He protested, looked anxiously back and forth at the two of us. She knelt down, kissed him on the forehead and gently led him out of the kitchen. Her lightly swaying gait once Lasse was out of out of reach. She opened the refrigerator, grabbed the Sauvignon and poured herself a glass. Coming back to the counter, I winked at her, at that point I wanted a peaceable end, we were both spent. Over the last few months, Hedda had grown sharper, I didn't hold it against her, those who are in love are unfair, but Hedda liked to hurt with gusto, as if she had no other plans in her life any longer.

'Some day you're going to be ridiculous too,' she said.

'Of course, Hedda, whatever you want.'

Hedda raised her glass as if she wanted to throw it at me. Then she put it to her lips, took a long drink and placed it back on the counter. She'd been drinking a lot recently, I'd told her so one morning when she spent too long in front of the mirror. 'Hedda, don't kid yourself, it's just like you see it, and you know what's going on.'

'I haven't wanted anything for a long time. But I have a son, and at some point I understood what responsibility is. Otherwise, the two of us would've been long gone by now.'

I let myself sink onto the barstool, played with the crumbs on the colourful paper plate and exchanged deep looks with the face of the clown who, even after all that cake, had not lost his wild grin.

'You'll soon be rid of me. When I'm in Rome,' I said.

'Why Rome?'

'A research project.'

'And? I'm just learning about it now?'

'I thought I'd alluded to it.'

'Alluded?'

'I've got to go to Rome, Hedda, there's nothing to discuss.'

'You've got to?' Hedda asked in her haughty way as if I usually spent my time doing nothing.

'Rome,' I repeated, 'for quite a bit this time.'

'Is this an exodus?'

I shook my head.

'How long?' Hedda asked.

'Four weeks,' I said. 'To begin with.'

'To begin with?' She took the paper plate from beneath my fingers and let the lid of the trash can bang open. 'Why not four years right off the bat?'

'Is that what you'd prefer?'

'There are a few things that I'd prefer, but that's no longer an issue between us.'

Another drink from the glass, once again too deep.

'At least think of sending Lasse a card,' she said. 'But don't even think of showing up for the first day of school. For once I'd like to celebrate with my son in peace.'

She grew fierce again. She was no longer in control. The worst thing about someone you have a child with is that you have to deal with them your whole life, and I really didn't like seeing Hedda growing helpless and absurd. But I was just too far away from her to give her support. I looked at her, her perfectly made-up mouth, her too-expensive dress billowing out around the low-cut neckline. I neither liked nor disliked the way the black fabric framed her bright skin. I was uncomfortably indifferent. There was nothing left between us. What was there supposed to be? The moment for me to be sad was long past. The beautiful moments too.

XII. WORLD REVOLUTION At the Hotel Lux in Moscow, in the winter of 1922, there is a moody night watchman, water damage and room for the most important communists in the world. On 4 November, the IV World Congress of the Communist International will be opened by a speech from the absent Vladimir Ilich Lenin. The Soviet power is celebrating the first five years of its existence, the supreme comrade explains to the IV World Congress of the Comintern, the Petrograd Soviet of Workers' and Soldiers' Deputies. It is more stable than ever. The Civil War is over. The first economic successes have been recorded. It is the greatest honour for Soviet Russia to help the workers of the world in their fight to overthrow capitalism. Victory will be ours.

Long live the Communist International!

Gramsci beats his hands together mechanically, they feel numb, he looks around the room and is surprised to find that he is still functioning in the row together with all the others clapping and glowing. The red of the flag pulses before his eyes, Terracini is trying to whisper something but he can't hear it. The next comrade in a rotten suit steps up, unbuttons his jacket. Giulia's laughter. She is a hundred kilometres away, *I'd like to write you thousands of things, Giulia, but it's not possible, a few of them you can possibly divine.*

But no! Giulia isn't missing a thing here. Gramsci tries to concentrate on the speech, his comrade up on the podium is like a marionette, his sentences swish arduously and unclearly out over the hall. 'Everything is there and possible,' the speaker, 'we only have to grab it, form it, we cannot allow ourselves to become weak in that very moment in which a new reality, a new world, is being born.' He swings his hand in order to draw an image of a world in the air for his listeners.

Giulia's face. Gramsci cannot remember it exactly, has even forgotten some of the most important features: the transition of the bridge of her nose, the height of her forehead, her proportions when he looks at her close up, how her profile appears to everyone else.

What he remembers: how big her eyes are when she wants to convince him of something and how she draws the lids tight when she's trying to find a way to express herself. The height of her forehead, a hand's width, when he checks to see if she has a fever or not, and the curve of his fingers when he runs his hand through her hair. He could gaze at her forehead for an entire afternoon. The slight wrinkles, not yet buried deep in the skin but above it, like soft caresses. The inlets of her temples. The muscles playing beneath. He knows the colour of her tongue and the form of her lips when she speaks, and as long as she speaks—and later too, much much later—her voice ignites a fragile euphoria in him.

He must lean against someone and that happens to be Umberto Terracini who does not understand what's wrong with the man he has known for so long! Terrifyingly independent, a sharp thinker, amusing, charming and bound to nothing and no one, that was Gramsci. But just what in the world was this little heap next to him now, sunk against his shoulder?

Later, at dinner, Gramsci seems tired, ill and worried about what's happening in Italy. Following the march on Rome, Mussolini was arranging his empire. Communists were being assaulted, taken away, arrested, beaten to death. The Revolution that was right there did indeed come. Just from the wrong side.

'We have to get back with the socialists, alone against the fascists we are too weak,' he says to Grigory Zinoviev who nods and sticks a dripping *pelmini* into his mouth.

'Explain that to Amadeo. For him the socialists are no better than the fascists.'

'If we believe that socio-fascism is our enemy, then we are blind to that which will really kill us. We must fight against fascism. Against pure fascism. Against Mussolini's troops. Why can't you all understand that?'

'We're living on a volcano,' he explains to Terracini who is fanning himself with a napkin.

'The socialists are breaking our backs,' he counters.

'The socialists, at most, are hurting our pride.'

'Revolution in Hungary, Estonia, Ukraine. In Germany, Italy, France and England, do you all still believe that?' he asks Amadeo Bordiga. 'The World Revolution will not advance all that quickly from here. That's nothing more than a head game birthed in the halls of the Comintern, in the rooms of the Hotel Lux, over the map lying next to Lenin's sickbed.'

'If we buckle, then it won't succeed,' Amadeo replies. 'No, it won't. But if we remain steadfast, Antonio, the state will hollow out the fascists, just you wait, the Revolution will be inescapable. And you want to deal with the socialists now? Bravo, dear friend, then you are prohibiting everything yourself.'

'You're still trying to compare Italy with Russia. Give it a rest. Here all it took was taking over the switchboards of the state. Russia was a dying, feudalistic empire. Freeing a country from tsarism is completely different from toppling a bourgeois society. The bourgeoisie doesn't control the instruments of power but thinking itself. That's the difference, Bordiga, accept it. Even if we had the communists in the Quirinal, they still wouldn't have won over the people, not by a long shot. They'll continue to play cards on monstrously large oak tables, curse the heat in August and not change a thing about the domination of the bourgeoisie— which, outside the ministerial bureaus, continues to exist in people's heads—while sealing deals with Mussolini and celebrating the Assumption on *Ferragosto* at their summer homes. At this moment, we cannot fight for the dictatorship of the working class,' Gramsci says, 'we have to do it for democracy.'

'The socialists, Antonio, are in the same boat as the bourgeoisie,' Bordiga counters. 'If there's anything red about them, it's their lifejackets. That's how cowardly they are. At the first hint of high waves, they'll negotiate with anyone offering them a safe ship. With them, you're just inviting the enemy into your own home.' And with that Bordiga slips off to get some fresh air.

Comrade Rákosi, an idiot without an ounce of political understanding, sidles up to them. Gramsci should become chair of the PCI, he explains, laughing behind an outstretched hand, he should depose Bordiga. In any event, people wanted Bordiga out of the Comintern, he talks Gramsci into believing.

'What rubbish, and dangerous on top of it! Bordiga will step down and trigger a crisis within the Party. And what will *Avanti!* do? It'll whip up any and every difference of opinion and the Party will split apart once and for all.'

On 13 November, Vladimir Ilyich Lenin approaches the podium of the IV Congress of the Comintern. His appearance is greeted by thunderous applause, the comrades stand up and sing the Internationale. *This is the final struggle / Let us group together.* Lenin himself hears but little, he doesn't look good and will not live to see any more struggles. His face is pale, his skin like paper, he looks as if he wanted to lend the decay of the class system and reactionary, petty bourgeois corruption a physical manifestation. Not disgust, but weakness; not shame, but frailty.

He is to speak about perspectives of the world revolution, but the topic is too broad, too large to tackle in one speech, the highest comrade decides and talks instead about the mistakes of the last few years, of the hasty outlines of the new economic policy that were to be the darkest hours for Soviet Russia and that almost meant the end of the victory of the revolutionaries. The workers were unhappy, the peasants rebelled, the famine remained. A crisis that almost destroyed the newly created organism. Our enemies will use these weaknesses and shatter and smash the masses, those who had simply hoped for a better tomorrow. Now barricades must be erected for the economy. State capitalism is a small, necessary place of retreat on the path to socialism.

'I think we can say that Russian roubles are famous,' Lenin explains, 'if only for the reason that their number now in circulation exceeds a quadrillion.' Laughter in the hall. 'That is something! It is an astronomical figure. I am sure that not everyone here knows what this figure signifies.' Laughter. 'But we do not think that the figure is so very important even from the point of view of economic science, for the noughts can always be crossed out.' Laughter.

But that's not only something to laugh about, Gramsci thinks, and once again feels the cold in his head. Why wasn't there anyone here to rub a hand across his back, to support him?

'That is why I think,' the head comrade explains, 'that the outlook for the world revolution—a subject which I must touch on briefly—is favourable. And given a certain definite condition, I think it will be even better.'

We cannot allow ourselves to believe in a kind of determinism, Gramsci thinks. When we cannot negotiate with history, we will become apathetic slaves.

'The most important thing in the period we are now entering is to study,' Lenin says. 'We are studying in the general sense. They, however, must study in the special sense, in order that they may really understand the organization, structure, method and content of revolutionary work. If they do that, I am sure the prospects of the world revolution will be not only good but excellent.'

Deafening applause.

That night, Gramsci lies awake in bed. Lenin's words echo through the darkness. The outlook for the world revolution. Not only good. But excellent. Excellent. Excellent. He sees Lenin's elongated chin, Chicherin's big, round, Chechen eyes, Eugenia with a flagstaff affixed to her shoulder, a red flag fluttering, then a shot, smelling like blood and rust, comes out of the rod and melts. 'The organization!' Lenin cries. 'Construction!' 'Method!' His fist hisses through the air. A small, red bullet bounces over the wall, hits the earth and splits apart like a raw egg. Letters flow out and spread across the ground.

Sleep, Gramsci thinks. *Please let me sleep.* He is emotionally exhausted, thoughts continue to rush through his head, and then this emptiness, this continual loss of memory. The six months in Silver Wood have not helped him to get well, all of Reverend's pieces of advice have simply kept him from getting worse. And now he is lying here and cannot find a way to fall asleep, a building without any doors or windows. So much fatigue in his eyes, behind his forehead, so much wakefulness around him. So many thoughts. The same thoughts over and over again. Cold at his back. The mattress doesn't feel right, too soft and too hard at the same time. He tosses and turns. Outside, exuberant strangers are jeering. Young people. People in love. People swaying hand-in-hand across Moscow's cobblestones. Soldiers who just a few months before had crudely raped emaciated farm girls but now held dignified ones in their arms, carefully helping the latter up the stairs into bourgeois homes where all signs of former rule have been torn down: wallpaper, curtains, bookshelves.

Gramsci feels the emptiness in his back. There is nothing there. There is no one to lay their arms across his shoulders, run their fingers along his coracoid, and since learning it could be different, he cannot handle it. Perhaps it was only a moment, long gone, but he will not be able to fall asleep if no one is there and no one comes and lies down next to him and all the noise is pushing through the glass, the jeering of the love-struck soldiers, the war is over, the war was victorious, the war had destroyed their lives, and twists and turns in Gramsci's head.

GiuliaGiuliaGiuliaGiuliaGiuliaGiuliaGiuliaGiuliaGiuliaGiulia
GiuliaGiuliaGiuliaGiuliaGiuliaGiuliaGiuliaGiuliaGiuliaGiuliaGiul
iaGiuliaGiuliaGiuliaGiuliaGiuliaGiuliaGiuliaGiuliaGiuliaGiuliaGi
uliaGiuliaGiuliaGiuliaGiuliaGiuliaGiuliaGiuliaGiuliaGiuliaGiulia
GiuliaGiuliaGiuliaGiuliaGiuliaGiuliaGiuliaGiuliaGiuliaGiuliaGiul
iaGiuliaGiuliaGiuliaGiuliaGiuliaGiuliaGiuliaGiuliaGiuliaGiuliaGi
uliaGiuliaGiuliaGiuliaGiuliaGiuliaGiuliaGiuliaGiuliaGiuliaGiulia
GiuliaGiuliaGiuliaGiuliaGiuliaGiuliaGiuliaGiuliaGiuliaGiuliaGiul
iaGiuliaGiuliaGiuliaGiuliaGiuliaGiuliaGiuliaGiuliaGiuliaGiuliaGi
uliaGiuliaGiuliaGiuliaGiuliaGiuliaGiuliaGiuliaGiuliaGiuliaGiulia
GiuliaGiuliaGiuliaGiuliaGiuliaGiuliaGiuliaGiuliaGiuliaGiuliaGiul
iaGiuliaGiuliaGiuliGiuliaGiuliaGiuliaGiuliaGiuliaGiuliaGiulia
GiuliaGiuliaGiuliaGiuliaGiuliaGiuliaGiuliaGiuliaGiuliaGiuliaGiul
iaGiuliaGiuliaGiuliaGiuliaGiuliaGiuliaGiuliaGiuliaGiuliaGiuliaGi
uliaGiuliaGiuliaGiuliaGiuliaGiuliaGiuliaGiuliaGiuliaGiuliaGiulia
GiuliaGiuliaGiuliaGiuliaGiuliaGiuliaGiuliaGiuliaGiuliaGiuliaGiul
iaGiuliaGiuliaGiuliaGiuliaGiuliaGiuliaGiuliaGiuliaGiuliaGiuliaGi
uliaGiuliaGiuliaGiuliaGiuliaGiuliaGiuliaGiuliaGiuliaGiuliaGiulia
GiuliaGiuliaGiuliaGiuliaGiuliaGiuliaGiuliaGiuliaGiuliaGiuliaGiul
iaGiuliaGiuliaGiuliaGiuliaGiuliaGiuliaGiuliaGiuliaGiuliaGiuliaGi
uliaGiuliaGiuliaGiuliaGiuliaGiuliaGiuliaGiuliaGiuliaGiuliaGiulia
GiuliaGiuliaGiuliaGiuliaGiuliaGiuliaGiuliaGiuliaGiuliaGiuliaGiul
iaGiuliaGiuliaGiuliaGiuliaGiuliaGiuliaGiuliaGiuliaGiuliaGiuliaGi
uliaGiuliaGiuliaGiuliaGiuliaGiuliaGiuliaGiuliaGiuliaGiuliaGiulia
GiuliaGiuliaGiulia. Unbearable.

'It is simply the following, Giulia,' he writes the next morning. 'I am exhausted. The days and hours and speeches are wearing me down. I cannot think clearly. When you are away, I come apart like a rotten mushroom. If I wanted to put it coarsely: You are not good for me. A man cannot be everything in life: a happy man and a driven one. A love-struck idiot and a clever revolutionary. Can you understand that?'

He must get away from her, she isn't good for him, she isn't good for his work, and what's more important: his work or Giulia? The world or the head of a pin? The prospects for world revolution will be excellent. Study. Giulia is pushing all of that away from him. Because she has to be everything, because she cannot handle simply being a part to join up with all the others. Giulia is every-where, she is sitting between the lines he writes, she is sitting in the papers he reads and barely does he move to take hold of her, she turns away and is gone. In the end, what is he getting done between so much of Giulia, between so little of her? His thoughts had been clear, his theses brilliant, but now he is stumbling about like a three-legged dog in the bushes. It is madness, the past num-ber of weeks have completely wiped him out. He has no longer been able to think, to sleep, to push forward what should have been pushed forward. He has simply staggered between his slight happiness, his slight unhappiness. But we cannot be everything, Giulia my child. There are more important things. There is the Party, there is work. We cannot forget the world around us.

He takes a deep breath. He thinks he is taking a deep breath. That's right, he has a duty, by now this is his life. And Giulia does not fit. He looks out onto the snow-dusted street before the Hotel Lux, he thinks about Lenin's speech and his thoughts are once again as cool as winter air. Then he takes the letter and burns it over the ashtray.

XIII. BOURGEOIS LIFE   We'd only been together a couple of weeks. I was waiting for Hedda at the museum where there was an exhibition on great forgeries, and she was late. Under certain circumstances, even the slightest delay can be awful. In order to cover up my insecurity, or even my fear that she might not show, that she might fall back out of my life like a bird from a nest, I tried to concentrate on one of the panels telling me about a Neapolitan forger. Born at such and such a time in X, he accumulated, bluffed and established connections in Y, I read as in the room a swishing and rustling began to be noticeable—subtle, but noticeable—and all the men shifted their positions in front of the paintings a bit, one leant a little backwards, another forwards, not enough to see Hedda but enough to get a hint.

She sauntered casually over to me, something I was certain she'd practised for a long time. The blue-black dress made her appear thinner, just a bit, she'd always been slender but on that day more than usual. Although it was only August, an autumnal light fell through the window. Hedda stood close to me, I could feel the trembling of her hair, I reached for her hand, attempted to grab her hips but she slid away.

The guard swept past us, I thought I could recognize something lewd in his face, Hedda didn't notice, or at least acted excessively innocent. He spoke to her, told her she needed to step back from the paintings—his glance palatably sliding across her body —even though she was standing far enough. I could've elbowed him off, but it seemed too absurd. Of course, everything was a danger. As soon as you possessed something of worth, most things fell apart, situations and relationships and convictions, and that was the reason I believed so strongly in the moment. It was over before it could break. Hedda, however, was no longer a moment and I had no idea how I was supposed to handle that.

We'd only recently spent a few nights together, it was still at that wavering time when we could have left each other without causing too much pain, we're always leaving people without even noticing, perhaps we could even have been successful, perhaps the fact that we didn't stop seeing each other, that we couldn't walk away, was a fluke, and I mean that I was in control of the situation, I sucked up her caresses inside me as if I could save them for worse times, I kissed her neck, her back, her collarbone, spread her legs, pressed her hips to mine, and later in the night when her hand glided across my back I felt so protected against that monotony of bodies and words that had indifferently rolled past me that I didn't know if I'd ever make it back.

I looked round to Hedda. She wasn't standing in front of a painting or in front of the window with a view onto the ramparts but out by the corridor that led to the bathrooms, one of the ugliest parts of a museum. But what difference did that make? Seemingly in passing, she turned her head towards me, but by that time nothing was in passing any more, not for her either, and I admitted that this one here could last a little longer, that, as one says, it was serious and that a body couldn't save a single caress but became addicted.

I was thirty-five that summer—not ridiculously old to begin getting serious—and the image of a middle-class marriage had always appealed to me as much as middle-class life in general. But, as I was incapable of being serious to the degree that Hedda understood it in terms of emotional balance or peace (as she would later accuse me), I constantly had to want someone or something. Stasis frightened me. But all of that—the accusations, I mean—came years after our visit to the museum and back then, that day in the museum, everything was easy; how gladly I would have grabbed her right there where she was standing, the green sign above her head, a man and a woman standing there, those sexless characters of lines, and in contrast to that image, no, even without it, *you shone, Hedda*.

Around us were Brueghels, Rembrandts, Picassos. Stories of auction houses and private collectors who had lost their reputations as well as their minds thanks to a pair of extremely talented charlatans. Life stories so insane you could hardly believe them and yet more real than the paintings on the walls. Of course, it had to do with one's imagination, as you'd expect in a historical museum, feeling the age of the items on display, the weight of the centuries deposited upon them and which from there shone onto us. We were surrounded by a few of the most beautiful pieces in the history of art, and the fact that all of it was bogus, was only a lie, a perfect illusion, nothing at all to do with the hands of Brueghel, Rembrandt or Picasso, was what made it so exciting. Something fake shimmered through the air. We were being betrayed, and we enjoyed it.

I walked behind Hedda, pinched her side, she shrank from me laughing. In front of us was a moon. The first scientific depiction of a moon. Scarred like the skin of an orange. It'd been done by Galileo Galilei. Or by a portly middle-aged man sitting under house arrest in Arona.

'Be honest, we're fascinated by betrayal.'

'I find it distasteful,' she said.

'But what's worse: rejection or betrayal?'

'Rejection is a punch in the face,' she said. 'Betrayal is war.' She took a step away from me and observed the image of the moon from closer up. 'War in a single unity. Civil war. Your neighbour places the enemy between you and them, you feel him, but the other person denies his presence. You think you're going to go crazy, but it's the world that's gone crazy.'

I softly caressed her cheek with the back of my hand; it amused me to hear speak so earnestly.

'Why do you take it all so personally?' I whispered.

'I'd like to leave now, Anton, I can't take this air-conditioning any longer.'

On the street she said goodbye, I knew that we'd see each other again in two days but it was as if she were abandoning me for ever.

'A family dinner, Anton, just a family dinner.'

I laughed, more out of fright than embarrassment. I hadn't thought that I could feel jealousy. Hedda walked upright, her bag tossed over a shoulder, and I felt uneasy. Something was hoisting me up over the edge of my life and letting me have a look down. I didn't recognize a thing. Only a massively gentle chaos.

Up until meeting Hedda that summer, I'd been certain I'd get married soon. Thirty-five was an age that, when I was younger, I would've long imagined myself to have been married by, in a middle-class life with a wife, a secure income, a house at the edge of town, one to two kids, two to three affairs. I'd always wanted an ordered life, that suited me, and Hedda was a good choice, I was in love, she was attached to me. Naturally, she wasn't too bourgeois, she stubbornly held on to her leftist ideas but that would all settle down in a few years. Who in their early thirties would still want to hitchhike to the Rosa Luxemburg days? But that's not why I hesitated, why every now and then I thought I had to walk away from her, even though I already knew I wouldn't be able to.

I wasn't in control of what was going on with me, or, rather, with Hedda and me, any more. Even for a few days I could barely do without her. When I was at home alone, the walls closed in around me cold and hard, I did things simply to make an impression on Hedda; and without her, nothing had any meaning. When

I had trouble finding an answer, I began to ask her questions in my mind, and that should've told me that, pretty soon, I wouldn't be able to get by without her, and that that would continue, not for weeks or months but for longer than I would be able to ignore, and how often had I felt overwhelmed by all the moments with her, *but what is a moment, Hedda, when you have your whole life ahead of you?* As I walked past the old police station—a grey, worn-out thing my parents had drilled into me as the epitome of state repression—two sentences hammered through my head: Let it go. This one's too big for you.

IV. CHANGE OF SEASON 'That of all people *he* turns out to be a Casanova. One-fifty is nothing I'd recommend!'

In the nurses' room, they are letting their tea cool in the small, calcified cups, ordering aprons and caps and desperately chirping among one another in the hopes of finding some kind of explanation.

'The invalids, I'm telling you, the invalids,' one warbles.

'Well, two of them have found each other,' another one adds.

'But who did he find? Eugenia or her sister?'

'No, no, she's too attractive for him, that won't turn into anything.'

'But isn't he back in Eugenia's room again?'

'What's he got to tell her? Nothing goes on here. Not a thing.'

'He's in her room but guess who he came with.'

'You can't be serious!'

'Indeed, indeed.'

'Something fishy's going on! The Party's behind it,' one of them says, spilling cold tea in fear. The others look at her and her chubby cheeks grow red, a red the hollow faces of the patients could never turn, not even if they had fevers.

'Indeed, indeed.' The oldest breaks the silence. 'That's how it goes. The invalids. They play by different rules.'

All of them nod, relieved, pour themselves more tea, and the clatter of cups and spoons and voices again fills the room. They, the nurses from Silver Wood, know it better than the people outside: in the end, the softest hold out the longest. Their intellects are transparent for feelings, something they have in common with the mystics alone, and their misty presence draws everyone's eyes but their true paths remain unknown. Invalids are never completely present anywhere, but they are never entirely absent either, with their hazy corporeality they manage to penetrate there where for other people are only walls, and that is why they remain irreplaceable for the Party. They build, if not the spine, then the fine nerve pathways along the vertebrae that, once clipped, bring the whole system down.

'I don't know, but this gnome scares me,' Vera starts up again.

'He's better than the two bearded ones, that's for sure,' Polina says.

'No, no, they're harmless, they only want their soup and to play cards.'

'You can't trust the bearded ones at all,' Polina says definitively.

'What they want is to eat and to sleep and perhaps a woman. Or what they understand to be a woman,' Anastasia counters, and Anastasia should know. Her grasp of what goes on in Silver Wood is better than all of theirs. She knows the patients' and personnel's and even the visitors' dispositions, she knows their stories and even the rumours that they bring: in summer, it had to do with the lack of nutrients in the food, that is, if you could even get any food around the corner. Now, in winter, it's the burnt leather breaking apart in all their ovens and shrinking since, due to a lack of wood, they're burning furniture and books too, soon they'll be burning air and the cold itself.

'And what's he got to do with Lenin?'

'The little guy? He's on the executive committee.'

'Eugenia and Lenin. I'm telling you. Eugenia and Lenin. The Sardinian is simply their little plaything.'

When there's a knock at the door, the nurses break into nervous laughter. They don't know why. Anastasia sips her tea. Sofia orders her clothes another time. Vera opens the door. Gramsci.

He is standing there sheepishly, a pair of pine branches in his hand.

Did they perchance have a vase?

The nurses rush to the door, Polina and Anastasia and Darya, even the hulking Sofia gets up from her chair. Gramsci looks from one to the other. Light reflects off the edge of his glasses. When you look him in the face, you forget how small he is. But other than his height and his eyes, what is there to say about him with any certainty?

Hardly a thing.

Eugenia awaits him with the same severity with which he left her behind in her Silver Woodian bed. She is sitting there as if he'd only been gone a few minutes, and perhaps that's how it is here in Silver Wood, a safety zone which gives time but doesn't take any while all around in the new Russia things are happening thick and fast.

But here too things have happened, Gramsci learns from Eugenia while trying to affix tiny candles to the fir branches. Head physician Reverend has disappeared like a fugitive landowner who all of a sudden has no past. And a small rebellion has begun, up on the top floor in the room of the two bearded men from Novograd who, since being admitted, have just sat there playing cards, neither of the two ever win, neither of the two ever lose, they simply quit as soon as one of their fortunes takes a turn for the worst and then start reshuffling the cards like mad. They are uninterested in the nurses or the garden paths, in the woods or in the food they receive three times a day.

'Three times a day, but always at the wrong time,' they'd mumble together in one voice.

While the Red Army was busy pushing on towards Novograd, the two were sitting with a sour soup of leftovers, hot beet-coloured water in which they placed their spoons and pulled out giblets, but they did not know whether they were of plants or animals, nor did they know what they thought about the Bolsheviks. Better than the tsar, worse than peace. Or the other way round. They didn't know. The soup was only halfway gone when the cobbler from across the hall was standing in the doorway, his shop window empty a week now. Up until yesterday, there were twelve pairs of uninhabited shoes on his shelves, but now they had been plundered. They didn't protest, they just left, were recruited, like the soup, that's just what everything looked like in war. 'Red giblets,' they say.

'They were mistrustful of everything,' Eugenia says and sceptically observes the candles wobbling on the branches. 'But most of all of Reverend. They just could not accept having someone like that dictate to them how to live. Someone like that who had not been in the war.'

Eugenia's shoulder bone stands out beneath the fabric of her blouse, a small bight for a gun barrel. Gramsci is always embarrassed in her company, for while he was sitting in Turin writing his essays she was busy watching firefights and death between besieged forests and empty shoe-repair shops. And he cannot even decorate a fir branch.

'And then all of a sudden it turns out he had been in the fight,' Eugenia says. 'It's just that he was on the wrong side.'

'With the White Army, really?' Gramsci wants to be sure but then Giulia is standing in the doorway and the bearded men, the White Guards, even the candles, become unimportant. She smiles at him shyly and then looks at her sister.

'Did the concert go well?' Eugenia asks.

'Yes, it . . . they were very happy.'

She lays the violin case on the table, opens it and checks something on the strings. He sees the light down on her neck, her tied-up hair—bent as she is over the case—fall across her cheek. He would like to take her in his arms, kiss her skin which smells faintly of pears and wood.

'It must have been outstanding,' Gramsci says. Giulia turns back towards him. She is glowing and he wonders if it's only because of the Christmas concert she has just given, the patients' applause, the appreciative nod of the new head physician that the Party has sent.

'Everything that Giulia does is outstanding,' Eugenia says, a bit too loudly. 'Giulia herself is something rather outstanding. No? That's what Papa always said.'

Gramsci and Giulia look at each other furtively.

'We could light the candles,' Gramsci suggests.

'We will light the candles,' Eugenia decides.

The room has cooled thanks to the cracks in the ceiling, the frost has spread across the windowpane and shares the view with its white crystals. Gramsci wakes up next to Giulia. Her whole body is visible, her ribs, her spine, the whole derelict, wonderful terrain, barely covered by a sheet, she should have woken up a long time ago on account of the cold but she continues to sleep with unbearable tenacity. Gramsci runs his hand carefully across her back, lays his hand in hers, her fingers soften, she lays sprawled, appears to wake, but then her breathing turns deep and even again.

He gets up. All at once having this woman so close to him seems strange. Unlike a few weeks ago, the overpowering sensations no longer make him nervous, the sense of distrust that everything could be a dream, a hypoglycaemic slip of his brain that, back in his student days, made him hallucinate an enormous spider on the ceiling. No, this here is, if anything, no hallucination. This woman has been involved with him too long already, stays by him even though he sends her away in his letters, constantly sends her away, makes terrible accusations when they see each other and no matter how harshly he shoos her off, she always comes back.

He quietly paces back and forth, looks at Giulia so harmlessly asleep, her too-beautiful face, her too-smooth body, her too-soft skin. She's not here because of me, Gramsci thinks. That kind of woman doesn't fall in love with a man like me.

Coming into her guestroom in Silver Wood's visitors building, he found her under a blanket, her cumbersome bustier wedged into her chest. He had not turned on the light, had quietly gotten undressed, hung his suit over the back of the chair, his underwear, lifted up the blanket and crawled into bed next to her. She turns her back to him. With raw fingers he undoes the loops of her bustier, stops himself, kisses her shoulders, nestles up against all the lace and eyelets, it finally gives way, Giulia's chest expands, he can still feel the incisions on her skin, she turns onto her back, looks to the wall. With his arm around the middle of her body, his thumbs stroke her stomach, circle her navel, her thighs open slightly. Giulia's eyes are closed as he kisses her forehead, her temples. He rolls down her scratchy woollen stockings, moves his hand up her thighs, runs his fingers through the short, curly hair. He moves along the edge of her lips with his tongue, comes up against her teeth, then the tip of her tongue and deep and soft her mouth. He lays on top of her, Giulia winces when he enters. Her faint, fierce, compacted breathing. He grabs her hands, moves inside of her. The numbness in his head subsides. His body is no longer wrong, but collapses into a single point.

Giulia's hands on his shoulders. She bites her lower lip, leans her head back. He remains on top of her, feels the throbbing of her body, raises himself on his fists and looks into her face. Her eyes are still closed. He slides away, lays down and hears her begin to cry. Every time she has to cry. Because everything's there again, she says. Because she can see again. Because she once again knows what she has seen. Because she once again is alone with the huge and horrific world.

'We have all seen things,' he chides her and sits up. 'Think about the ones who fought for us in the Civil War, you're not the only one who's close to the abyss, our times are challenging us to the very last, that's how it is.'

She doesn't answer, he just hears her soft, even sobbing. He would prefer to push Giulia away. She breaks too deeply into him and he wishes he could go back to the time when he only lived in his mind, in his first years in Turin when he never laughed but never cried either and believed everything could be overcome through work. Back then, he had lived so far removed from reality, outside of the world.

At last, Giulia opens her eyes, her gaze is glassy and absent as if her whole being were retreating, clotting around the last warm beat of her body. Gramsci turns his face away and stands up.

She never loved me! he thinks suddenly. It comes to him in an uncomfortably clear, simple and logical way. He walks up to the window, close to the cold, white January morning. She just couldn't. One cannot fall in love with a man like him. He'd always known it. And this here, the fact that she was lying here, that she has kissed him and slept with him, this is all a sham, an enormous fraud. He should never have allowed her to come close to him. He sees Eugenia standing at the fence, their first meeting and how interested she was to learn he had never been in love. Why had she asked him about that? And why had he, hardly knowing her even an hour, answered?

He feels how cold it is in the room, but the sweat is streaming down his chest. Giulia has a purpose here. He knows it, how could he think for so long it was anything else? She does not fit into his life, between those houses eaten away by the salt and humidity, those open hillsides that emerge a marshy green. Sorgono, a tiny burg in the middle of nothing, where as a child he hunted little animals. On those late autumn days that hang mild and melancholic across Sardinia, he hunts hedgehogs and sits out in the fields under apple trees, quiet and hungry, sits there until the darkness falls between the houses with such a vehemence that the soup spills onto the plates and the sheep become mutinous in their stalls. He scurries home through the shadows, a dwarf, a cripple, a wisp through the landscape, and the quicker he runs the more he resembles a beetle that has fallen from a tree and is scuttling confusedly through the area. In the distance, the light from a house, forgotten halfway between one village and another, and that is Gramsci's mother. Peppina presses herself against the walls of reddish lava rock, she's always in the shadows, always on the lookout for glances, she does not want to be seen, she is ashamed to be the wife of a prisoner, not even drunk workers walk through the town at that time of day, there was nothing there but farms, pastures and a land-registry office that measured the size of the pastures. One slept when one found the time. The county seat was responsible for everything else.

She drags her escaped son home by the arm, she curses him in a hiss, was she supposed to go looking for him everywhere? He's sent to bed without anything to eat. Then it is quiet, Peppina picks up a piece of needlework, bends over the thin light of an oil lamp in order to have somewhat of an idea of what she is sewing. Something is always broken, stockings, shoes, a chair leg, and she can no longer keep up with repairs. There is no money for anything new. Ever since his father has been in jail, their income has been blocked for the unforeseeable future. After an hour her eyes hurt, she is so tired that her hands tremble. Before going to bed, she looks at herself for an endless second in the bedroom mirror. Seven children. The oldest fourteen, the youngest still in nappies, in-between one who is growing into his breastplate. Both Peppina and his siblings are watching the metamorphosis, they don't speak about it but their eyes betray the disgust they feel when they touch him by accident.

That was a long time ago. He survived it all.

This, here, he will not.

Gramsci thinks about Eugenia and how well she understands Lenin, she is almost on intimate terms with him. Giulia's face turns into the pillow, her lips lightly spread, he thinks he can hear her inhale and exhale. Her naked shoulder protrudes from the blanket, he had just had his hand stretched out upon it, yesterday had told her—body to body, head to head—about his worries. By now what Gramsci thinks, what he really thinks, goes through all of Lenin's offices long before he speaks before the Comintern. From now on he will be calculable. And that is essential for the survival of the Party. At any point the whole thing can start to crumble. With any comrade. Someone has to hold the thread. Someone. Giulia lolls about and her pale body slides even further out of the blanket.

Oh, let her sleep. He takes her hand, bends over her and kisses her fingers. He had not been able to get what was going on around him under control either. On 30 December, the Union of Soviet Socialist Republics will be founded, Lenin, paralysed and with a weak voice, announces. The new world order, this standing-on-its-head, will stretch from Samar to Odessa, from Kamchatka to Yerevan. No one knows what is to come, what will happen with the brand-new republic, this delicate web of communistically sub-jugated countries, people still believe that something is arising and not about to go down. History has not come to an end, it has not even reached a new level but will run amok for a few decades. Gramsci feels Giulia's shoulder on his chest. Slowly he sinks into a brief, far too brief, sleep.

XV. FOLK DANCES   There was a rattling at the door.

'Anton, I must speak with you,' Brevi ordered. I opened my eyes and saw a scrunched-up sheet in my arms. My head hurt, my tongue was sticking to my gums. The evening before, not wanting to go back to the palazzo that smelt of old people and even older books, I had stayed in a bar. Watching the young, seemingly endlessly colourful women, I'd had a glass of wine and then another, and thought about Tatiana walking away in her too-wide trousers, one hand on her pinned-up hair like a nest made by crazy birds. I'd continued to stare at her through the window of the bus, had wanted to get back out, rush after her. Then the bus stopped, but I just stood there, incapable of deciding whether to do something. Once it got moving again, I kept looking out the rear window as the street corner grew smaller and smaller.

'Anton, are you still asleep?' Brevi sounded brusque this morning or maybe it was already later. I felt for the clock on my night table. It was a little past nine, no reason to be alarmed, but Brevi was knocking at my door again, so I tumbled out of bed. Apparently, the night before, I'd ordered a fourth glass of wine and even a fifth. Though I usually avoid wearing shirts twice as I like the feeling of freshly starched textiles on my skin, seeing that Brevi seemed to be in quite a huff, I grabbed my shirt from the back of the chair, pulled it on, then slipped into my suit pants and in the end found myself standing rather poorly—and, in any event, not my usual self—in front of him.

'Listen, this won't do, Anton.'

'Sorry, but you couldn't wait to speak with me,' I answered, defending my neglect.

'What have you come to know by this point? How have you been getting along at the institute?'

'I have . . .'

Tatiana's steps in the hall. I tried to remember what had happened before and after. Tatiana's steps.

'I've sifted,' I answered and pulled my shirt a bit straighter.

'Sifted?'

'Explored.'

'Explored? Listen, Anton, we don't have any time to explore, we've got to make a find. Bunotti is here.'

'Here?'

'In Rome. Not he himself, but one of his followers, and that is even more disastrous. You know how quickly these little academic truffle hogs rummage through everything, greedy for recognition and unearthing whatever they need to survive.'

'Bunotti could be involved in just about anything,' I argued.

'But he's not. I heard it from Vacca. Or, rather, his secretary. To be precise, from one of his secretary's acquaintances. Bunotti is in Naples and his colleagues are here in Rome. If we are out of luck, the whole Gramsci world is already against us. We have to be the leaders,' Brevi explained, 'and not the subordinates.'

'Indeed,' I mumbled and thought of Tatiana's slightly red forehead, the way she moved her lower lip so she could blow against her fringe.

'To be brief!' Brevi called out, 'I've organized a secret meeting with Alexander Golubev at the Russian embassy.'

A secret meeting! And so we were stepping back into the early half of the twentieth century.

'Did you know you can recognize a spy by the way they walk?' I asked.

'No, I didn't. But you mustn't worry about your gait, they'll recognize you anyway. You have been ordered to be at the embassy for ten-thirty, and, Anton, we cannot allow Vacca to lead us around by the nose. And by no means whatsoever Bunotti. We've got to be quicker. And you're not even completely awake!'

The embassy was in a crème-red building with a slack flag out front, located in the area around the train station, where street after street of cheap guesthouses and grubby Internet cafes pushed up against one another. In front of the gate was an SUV from the Carabinieri and a young officer in camouflage, more illuminated than hidden, playing with his mobile phone. Across the road, an ad praised the best phone contracts in all of Italy.

A female porter turned towards me as I entered. The glass doors were open and I quickly made my way past, for I knew that, most of the time, you could only expect indignant questions and delays from such people. Her hair was pulled back under a dusty net, and the collar of her blouse faded into her wrinkled skin. Once I was almost past her area of responsibility, she hissed a rough *'un attimo!'* after me. I turned around. She looked at me threateningly from her glass box. 'ID,' she snapped.

I rummaged in my rear pocket, pulled out my wallet and handed it to her.

'Who are you here to see?'

'Glbeff,' I mumbled.

'Appointment?'

'Half past ten.'

'Please have a seat in the reception room. Someone will bring you to Counsellor of Legation Golubev.' Then she turned and noted something in a tattered notebook.

I'd barely made it through the glass airlock when a spindly woman walked up to meet me.

'Herr Stöver, I am happy to be allowed to greet you as a guest of the Russian Federation,' she said with rigid kindness and led me through a corridor while I pondered what exactly was secret about this secret meeting. On the walls hung portraits of Russian statesmen. Putin looked like an overly decorated clerk from the '70s, Medvedev like a news anchor on public TV. The woman made me wait in one of those typical state-decorated rooms full of Corbusier-like furniture.

'Mr Golubev is still on the telephone,' she explained and disappeared into another hallway, which, I'd noticed, led to even more hallways and rooms. The space around the Corbusiers was so grey and cheerless, it was just like we'd imagined the East to be back at school. An air-conditioner wheezed above the window. I took a brochure touting the beauty of west-Russian folk dances from the rack. Men in colourful pants drifted across the stage, young women with thick, blonde braids smiled at me. How gladly I would have climbed into the photograph with them. And why not?

It was ridiculous enough, no doubt Golubev was a grey-tied embassy employee from Nizhny Novgorod, and the story he wanted to serve up would have to do with Piero Sraffa and his trusted friend, Raffaele Mattioli, president of the Banca Commerciale, and nothing to do with reality at all. What could this gangly clerk know? At best he was interested in salary grades, savings deposits and a few EU guidelines, but not a bank safe from 1937 that possibly (possibly!) contained a few of Gramsci's fictional pages.

I walked to the window and looked at the battered cars and the dead concrete square where some kids were playing football. A young couple shared a cigarette, leaning against a streetlamp. In the trunk of a palm some pigeons had made a nest. They appeared to be sleeping. But right as I was about to turn, they began to coo, with a deep and guttural sound.

I'd had no idea pigeons could sound so good, it was almost a female pitch. I let myself sink into one of the Corbusier chairs, stared at the ceiling, at the dirty insulation panels, and heard the sound from outside became more urgent, almost imploring. Then a door opened, then another and a massive rush began. People spun around me, but not with the beauty of the west-Russian folk dancers, it was severe and tense in a way usually reserved for supervising teachers. Doors slammed, footsteps pounded. I didn't know what was happening. Had Ukraine won the war? Had Putin disappeared, perhaps in as obvious a way as the Polish president in his foggy aeroplane?

A giant in bright morning dress shoved my chair so that I made a quarter turn. Three muses slithered across the room on glossy pumps. Taller and shorter, younger and older suits of higher and lower service grades filled the room and then disappeared. Out of the chaos stepped a man with a pocket square and a bald pate. His massive nostrils impressed me.

'Golubev,' he said and held out his hand. 'We shall go to my office—this way, please.'

He directed me softly, almost like a girl, through one of the hallways until we stopped in front of a streaked glass door. The room was crammed full of old files which seemed to come from pre-Soviet times, a photo of Nabokov hung next to the door and an icon stood on the desk, there where you most often encountered family photos. The huge, dark-wood conference table almost took up the rest of the room, it was circular and no matter where you sat you were forced to the edge. Here too you could hear the pigeons cooing, which, alone as I was with Golubev, moved me in an embarrassing way. We sat across from each other and had so much cherry wood between us that we had to raise our voices when speaking.

'Gramsci!' he cried and lifted his little hands as if meaning to clap them above his shining skull. Through the glass door behind him I could see into the hall. A young man in baggy clothes hurried past, a stack of papers in his hand.

'Professor Brevi has already told you what this is about. It has to do with the mailing of the notebooks,' I called across to him.

'According to the present state of research, which Professor Brevi and I believe—'

'And that's what I would like to—but please, do continue,' Golubev interrupted.

'According to the present state of research, it seems as if Tania Schucht did not, as some sources hold, have the notebooks mailed to Moscow after passing through a safe at the Banca Commerciale, but in 1938 handed them over to the Russian embassy in Rome.'

'May I offer you a coffee—' Golubev asked, and poured me a cup. He craned over the table in order to place it close to me and I stood up and stretched forward but it got lost in the middle where neither of us could reach it.

'In any event, it cannot be excluded,' I continued, 'that, in the then tense situation, some of the notebooks were overlooked.'

'You do not mean to imply—'

'It is possible that some of the notes remained in Rome, that they are not to be found in either the archive in Moscow or the archive in Rome.'

'Now, I do not believe that on Russian territory, and the embassy counts as such, something of the public—' Golubev said and raised his cup. 'Let us drink to the friendship between Italy, Russia and Ukraine!'

'Ukraine?' I asked uncomprehendingly.

'Do you mean to question something?'

'Not at all,' I answered quickly.

'Even if in the local press from time to time—to my great regret.'

Behind him, in the glass door, a light went on, the morning dress goose-stepped past.

'I think that the misunderstandings, upon closer inspection— but you've known that for a long time by now.' Golubev smiled warmly at me, the backdrop of the hall sank away behind him and I tried to concentrate on his soft, constantly moving mouth.

'You and Mr Brevi are of course exceptional researchers, and I say that with complete—'

Then I saw her. Tatiana. She was carrying a stack of files and seemed to be trying to catch up with the morning dress. Golubev murmured on, I wanted to wave to her, make a sign, *can you just wait*, but she'd already disappeared behind an iron-grey door.

'But now, that's how it likely is,' Golubev explained decidedly.

'Sorry?' I asked, confused. I pointed towards the glass door behind which Tatiana could no longer be seen. 'Was that one of your employees?' He looked around, found nothing noteworthy, and turning back to me asked, 'Do you know Tyutchev perchance?'

'Tyutchev?' Perhaps I'd heard of him once. Was that important? Tatiana was walking around behind that door, maybe she was Russian without my having noticed, and what else could she be on top of it?

A suit came down the hall tearing at the plastic wrapping of a Müsli bar and let it fall where Tatiana had just been standing.

'One cannot understand Russia, one can only believe in it,' Golubev intoned and fingered his pocket square. 'Tyutchev wrote that in his famous—'

The suit disappeared into his office, letting the door close behind him; the plastic wrapper was caught by a draught of air and flew out of sight.

'I appreciate your great countryman Rilke on a much different —but not less,' Golubev assured me. I nodded and looked past him into the hallway once again bathed in a cold, energy-efficient light. The roll carpet was fading, the metal shelf held a thin ficus and I felt like I'd gone back in time, back into the hallways at the University of Göttingen I used to walk up and down, there where I lived and dreamt and spent the nights researching, where I warmed myself with instant chocolate milk out of the machine long after my colleagues had called it a day and headed off for their tenuously happy weekends that stretched from Thursday afternoon through Tuesday morning.

'We find ourselves in a time which successive—' Golubev whispered and bent forward over the cherrywood table with the whole gravity of his seal-like body. 'We must have more understanding for one another—otherwise I see a whole lot of harm coming. And who would wish that to happen?'

I started as the spindly woman appeared behind the glass pane.

'For you must consider what great, bilateral rapprochements—!' Golubev said. 'What hopes we in the last twenty-five years—!'

The spindly woman stuck her head into the room at an angle. 'Mr Golubev, it would be about time,' she said rigidly.

'Ah, of course.' Golubev fell back into his chair and assured me with a warm voice, 'Herr Stöver, it was a great—!'

He stood up, walked around the table and pressed his small fingers around my hand. His nostrils quaked.

'And Crimea—' he said on parting.

'And Crimea?'

'I simply wanted to have said it. I wish you all the best with your work.'

I lingered for a little while longer in the area around the embassy, observing the round screen walling beneath the balconies, the cast-iron arabesques decorating the premises, the huge, shiny-in-the-backlight black windows behind which Tatiana was probably still roaming about. At some point she'd leave the building too, I'd just have to wait long enough. And even if that meant waiting until late at night when she left with the last clerks, what did I have to lose?

I sat down on the kerb on the other side of the street, watched the hedge wave in the light breeze and longed for Tatiana's body, longed for the heat driving against me from her small, taut body, longed to lay my head on her stomach afterwards . . . she would run a hand through my hair and talk to me soothingly, she would brush off all the unease Golubev had instilled in me—or Brevi or Hedda—like dust from the arm of a coat.

'Excuse me.'

The young *carabiniere* was standing in front of me, looking down.

'What are you doing?'

'I'm waiting,' I answered, shaking with rage inside. What did this camouflaged kid have to do with a story that was far too important for his ridiculously low rank?

'Waiting? For that you'll have to look for somewhere else,' he explained. 'If you continue to surveil the embassy, I'm going to have to take your information.' He glanced at me with a look that had no interest in getting to the heart of the matter but just wanted to oversee it.

'Please do, if you really must,' I answered and handed him my ID.

'Hmm, beh,' he said and padded his pockets for a pen but without any success. He walked back to the SUV, leant over the driver's seat and rummaged for a piece of paper. He wrote down my name on the back of a torn envelope which he would no doubt lose as soon as he'd finished.

'It is our duty to protect the embassies in Rome,' he said. 'We provide security. State security. What would happen if there was a terrorist attack?'

'I'm not a terrorist,' I defended myself. 'I don't even have any convictions.'

The official laughed arrogantly which was probably the most human impulse I could expect.

'I wouldn't have thought so. All the same, go somewhere else. Make sure you get out of here.'

He gave me back my ID and wished me a good day.

XVI. TICKETS   Serrati has been arrested in Italy, Tasca has fled to Switzerland, Lenin has had a stroke and lost his power of speech. All that seems marginal to Gramsci. He's walking with Giulia down Tverskaya Street. The young women are wearing rouge on their cheeks, and the men are relaxed. Life here is quieting down, the city is growing used to its new administration and Giulia laughs when he sticks out his tongue at her. He caresses the bridge of her nose, she keeps laughing, runs ahead of him only to stop at the end of the block, then turns around to wait. After 20 metres, they finally, finally fall back into each other's arms. He holds her hand. He holds her elbows. His fingers run up and down her back. Giulia's vigorous and softly pulsing veins at her temples. Her cheeks. The half-moon of her jawline. Her chin. The cheekbones below the bright, silky skin.

What had summer been up until this summer? A collection of hot and too-hot days. Dazzling bright light when he tried to read. Mosquitoes circling his bed when he wanted to sleep. How beautiful Moscow is now. More beautiful than in autumn when the red leaves cover the walkways and Giulia is walking next to him through the grounds of the sanatorium, their touches still hidden and new. Had he known Giulia already? Just a hair's difference from what he knows now.

Right on time, Giulia pulls him back by the arm. A hackney carriage rushes past and almost pulls Gramsci along with it. It stops a few houses later, and a man in an English suit steps out. He snarls at the carriage driver and disappears into the elegant entrance.

'Sometimes you don't know who's actually in power,' Giulia says. 'Why does someone like that think they can still do whatever they want?'

'Because he gets away with it,' Gramsci answers, 'and the workers continue to cringe.'

'Then what's the whole point? In the end, the tsar's palace simply has new inhabitants. Outside, everything looks exactly the same.'

'It takes time. You all think that the workers won a long time ago, but they are just on the alert.'

'But the rulers live worse than the ruled!' Giulia cries. 'Some see that. They simply won't prevail, perhaps for that very reason. Because no one wants to see something like that.'

They turn into the park. Children run past them. The noise from the main street reaches them in dampened tones.

'You know, on the islands, people are still dying of malaria,' Gramsci says, 'and in the mines they beat out stones fifteen hours a day, seven days a week. In northern Italy, they've founded a parliament and are building one factory after another. For the people in Turin, the south is just a supply of cheap labour. And the people there have heard it so often that they believe it themselves. Those who have never been told they have rights first have to learn to be able to speak for themselves.'

He thinks about Sardinia, about the eternal noontime when nothing grows because of the heat pressing down on everything. This is the famous Italian shoe, he thinks, this half-island dangling into the Mediterranean and rotting at its sole. Giulia's collarbone gleams in the sun. One cannot understand Russia, one can only believe in it, Tyutchev had written. And that's how it is with Giulia. Although she is next to him now, is running a hand through his hair and talking about her father who had called in on the sick Lenin, he misses her, he misses her for all those years he was not with her because for twenty-six years she wanted nothing to do with him. Twenty-six years of her life. In his own life there were thirty-one.

'Lenin is worse off than they are saying,' Giulia says. 'And Stalin is coming to visit and acts like his heir.'

'You don't like him.'

'Stalin is sinister.'

'Do you know him?'

'No. But he's up to no good,' Giulia says emphatically.

'Please, what are you afraid of?'

'Sometimes I am simply afraid, I cannot explain it to you. Go ahead and laugh at me.'

'I'm not laughing.'

She edges a bit closer into him.

'I see a scene in front of me. We are sitting there in our day-to-day, and there's a man walking around, a stocky man in baggy trousers with a tired face. He's collecting our tickets and saying: "So, that was it, folks. The ride's over." But the train has not even left yet.'

As she speaks, she keeps putting her hand in front of her eyes, as if something were blinding her.

'We look at ourselves in irritation,' she says, 'a few strangers sharing a compartment, then look out of the window onto the empty wagons standing on the rails. The man opens the door, *please come with me, Madame*, he says and takes a deep bow. I slide to the exit, step outside, but the metal stair has disappeared and I fall into nothingness.' She hunches her shoulders as if protecting her neck from an attack. 'It's nothing, it's just an absurdity, forgive me,' she says. 'But I'm afraid that the man with the tickets will call after me: "It's your own fault."'

In front of the Executive Committee Building they say goodbye. Gramsci has to go back to his work, he has a meeting, he has to get to his desk which is piled up with papers, he has to speak with Togliatti. As he climbs the stairs, the train in which Giulia was sitting among strangers comes to mind and he thinks of Stalin. Lenin won't be around for much longer. He hardly appears in public any more, they push him out into the garden in a wheelchair, wrapped up in blankets he smiles at everything and has fallen back into his childhood. His mind is dying and you can see it. His empire is little now, two squares on the blanket along which he runs his finger over and over again. In the postscript to his will, Lenin wants Stalin to be removed from his position as general secretary. He is too coarse and that cannot be tolerated in such a post. They should put someone else in his place who differs 'in having *only one* advantage, namely, that of being more tolerant, more loyal, more polite and more considerate to the comrades, less capricious'.

Sitting at his desk, which is too small, new papers keep coming and coming, a comrade tells him about the results of a special session and in the background the telephone is ringing. He wants to be holding Giulia's hand. Or her hair. Nothing else. And regardless of whether they're successful or not at removing Stalin from his position, as long as Giulia is there everything will be fine. She appears in the notes Gramsci takes during the Executive Committee meeting, she is sitting next to Trotsky, she is looking down from a balcony onto the whole group, and then she's simply there, without any backdrop, without Trotsky, Mussolini, Stalin, Lenin, Zinoviev, Bordiga, without any roads or country or sky above her. He can see her hand. Her watery eyes. He hears her thoughts or what he imagines her thoughts to be. But if she isn't there, if she were to disappear (he cannot allow himself to even consider that), the world would only be a stone falling through the void.

XVII. LOVE OF ONE'S NEIGHBOUR   During one of my visits, Ilsa asked me how I ended my affairs. Once again my money situation had grown tight, once again I'd travelled to Ilsa to fill out one of her bank-transfer slips, once again my financial difficulties had to do with overly expensive restaurants and hotels which I admitted to Ilsa after she'd triumphantly figured out exactly how my finances would look if I was only taking care of my family.

Ilsa considered it progressive to go straight into those things that usually required a tad more tact, and often confused shamelessness with openness. Be that as it may, that is where her progressiveness ended and began to suffocate under lectures on Rasputin. For after tossing Thomas Aquinas to the side as a clever but fainthearted copyist, she'd spent that summer with Rasputin. And the only reason she read Foucault was because she thought that she might finally be able to get me, my interest in power, my dictatorial genius.

'As I am already paying for your escapades, I'd at least like to know what they look like,' she demanded, leaning back on her Biedermeier sofa. Having recently had it re-covered in an even bolder yellow than before, she seemed somewhat awkward against all the blaring material. A pile of books tottered on the side table, topped off by a plate of cookies. The only place for the coffee cups was on the floor.

'And so?'

'Come on, Ilsa!'

Naturally, I didn't tell her a thing about my affairs. I had trained myself to be tactful, which, in my family, was a real work of art, and I was quite proud of it. In Ilsa's circle, no one understood the difference between eroticism, lust and apathy. Whoever lost a sense of shame could say goodbye to desire too. Whoever got rid of taboos annihilated lust. So much for *Kommune Eins*. I ended my affairs with an explanatory talk. Ilsa uncorked a bottle of grappa.

'I told Hedda to leave you years ago,' Ilsa said and handed me one of the mouth-blown glasses she'd picked up in Murano or Venice with one of those lovers of hers with whom she shared reading materials rather than the bed.

'How lovely to learn she still possesses her own willpower,' I answered.

'You decimated her willpower long ago. You treat her miserably, my dear, and she allows you to do anything you want with her,' Ilsa, schooled in strategies of annihilation against me, said.

'I made an effort with her for a long time. Now it just doesn't work any more, Ilsa, and there are reasons for that.'

'Yes, reason, that's a good word. I have never liked seeing this ... your women stories. This risible conquering thing.' She held out the glass to me more as a challenge than an offer, and in her gesture I could feel how unyieldingly and deeply she still despised me. But I couldn't do a thing: what Ilsa held against me, what she couldn't stand, was that I understood desire whereas she only understood control. Whereas I was able to enjoy, she was merely clever. And whereas she was idolized, I was loved and had even loved myself, not for long, true, but uncontrollably and abruptly. Ilsa, however, was far removed from those experiences.

'You never let Hedda say a word,' she said after downing her grappa. 'You stifle her, you run roughshod over her before she can express her own opinion, and when she does, she's worse off! That's when you put her up against the wall. You're always right. You refuse to entertain a single point of view outside your own. You're a dictator due to your helplessness, my dear. You know what, Anton Stöver? You simply did not deserve Hedda.'

'Did not deserve!' I called out in amusement and thought about my father who, once outside her gravitational field, had managed to become a bureaucrat in school administration, maltreating everything and every one with prescriptions. What had she made of that man? How he had degenerated into a nothing on her leash.

'You were never interested in Hedda,' Ilsa stated with her inquisitorial charm. 'But what am I saying—you were never interested in women.'

At that point I downed my grappa too. What kind of abstruse allegation was that? I was interested in women, constantly and all over the place. A lack of women was something you really could not accuse me of, and I wasn't interested in their bodies but what was going on in their heads, what they thought about before falling asleep, when they woke up, when they got bored during their lunch break. I was interested in everything about them, I just wasn't interested in one of them exclusively and that's what Ilsa's damned communism should have taught us. The removal of any exclusivity. The love of a class or, even better, unconditional love of one's neighbour. Because what else was the thought of the collective good for? Why hadn't it brought us anything other than the expropriation of land, the five-year plan and a few scruffy leftwing group flats?

'Göttingen is just too small for me,' I said.

'Is that right? But it's thanks to you that you went to Göttingen in the first place. Hedda had been offered a fantastic position at the Fine Art Museum in Bremen. And she said no, for your sake, because of your paltry job as a middle peasant at the university. Did you ever have an eye on a professorship?'

'Of course I did.'

'You're the only one who believes it. Now Hedda is wasting away in that gallery which is far below her capabilities.'

'As if you would know what her capabilities were.'

'You ruined her life.'

'You can only ruin your own life. And Göttingen is too small for me.'

'Because your lovers keep running into your wife.'

There she was not completely wrong. There was precisely one cafe I could go to with women, it had been there for years and for years it had been the only one. In any event, it was odd that these women often spoke of abandonment when I said goodbye. The term 'affair' seemed to be understood less and less, which I held to be proof of the decline of culture, and an affair was the limit of what I shared with these women, and only because I enquired into what was going on with them, apparently no one else was interested, but that does not mean that we ever had anything like a relationship.

Göttingen was too small for my needs, and that was not the only reason I had suggested to Hedda again and again that we move to another, bigger, more culturally inclined city. Well. Hedda's gallery. The gallerist was one of the few women who couldn't stand me. Whenever I entered to pick Hedda up or tell her something, she cast me scathing looks, and the only reason she'd kept Hedda from going was because she knew that her full-time position screwed up my plans.

'Have you ever thought of anyone other than yourself? Of your son, for example?' Ilsa asked.

'The way you think of yours?'

'Do you not have even the slightest spark of morality within you, Anton Stöver?'

'Morality? Your morality is nothing but an enormously formed provision. All of you with your romanticism of bureaucracy. Love is *always* amoral. You know what, Ilsa, what you're talking about doesn't have anything to do with love, anything to do with Marxism, at best it's just Christian Democracy. Little shepherd's hour at Ibis level.'

'But for your affairs it's always got to be Gebhard's Hotel, of course. Nothing less will do for my son.'

'I looked for alternatives, Ilsa, I'm sorry, but by-the-hour hotels in Göttingen are unacceptable. I can't go with any woman there. If were in Cologne or Munich though—'

'By-the-hour hotels! I'm disgusted, Anton. Your lifestyle disgusts me.'

'My lifestyle can be of no interest to you. Where I go with women can be of no interest to you. And your Antonio Gramsci, by the way, was no poor guest with the prostitutes of Turin.'

'He didn't have the means,' she defended him. I raised my eyebrows and looked at her amusedly, and, when it became clear to her that it was no defence to me, she added: 'And no interest, either.'

'Gramsci was a human being, Ilsa, not a holy pillar. Give him that much.'

'Your by-the-hour hotels are the epitome of the bourgeois!' she yelled.

'And all of your communes were the epitome of prudery!'

'I think you'd better leave now,' Ilsa said, and her voice suddenly sounded unbearably cold.

XVIII. VIENNA   On 3 December 1923, Gramsci arrives in Vienna, sent by the supreme authority of the Comintern. Giulia has stayed behind in Russia. After a year in which they had become so close that neither of them could any longer say whether they had truly grown up without the other, he is again alone for an indefinite period of time.

If only he'd been separated from her in Rome. But in Rome Mussolini's *squadristi* are securing the streets, not only the socialist Serrati but almost all the leading communists in the country have been arrested, all of those who could not take off or go underground quickly enough. And after the communists it was the turn of all the others who'd opposed the fascists and therefore been made to disappear. Mussolini is rearranging the republic according to his own standards. He is weeding out, locking up, allowing anything that could be dangerous to him to be removed, and Gramsci wants to get back to Italy as soon as possible. He wants to see what is happening in the flesh, he wants to negotiate. Now it is more important than ever.

'You cannot be closer to Italy,' they said when choosing Gramsci, 'than Vienna, but you cannot be any further away either.' From here he is to peek into the neighbouring country, push ahead with the founding of the Party newspaper *L'Unità* and snap up the few bits of news that come up through the Tyrol, report on an unsuccessful strike in Milan or those former comrades in Trieste who moved over to the fascists or a burglary in Naples where a printing press was destroyed. His comrades never deliver any good news, nor is it ever precise. Often what they know is second-hand or long obsolete. Gramsci doesn't know what he's supposed to be doing. In the meantime, the authorities are already pestering him, fussy Viennese clerks who moisten the tips of their pens with saliva in order to penalize anything that does not fit into their worldview in an embarrassingly precise way.

Gramsci is living in a room on the outskirts, he can reach Schönbrunn Palace on foot, the city is far away. The flat is cold, Vienna is cold, and though he cannot say where the city begins, once he stepped onto the wrong tram and ended up in an area with a desolate wine tavern out of which the first drunks were already tumbling into the early evening and the white hills around reminded him of the Saline hills in Cagliari and the countless emaciated convicts working there.

'Still better than Schönbrunn,' he thinks.

Josef Frey, his host and general secretary of the Austrian Communist Party, is a melancholic, and the grey of the clouds which hang over the city have made its way into the colour of his eyes. His wife looks at Gramsci sullenly. And he understands her: as if her husband weren't a terrible-enough fate, the Party has forced her to take a dubious lodger who might cause her to have problems with the authorities.

But Frau Frey is an upstanding person. A bit mercurial perhaps, but upstanding. Years earlier she'd given up her Jewish faith in order to become a Catholic with heart and soul. The liaison, though, did not last too long, for her heart soon wearied of the host and genuflexion, and because comrade Josef Frey set to wooing her with puffy charm and a few flowers now and again. She did not hesitate, but converted to the communistic faith in order to bind Frey-Josef to herself in accordance with the provisos of the councils and five-year plan. But as soon as he was legally married, he began to overlook the flower shop, remembered a flattering turn of phrase very infrequently indeed and went to meetings every evening, soon he even began to go in the afternoons and mornings and Frau Frey for her part grew lonely with communism. She missed the faces of the saints covered in oil. Here there are only fur caps, Lenin and his goatee, and Engelsmarx. In the long run, who can take all of that? On top of it, people have been putting their noses into their business, and Frau Frey has never liked being a stumbling block. She is an upstanding person. Upstanding through and through. Secretly, she begins to practice her Catholic magic again, buries herself defiantly in her Ave Marias and longs for the return of the kaiser.

Gramsci would like to get moving again. Everything he sees in Vienna displeases him, the last remnants of the bourgeois epoch punting out of a drift of snow. The streets seem sombre and pretentious, people wear their *noblesse* like a death mask and the Hotel Sacher is sinking into upper-class decadence. He thinks about the hunger of his childhood, which almost killed him, about how the Sardinian spring hangs mild and placid over the land and knows nothing about the ecstasy a piece of cake can trigger when it runs from the tongue into all of one's senses. Outside, all that awaits him is a rough tongue, passers-by ducking dejectedly into the snow-rain and horses trotting in three-four time in front of their Fiaker carriages. In Vienna, he thinks, the people creep into your soul because, otherwise, you simply could not handle the city.

What is Moscow in comparison? Snow-white and happy, sleds and laughing people with frozen red faces. And even though he has never been on one of those sleds, and even if not a single one of those faces really laughs, and even if Moscow is generally anything but happy but, rather, a collection of overstrained revolutionaries, penny pinchers, starved schoolchildren and an upper class still clinging to its privileges, Gramsci can only remember it in the most beautiful of colours there in his room in Vienna, there in that way station from which he can neither return to fascistic Italy where Mussolini's faithful would continuously arrest him nor to far-away Russia where Giulia is waiting. Or is not. But that is something he cannot think about at all.

Two thousand kilometres from Vienna to Moscow. Two thousand kilometres are too far for anything, and now he is stuck with Frau Frey bringing him slippers. What about the neighbours! The good parquet! What a life, where people just want to have everything ordered and not stick out in any way. He is standing in his room, looking at the picture of Saint Agnes. When it's six degrees, he lies down in a very hard and very uncomfortable German bed. He hardly sleeps and feels as lost as he did when he first arrived in Turin. So there he is again, back in the past, as if nothing had happened, as if he had never got free of the monotony of his life. His room smells like the sweaty cheese he'd kept for too long in Turin because he hadn't dared to touch the little he had, there is a draught from the window, his suit is too thin, he doesn't want to think about it, he doesn't want to go back there, to Turin, to those years in which he was so unconscious, and he presses his face into the pillow Frau Frey has made extra-hard, tries to concentrate on the good moments: when he used to play harmonica for his guests squeezed together on his bed and on the floor, there were so many of them and his room was so small. When his first article appeared. When he saw Ibsen's *Doll's House* and got angry about the how the audience found the third act, Nora's going away, offensive as they could not understand how deeply moral Nora's compliance with her duty was, the duty everyone had to themselves and only then to others, namely, to create a world for oneself in which one can be human.

Giulia sends a letter from Russia where visitors to the Kremlin are now making their way through a new mausoleum in which the dead Vladimir Ilyich Lenin is lying in state. He died on 21 January. Frau Frey had brought the letter to him with an inquisitive air. She remains standing next to him, stares at his finger that's supposed to tear open the envelope, and only when she finally leaves does Gramsci carefully open the envelope and pull out the piece of paper, has to read the lines twice in order to understand, or at least have an idea, of what Giulia wants to tell him. He is dizzy, had he eaten anything today? Agnes smiles at him sanctimoniously from the oil painting. 'What do you know about it?' he hisses at her. In Moscow, Zinoyev has positioned himself, Stalin is still keeping his plans secret but he's long had something in mind that is stronger than Lenin's postscript, but that is all nothing compared to what Giulia has written him. 'What do you know,' he hisses up to Agnes, 'about the fact that Giulia is probably awaiting a child?'

He must answer her, he must have her close to him right now, not this insufferable and sacrosanct Agnes, he wants to take Giulia by the arm, but how do you write about something like that from 2,000 kilometres away? 'I'm going to make clocks out of cork,' he writes, 'and papier-mâché violins and wax lizards with two tails. I am going to recite poems from my childhood which was a bit wild and primitive—very different than yours.'

XIX. TERESA   The traffic report mentioned a 10-kilometre bottleneck on the A1 due to construction and an accident near the Maschener Kreuz interchange. Then Chopin came on, a series of dribbling piano notes, terribly sentimental. I turned off the radio and listened instead to the monotonous noise of the car.

Hedda was waiting for me at home, probably flipping through a book on the Russian Futurists. On my suggestion, she'd had her hair cut in a severe bob which made her look more elegant and a bit more mature. At the time, she was thirty-two and I was on the staff of the University of Göttingen. We'd been arguing a lot. About her colleague Karsten who she had lunch with every day at Café Schroeder; about her doctorate which wasn't getting anywhere; about the colour of the sheets and the colour of the sky. For a few weeks, being with Hedda had been unbearable, she was more moody than ever and would start to cry in the morning for no reason at all, as soon as she woke up next to me. I'd ask her what was wrong and she wouldn't answer. I just wanted out of that cage and, I have to admit, it didn't just have to do with her. Someone honked. I slammed on the brakes and swerved back into the right lane.

One of my affairs had become more important than I'd expected. Her name was Teresa. She was frighteningly beautiful, and in bed possessed the eternal fervour of the inexperienced who you could surprise with anything. In short, I couldn't drag myself away, and she'd begun to make demands. Usually, this was when I politely explained to women why things between us would go no further. I was always polite. Losing your manners was vulgar. I was never vulgar. I acted politely, I paid attention to my body, I showered for a long time after sex with every woman and, regardless of where we were, picked up the bill for us both. All in all, I was an ideal lover, and Teresa could have been more than happy about our having met, that meeting which was fleeting and straightforward and markedly beautiful. But she was damned determined to hold on to something that it's better not to try and hold on to.

I parked the car in a small side street, for though I knew that Hedda, at most, would go to her gallery (if she left the house at all), I was careful. In some things Hedda was really sensitive and I wanted to protect her. I hurried the last few metres over the pavement, went up the un-renovated stairwell, and Teresa, who must have already been waiting for me, opened the door before I'd even rung.

I remained in the hallway, I liked to tantalize her, she hung back, playing the ice queen, but then grabbed my hand and we hurried through the narrow corridor to her bed. Or, rather, what she considered to be her bed, just a slatted base balanced on a bunch of old bricks. It creaked and groaned and was extremely uncomfortable.

'You could buy yourself a decent bed at some point,' I said. She looked at me offended, though I really meant well; after all, she had to sleep there at night too.

'Well,' she said, 'let's go to yours then.'

I dodged. 'We could get a hotel room.'

'A hotel? In the town where we both pay rent?'

'You're terribly parsimonious, do you know that?' I said and ran my thumb along her chin.

'Always these secret meetings here,' she said.

'Always your questions,' I said.

The only thing I could do to get her to terminate her inquisition was to kiss her and place my hand between her thighs. She was sullen, she was anxious, she was wonderful. She moaned roughly, which made a mockery of her shyness, flouted her subtle inhibitions, and every time I made her submit anew. It could all be so easy: her flat was small, but with a few new pieces of furniture, a bit more order, we'd have a nice place for the two of us. I'd have a key and would come by between appointments at the university, would quickly take her clothes off in the hall, or she would come to meet me, naked already, maybe in fishnets or yellow lingerie. In itself yellow lingerie was tasteless, but on her olive-coloured skin it would have an absurdly exquisite charm. Teresa in yellow lingerie. It could go that way for months if she just gave up her unnecessary questions. Why I was so closed about certain things. Why I didn't want to go out in public with her. Why I didn't talk about my early experiences.

'Always this curiosity, dear Teresa,' I whispered.

'I'm just interested in you,' she answered.

You couldn't get anywhere with that crap. Didn't she understand that in asking these questions she was letting the beautiful thing we had die? She was simply letting it go bad, as if it didn't matter. I didn't want it to end; for the first time since I'd been with Hedda, perhaps for the first time in my life, I wanted to preserve my relationship with a woman even though it went against my own rules. I knew that I had to end it, that it was beginning to get tricky for me. But every time I was with her, I just couldn't bring myself to do it. I was subject to some kind of mysterious force that sapped me of any free choice.

'You're already imagining odd things with me,' I said.

'You know what, Anton?' she answered laughing. 'I think you're completely in love with me.'

'You think so?'

She kissed me on the chin, the neck, her lips crept across my shoulder, her tongue licked the groove of my jugular.

'I'm going to have a quick shower, if that's OK with you,' I said, pushing her away.

Teresa didn't answer, just pulled the blanket up to her collarbone. All of a sudden I found a satin landscape blocking my view.

I looked at the clock in the bathroom. It was just after six, in half an hour Hedda would be waiting for me. It was our anniversary, and even if Hedda maintained that she didn't care about such things, I knew it was only unimportant to her so long as I was thinking of it. I washed carefully, looked at myself in the mirror, and the more the mist cleared the more I had to accept how positive my affair with Teresa had been for me. The skin beneath my eyes was soft and bright. And though I was sleeping less than ever, I looked rested.

As I was getting ready to leave the bathroom, Hedda rang. I terminated the call, but she didn't give up and my mobile rang once more with that hideous sound she'd programmed. I terminated it again, but she called back.

'What is it?' I hissed.

'Anton?' Hedda stammered. It sounded as if she'd just been crying. 'I have to see you, right now,' she said, and I noticed that I'd been mistaken, she hadn't stopped crying, and one thing I cannot stand is when grown women cry. It's such an infantile move.

'Listen, I can't right now,' I said.

'My mother's had a stroke, she's in hospital, I don't know how she is.'

'It's really not a good time.'

'I don't know a thing, we have to go see her. Now.'

'Don't put me under pressure, Hedda. We were supposed to see each other at seven,' I said somewhat louder.

'Anton?' Teresa called from the hallway. 'Everything OK?'

'Where are you?' Hedda asked.

'At the university. I told you already.'

'No you're not. I'm at the university. I'm standing in your office.'

'What's with the haughty tone?'

'Anton, sorry, my mother's not doing well, I'm worried.'

'Then drive to the hospital. I'll cancel our reservation at the Italians.'

'I'm scared, Anton.'

'You always act as if you're the only one things happen to. Your mother's not the first seventy-year-old to have a stroke, you know.'

'Anton?' Teresa called from the hallway.

'Where are you, Anton?' Hedda asked again.

'Hedda, we already talked about that. Go see your mother, we'll talk later tonight.' I hung up, rubbed my wet hair with the towel and left the bathroom.

Teresa had laid back down, the blanket only reached her hips, I could see her white breasts, the violet-brown lace of her bra, and beneath the blanket her legs were spread and formed a triangle. My hand slid across the satin up to the spot. Now we had time, Hedda wouldn't be back before eight or nine.

'Who were you talking to?' Teresa asked.

'Someone from the university. They don't even leave me alone on Fridays.'

Her small hand crept into mine, and gripping it for a moment I thought it would have to work out, that nothing between Teresa and I would endanger my relationship with Hedda, not in any real sense, and anyway, you shared your life with so many people, why should these two rule each other out? Teresa kissed my neck, her hand stroked my hairline; I pulled her to me and kissed her breasts.

'You are so ridiculously clean, Anton,' she whispered. 'I can't taste you at all. Just soap.'

'Really?' I said and backed away. 'Does anything else about me bother you?'

'What's wrong? Why are you so pissed off all a sudden?'

'I'm a bit stressed at the moment, I have so much work, the edition of the letters, the articles for the Marxist dictionary and this whole Bachelor's nonsense, you have no idea how much work that is. Right now I really am just not interested in your mood.'

Teresa stretched out, naturally, only so that I would see her what she imagined to be irresistible body. Then she opened her eyes, such big round eyes! But, despite all her charm, the snappy tone did not escape me.

'Who were you talking to?' she asked. 'It didn't have to do with the university, be honest.'

'Are you implying something? Listen, Teresa, we can end this too, right now.'

I stood up and crossed my arms.

'Sit down, Toni, what's with you?' she asked and lowered her eyes, the silly fawn-like charm. I looked around the room, reviewed her whole slovenly day-to-day life, a skirt hung carelessly over the clothes rail, a shirt lying crumpled on the ground, Teresa probably didn't even own an iron, and then I noticed the white flecks on the fabric. I didn't flinch, for I had my body under control, but if I'd been a less composed man, I would have. I recognized those spots, I liked seeing them on expensive suits and business clothes. The more severe the outfit, the greater the excitement, and theoretically I would have liked it on Teresa's well-cut and well-ironed shirt too, which must have looked good on her, it's just that she'd never worn it around me and had likely never ironed it either.

'Please don't be so angry,' she said sweetly. What completely phoney innocence. She just had to make the little bit of emotion she felt appear absurd. Because she couldn't bear it. Because she preferred the safe, the safe and the dull.

'Did I say something wrong?' Teresa asked, begging for an explanation. She looked concerned, and when I refused to turn away from her gaze, she risked a smile. Of course she only wanted to hear that she hadn't said anything wrong. *Teresa, how could you of all people say something wrong?*

'Say something, Anton.'

I picked up her shirt and threw it into her lap.

'What am I supposed to do with this?'

'You should keep your clothes clean.'

'You can't be serious.'

'You expect me to put up with that?'

'Put up with that? Some yoghurt on my shirt?'

'Yoghurt?'

'Or toothpaste, I don't know.'

'Toothpaste?'

'You're nuts, Anton, you're really nuts.'

'Is that so? I'm nuts. And your accusations are, naturally, completely legitimate.'

'Perhaps you'd better go and we'll talk tomorrow,' Teresa said, knotting the shirt in her hands.

'Yes, of course. Always according to your rules. Do you know what, this game is far too idiotic. We can spare ourselves the call. Once and for all.'

Leaving the building I called Hedda. She'd finally got hold of her father. Her mother—hadn't I told her immediately?—was doing fairly well. 'You see, Hedda, it's not all as bad as you always think. I'll pick you up afterwards and we'll go to the Italians. No, not because of your mother. Do you remember that, as of today, we've been together for exactly five years?'

XX. ROME Under the protection of immunity, Gramsci returns to Italy on 12 May 1924. At the beginning of April, he was voted into parliament, and his comrades still believe that the fascists actually care about immunity and parliaments and the rights of their opponents, or still want to believe, or have long since ceased to believe, but what other choice do they have? There aren't any alternatives.

The fascists have been chasing Gramsci's shadow for years. In Turin, where in 1922 they stormed the editorial offices of many newspapers and beat up communists, they could not track him down but managed to find his brother and let their rage out on him instead. It cost Gennaro a lot of blood, as well as a finger. Then he fled abroad, with only nine fingers and a continual sense of anxiety that he could no longer bear Italy.

But Gramsci has to go to Italy, he is the one who can create a front against the fascists, beyond the Party ranks, he is the one who can speak with all the deputies and bring them together, there where everything is argued down to the smallest details. If anything, they had held out too long against the socialists and the bourgeoisie, perhaps he will no longer be able to overcome all the fissures. And he won't be able to bring back his brother's tenth finger either.

He walks through the market to Piazza Alessandria. The ground is wet from the water that's been tipped over the fish on display. There is the vapour coming from the *trattorias* on Via Mantova again. The flower girls in the Villa Borghese hold little bouquets of violets out to him. He buys three to dry out for Giulia on the windowsill of the new room he has taken, under a false name, with a German family, the Passarges.

The Passarges speak in a formal accent and refer to him as Professor because his second suitcase is stuffed full of books. Gramsci does his best to keep secret his activities as a communist deputy. They have great respect for titles. Frau Clara Passarge, who, because of her sincere reserve, was almost invisible, takes painstaking care to ensure that the Professor remains undisturbed. When they pass each other in the hallways, she shyly invites him to a coffee she prepares in the kitchen in the German fashion: with warm water over a paper filter she lets drip into the pot instead of heating it up on the stove until it hisses into the little metal container and is three times as strong and three times as hot. But in compensation the cup she gives him is three times as large as the cups he drinks his coffee from in the bars around Piazza Alessandria or on Via Mantova.

And naturally she's right, he needs his quiet, even if she didn't have to make it into such a general rule: those studying need their peace and quiet, Frau Passarge believes, they live quiet, they breathe quiet, they nourish themselves on quiet, that is what differentiates academics from other people who would rather eat, drink and be physical. Whenever her granddaughter visits, he hears a scratching at his door as she tries to reach the handle in order to worm her way into seeing the funny guest, but, at four years old and three feet, she's still too small, and she calls through the closed door in a childlike Italian: 'Stlivi?' Are you writing? And barely has he opened the door does she shoot inside, hold out her cheek to be kissed and ask: 'Do you want to play?' Gramsci pulls a piece of paper out of his stack, draws her a bird and then together they let ink drip from his pen and think what strange forms they make on the paper.

The Passarge's flat is in a side street off of Via Nomentana, near Porta Pia. Gramsci takes long walks down to the Colosseum with his comrade Felice Platone, and they laugh and argue and laugh some more, even if Russia is too important to joke about, as is the bureaucratic dictatorship spreading out of the offices and backrooms because no one knows how to control the country any more; for an entire country, one that's been turned upside down, must first find itself and yet it doesn't have the strength left to do so. They eat in a *trattoria* near the main train station, sea bass and pasta with a beaten egg, a few of their other colleagues join them, Alessandro, Federico, Lucca. Felice leans forward and looks at Gramsci for a long time, too long, and Gramsci knows he will have to swear it: yes, he still believes. In spite of everything. Even though the USSR is not always good for his faith. Stalin's faithful have fought the Zinoyevs and Trotskys to the death, as power will not simply let itself be switched in people's minds from one day to the next. Together they had won a revolution, together they had won a civil war, but winning over people's minds takes longer than winning the streets. Once Lenin's successor is named, everything will go well, Gramsci had hoped. Because this was a new era. Because this was a chance that could not be lost. The important thing was not to rush. Not to turn brutal with one's methods. You had to allow the opposition their space. At the thirteenth Congress of the CPSU, Stalin presented himself as the only legitimate successor to Lenin.

'He makes me uneasy,' Alessandro says.

For a moment it is quiet, then they can hear the scraping of silverware against porcelain. Strings of spaghetti hang from the comrades' mouths.

'I don't know, but there shouldn't be any power struggles between two comrades,' Federico answers.

'Power struggles as always. This isn't a new era at all—we just have new names. Everything will stay the same,' Felice grumbles and pushes her plate away. 'The food used to be better here too.'

'Nothing stays the same,' Federico counters.

'Of course not,' says Gramsci. 'We were asleep. We were busy focusing on Russia and forgot that Italy is a totally different country. That things here would go otherwise. Take a look around, Felice, it's long been worse than we ever feared. The fascists are in power. They've taken over everything. We depend on their tolerance. Do you understand? On their tolerance! We're dependent on them. And we didn't see any of this coming because we were too arrogant with our optimism.'

Federico nods. Amadeo looks at Gramsci blankly.

'Perhaps we've harmed the country more than the socialists,' he says softly. 'Perhaps everything we fought for was wrong, because we did it at the wrong time.'

After they finish eating they head back to the north of the city. Lucca says goodbye first, then Alessandro and Federico. Felice and Gramsci separate at the monument by Porta Pia. The stone figures stuck with their weapons in remembrance of the Italian war of unification follow Gramsci into his dreams, the seagulls circling above the Vittoriano monument swoop into his bedroom. Vienna disappears from his life as if he had never been there. The saints in Rome look at him less sanctimoniously than Agnes with her dust-covered hair, and Giulia seems to once again be closer even though there are now a few more kilometres between them. But who cares about geography? Gramsci wants to show her what the roofs of Rome look like from up on the Trinità dei Monti, she hasn't been here in such a long time, and maybe she's forgotten. He wants to tell her how green the Tiber is this year and how harshly Tiber Island splits the current, how the small waves fall over one another, eddy and swirl and can't take off quickly enough. And he wants to show her this too: the men standing around beneath the cypresses by the racecourse and making fun of politicians. One of them imitates Mussolini's grimace, then mutters his infamous phrase: *Me ne frego!*'

The first time they meet he doesn't see her. He sees Giulia. He sees a shadow that has broken out of his memory and become real. It is a smoky, foggy morning, people are pressed together in the tram, they have just passed Via Nomentana, they will soon pass through Piazza Buenos Aires, a charming little circle with villas and sandstone lions looking imperiously down on the wobbly, over-filled ride. Then along the edge of the massive Villa Borghese to the zoo, where, when the wind's just right, you can hear the elephants. The doors have just closed, it is sticky and people's arms are damp with sweat. He turns his head and sees a woman who, when she briefly turns her head towards him, looks familiar. He stops short, thinks of Giulia. Thinks of his son. 3,600 grams, dark hair, blue eyes, a nicely proportioned little head, Giulia had written him in August. 'It looks like he has been ripened in the sun.'

People push between him and the woman, arms brush him, damp impressions stay behind on his skin, he sees the round face with the sharp lines of the eyebrows, the delicate body, and asks himself whether his wish has become so urgent that it is actually standing in front of him, whether she has come all the way from Ivanovo without telling him.

No, that'd be impossible. A wish would have at least said hello.

And then he knows. Tania. He has just seen Giulia's sister, who he has been seeking for weeks, after the Schuchts asked him. When the family went back to Russia, Tania stayed behind in Rome. 'In order to finish her studies,' Giulia had said. 'That's only half the story,' Gramsci had answered. 'Natural sciences,' was all Giulia said in response. 'She was very talented.'

He wants to get out, he wants to follow her but the tram has separated the two of them. When he gets off at the next stop, he cowers like a beaten mutt and hurries along the rails in the opposite direction. The people on the pavement avoid him. He hardly notices any more, he has grown used to it, those looks, but today he can feel all the displeasure he has long felt directed towards him, towards that misshaped body.

He disappears further into his coat. All of a sudden he is freezing even though it is more than twenty degrees. The air seems leaden and over there, on the other side of the street, a door slams so loudly it's as if it wanted to reach all the way to Moscow. He's afraid, suddenly he is afraid of the hydrants next to him, afraid of the upcoming intersection, afraid of the thoughts beating him back into his isolation, into that cocoon through which nothing but letters and numbers pass. That stumbling of the nerves and thoughts which one calls love, but where does it lead? There in Rome it has no place nor goal, and he has to make his way to an assembly meeting, and Tania will have disappeared into one of the streets.

He already knows this much about Tania: she is registered as a citizen of the USSR at the embassy; in June, he learnt about a Roman address but by the time he got around to visiting, she no longer lived there. She had had to go to a clinic, the landlady had explained, standing before him in a blue-white smock and massive upper arms. Behind her, a child pushed itself into the doorway and looked at Gramsci with curiosity. 'The Bastianelli Clinic,' the landlady said and drove the child back with a perfunctory hand movement. 'Please give her our best wishes for recovery.' At the clinic he learnt that she was away for hydrotherapy in Pescara or Tuscany. She's doing well, Gramsci told his wife in July. In October, he heard that she was teaching at a private school on Via Savoia, but he had been unable to find the street as it had recently been renamed and was not yet listed on the city map.

'She's hiding from you,' Comrade Stuchevsky opines, 'otherwise you would have found her a long time ago. She doesn't want you to find her. She doesn't know what you want from her and whether it could be dangerous for her. Who knows, perhaps she's afraid of the fascists. Or us.' Gramsci nods, he can understand, he's afraid of them too, if not for himself. He often thinks of his son, he imagines him as a sun-ripened apricot with two eyes, a mouth and a nose.

140

Stuchevsky pats him on the shoulder. 'A female friend of mine can provide you with her new address, perhaps you'll get lucky.'

The building that Stuchevsky named is only 200 metres from the Passarges', across the Nomentana on a street to the left. He pays a visit in mid-January, but instead of Tania a man with a funereal expression opens the door. He is wearing a suit, but is barefoot and looks at Gramsci morosely. What did he want from Tania? He was her flatmate, neither a relative nor related by marriage. And him? Ach, a deputy in Parliament? A communistic one? He himself, Schreider was his name, was a social revolutionary. And so the deputy was in contact with her family in Moscow? Nothing good had ever come out of Russia, all the local representatives of the Soviet were corrupt scoundrels, and if the Revolution had broken out in Europe instead, things would look very different indeed. In Russia there simply could not be anything good, he had realized that by now.

'Yes, thank you, and please let Miss Schucht know that I would like to see her. She has nothing to be afraid of, we will not walk to Moscow.'

On 1 February, at four o'clock in the afternoon, Gramsci is again standing in front of her door, his shoulders back, he expects to be met by Schreider's gaunt face, but then it is Tania, Tania herself, standing before him. How similar to Giulia she now seems, outside of the narrow confines of the tram, outside of the shadowy morning light.

'So, you're here,' she says and lets her hand slip off the door handle.

'Yes, here I am,' Gramsci answers and squints towards her. The light in the corridor has just been switched on and is blinding. But this much he does see: Tania is wearing a bright linen blouse and a broche over her left breast, she seems vulnerable and determined at the same time, and the way she is standing there, she could also be a middle-class housewife, not upper-class of course, just a household with one maid, nothing more.

'You wanted to speak with me?'

'Yes, I did,' Gramsci responds.

He hesitates a moment, then sputters: 'You do not know it yet, but I am your brother-in-law.'

She raises an eyebrow.

'You also have a nephew, Delio, Giulia and my son.'

'Giulia?'

'From whom I send greetings. You are missed in Moscow.'

Tania abruptly turns away, he sees her neck and the slightly wavy hair, her thin neck which seems even more fragile than the rest of her.

When she looks at him again, it is almost shyly. 'Then please come inside, we cannot stay in the open door for ever.'

He looks around for Herr Schreider, either hidden behind the doors or perhaps not at home. They sit down in the kitchen at an old dining table, the water tap is calcified, the sink a stone trough. Tania opens the coffee pot and measures out the powder exactly, they can afford a few things here but never too much.

Herr Schreider had brought her here, she tells him, he looked after her, she wasn't to get involved with the wrong people, work for the wrong people, think the wrong things, he looked after her so much that in the meantime she could hardly breathe. Was all that care a waste of time? Work was fine, life was fine, not necessarily good but fine, and good, what does that really mean, who could define what a good life was, but she wouldn't call it poor either, for things were coming along and it had never got ugly, the fascists left her alone. She was teaching natural science at a private school just a few hundred metres away, she liked the children even though she remained indifferent to them in a pleasant way. In general, she was indifferent to many things; perhaps that was what she treasured about her life in Rome.

'Don't you miss your family? And Russia?'

'I hardly know Russia at all.'

'And do you agree with Schreider that nothing good comes out of Russia?'

'Does anything from Russia even come here?' she asks. 'Schreider has his ideas and I have mine.'

All of a sudden she looks very tired and Gramsci suggests they go eat. She nods silently, places the cafetiere in the stone sink and throws a thin shawl around her neck. Outside, it has just grown dark, they walk next to each other, and when Tania briefly puts her hand on his arm to stop him from walking into the street—'Careful! An automobile!'—he feels how thin she is.

In the *trattoria* she hardly eats a thing. Gramsci tries to convince her. *At least the meat*, he begs.

'I don't have any appetite,' she says stubbornly.

'It's got nothing to do with appetite, it has to do with you gaining strength.'

'That is all your lot ever thinks about, strength.'

'You have to think a bit about yourself.'

'I have never thought much about myself,' she answers gruffly, as if it were uncomfortable to her.

'One cannot only think about society, Tania. Without us it wouldn't exist. And without what we want.'

'I have no sense of what I want. I am not even sure if I have a sense of my own being.'

'You have to hunt after yourself like frogs in a meadow,' Gramsci says, laughing.

Tania looks away. He sees her profile which again reminds him of Giulia. Perhaps he has no sense of her being either, perhaps he only sees Giulia through her. They talk till late in the night, it is almost twelve by the time Gramsci says goodbye. He embraces her for a long time, or is it she who embraces him, who does not want to go back to Herr Schreider and all that loneliness?

'When will we see each other again?'

'Soon.'

XXI. GLANCES   The next day I waited in front of the gate to the Istituto Gramsci for the library to open with the first two mummies to have arrived. At nine-thirty, the glass doors slid open, and, though the sun was shining, the temperatures inside dropped to those of a wine cellar. The heavy tomes trapped the daylight, the halogen lights hummed like dying insects and one glance at the students already grinding their way through the tedium of term papers made me nervous. Tatiana wasn't there yet, perhaps she wouldn't show up today at all, all the same I took a seat, stuck with a book and looked towards the door when it opened now and again, even if only to let in some more sad PhD students. Then I turned and looked out the window onto the stem of the palm as it fanned out towards the top. I was looking for pigeons, but the tree seemed uninhabited.

Tatiana briefly appeared before my eyes, contemptuously wedging the pack of cigarettes over the edge of the rubbish into the bin. My hand slid across her hips. Someone bumped into a chair, a pile of papers plopped down onto a desk, a door closed. I started at every sound; Tatiana's curves flared up, then became blurry. She simply did not allow herself to be held in my memory. As if she were defending herself. As if she were forbidding me.

Maybe she was slinking through the corridors of the Russian embassy again. All of a sudden I was so sure of it that I wanted to jump up and run back to Mr Golubev, but in the end I stayed where I was, for I knew that as soon as I left she'd show up, sit down at the desk next to mine and look for me in vain while out in front of the embassy a kid-like *Carabiniere* would be attempting to take my personal information again. Everything seemed to be getting in our way, and ultimately we prefer to be unhappy among other unhappy people, which was precisely why the institute was allowing this courtyard—lost beneath the red plastic cordons and site fences and continuing to rust on unobserved—to deteriorate: it was a way to conceal the misery inside.

By the time I'd had another look through the room, Tatiana was there, at a desk, her face bathed in the unhealthy light of a halogen lamp and the room tingling like cat fur with an electric charge. I couldn't see what she was reading and maybe she was reading a number of different books, I could only concentrate on that little spot, on a point above her eyes where there was a wrinkle between her brows, and I didn't want to do anything else than run my fingertip along it.

I couldn't say how long I watched her. Mummies kept interrupting my line of sight, coming in with piles of grubby documents in their arms, and then a library employee informed me that the seats were reserved for working visitors.

A young student sat down next to her, holding a newspaper from the archive that had become transparent with the decades and threatened to blow away like an abandoned cocoon. Crumbs of tobacco stuck to the fluff of his sweater. I recognized him immediately. I knew his kind. Guys like him would stand at the edge of the smokers' area with their hand-rolled cigarettes, and show up in seminars with deadly serious eyes and overwrought papers. They read Camus and Foucault but could not put together a single clever idea about them and were nothing for women like Tatiana.

She slid him a piece of paper; he bent over it and scribbled something on the edge. She leant towards him as if she couldn't wait for him to slide the paper back. Their arms touched. It looked like she was whispering something to him. I bent back over the picture of the star athlete in the book in front of me, over her wiry, grey-striped upper arms. There was no point in getting upset about guys like him. He would never be a milestone in a woman's life, just a low point, and his whole life long he would probably never get it. I squinted over towards them. Tatiana's face seemed older and more angular, as if her neighbour's ashen skin was rubbing off on her. He was no good for her, I could see that straight away.

He stood up and moved behind her, bent so low that his chest touched her shoulder. He whispered something to her, but what? Then she stood up too. They were standing so close, one in front of the other, obscuring a few books on Palmiro Togliatti; then next to Tatiana I saw a title on the paramilitary organization Gladio. Gladio had been responsible for bombings in Bologna in 1980 and Rome in 1969 and, if you paid any attention to Ilsa, for Aldo Moro's death too. Tatiana's fingers drummed against the fuzzy sweater. A piece of clothing like a Shetland pony. I stood up. I couldn't stand to look any more. She deserved better.

On the left, a collection of speeches by Palmiro Togliatti and the Shetland pony; on the right, Tatiana and the bombing in Bologna. The guy eyed me irritably while pompously explaining something about the concept of the state to Tatiana, as if he were the first person to have read something about the integral state. He tumbled onward, dragging Tatiana from Gramsci to de Tocqueville all the way to Machiavelli before treating her to an explication of Venetian tax law.

'So, listen, it's not that complicated,' I interrupted. 'According to Antonio Gramsci, in the integral state we do not observe the political institutions alone but the private initiatives of civil society as well. And that's where the fight for cultural hegemony takes place, for the dominance of particular convictions. Or, as Gramsci explained in a short formula: "State = political society + civil society, hegemony protected by the armour of coercion."'

'German, eh?'

'What does that have to do with Germany?'

'You should work on your accent. You're too clipped.'

'And you're limping hopelessly behind scientific standards. There's no point. You're just wasting your time here.'

'Do you know each other?' the pony asked Tatiana.

She shrugged her shoulders. I was captivated by how nervous she was.

'In any event, she has talent,' I explained to him. 'As opposed to you.'

'You know that for a fact?' Tatiana asked.

'Tatiana,' I said and laid my hand on hers. 'I am doubtless not the first to compliment you for your intelligence.'

'Why's he calling you Tatiana?'

'Oh, leave him alone.' She tried to get rid of the pony. But the young lint-carrier didn't seem to understand. Some people were brilliant at blocking out reality.

'I think you are now truly superfluous,' I translated with an unmistakable bluntness.

'Is that so?' it asked.

Tatiana looked back and forth between me and the pony without saying a word.

'Well, I'm out of here. We'll see each other tomorrow. Or whenever.' The pony kissed Tatiana on the cheeks, left, right, then trotted towards the exit, the door snapped shut, we were alone. Only a few mummies were left, shrivelling up at their tables.

'Shall we eat together this evening?' I asked.

'Excuse me?'

'Or do you already have plans?'

'Wow, you're smooth. You just got rid of my plans.'

'You don't really mean that. You didn't really want to go out with him?'

'And why not? Do you know him?'

'You cannot honestly be telling me that you're interested in that kind of man.'

'He's smart.'

'Yes, just now I was completely won over.'

'Maybe he can't explain things as eloquently as you, but he's also only half as old.'

'So, he just turned fifteen?'

'And, you're insane.'

'Well, at his age he should have more to offer.'

'You were never his age. You were born old.'

For a moment I was confused, I didn't know what she meant until it became clear that she'd entered the game and was winding me up. I laughed and bent my head to the side. She turned and left the room.

The man at reception grumbled something to me as I walked past, the glass doors slid open and there she was, standing with her back to me in that wasteland of asphalt. She was not alone. I saw the pony and the pony saw me. It arrogantly ignored my presence and continued to speak to Tatiana in a quiet voice. She shook her head a few times, and, when the pony paused, began to gesticulate wildly, said something that I was too far away to understand. The pony rummaged about its pockets, pulled out a package of tobacco and grimly rolled a cigarette.

I took a few steps towards her in order to get into her field of vision but kept a good distance. I could feel how I'd struck the ideal balance between understatement and urgency on my face. Most people knew little about their own faces, they just rubbed peeling creams over their skin and bought expensive anti-ageing moisturisers, but as of yet ageing had never been stopped by glycerine and propanedial. They exaggerated their expressions, raised their eyebrows too quickly and either looked ridiculous or remained stony and invisible. The women I chose to look at never thought they saw anything special in my face and yet they still felt something, confusion, some kind of pull, never right away, it always took a few hours to develop. The night was important, the night is the incubation period for everything that touches us more profoundly than the everyday.

The problem was that Tatiana wasn't looking at me, though she must have felt that I was looking at her. She was keeping her eyes down to excite me, and I liked it, though it was a bit silly, I mean, how old was she? A young woman in her mid-twenties was still allowed to be silly, in fact, she *had* to be, anything else would just seem precocious and cold.

'We had a date!' she said so loudly that it made its way to me.

'This is too stupid!' the pony yelled back, then galloped past me and began tampering with a Vespa. Tatiana turned slowly towards me. I smiled; she sank her head. Her face looked fragile, as if she'd just been crying.

'You shouldn't get involved with those kinds of people,' I said.

'You don't have any idea what's going on.'

'Ach, Tatiana.'

'I can't get you to give up on that name, can I?'

'Let's go,' I decided. 'We're disturbing the saintly devotion here.' I cast a glance at the fluffy pony working on its Vespa, and delicately led Tatiana towards the exit. As I pushed open the door, my hand briefly brushed her shoulder. She lurched. I grabbed her arm.

'Are you OK?'

'Yeah, yeah. It's just . . . you just smell an awful lot of cologne.'

XXII. INDEED! INDEED! They briefly size each other up. The distance between them is only a few metres: Gramsci on the rostrum, Mussolini, his chin stuck out, at his usual place. They have known each other for years. Mussolini had run *Avanti!* before his expulsion from the Socialist Party, Gramsci *Ordine Nuovo*, but today is the first time that Gramsci will be speaking out against him, face to face. He has been waiting for this moment since returning to Italy, and, in fact, for much longer. Mussolini seems like a chimera, unreal, frozen into his pose. The prototype of the petit-bourgeois gone wild.

The socialists are unable to harm the Duce, they have only twenty-two seats while the fascists dominate the parliament with more than ten times as many. In the end, it was clear who was stronger, who was right, and little by little Mussolini will drive the last deputies out of parliament, including this strange little Sardinian he'd allowed to write a few articles for *Avanti!* and who now seems to think he can put something together with a little rhetoric. It isn't wise to turn against the Duce in parliament, the stage is his, as is the rest of the country, and the last time someone raised their voice against him in this room—the socialist Giacomo Matteotti who, after the previous spring's falsified votes, had accused the fascists: 'If you hadn't won at the ballot box, you would have employed sheer violence'—didn't end well. His corpse was found a few weeks later in a forest 25 kilometres from Rome.

The fascists could not control the usual parties, so they obscured their goals with arson attacks and deception, Gramsci hisses into the room. He tries to speak as loud as he can, but his lungs are weak and the speech exhausts him. Wearing amused and bitter expressions, the fascist deputies lean back onto their benches and yell: 'Indeed! Indeed!'

'What does one do against a powerful enemy?' Gramsci asks the assembled parliamentarians and, above all, Mussolini, Little Benito, who he wants to cut back down to size. 'First you break his legs and then you compromise from the superior position.'

'We're only doing what you are doing in Russia!' Mussolini yells. Gramsci turns towards him, and although he had been waiting for precisely that moment, he does not look at the Duce but over his head.

'In Russia there are laws, and they are obeyed,' he counters.

Mussolini stands up. 'You're very good at cracking down in Russia too,' he calls out.

'In reality, the national police apparatus already views the Communist Party as an underground organization,' Gramsci answers calmly and continues to look past the Duce, a small figure amongst other small figures.

'That's not true,' Mussolini thunders.

'Nevertheless, anyone who attends a meeting of three or more people is arrested without charge and thrown into jail for being a communist.'

'How many people are sitting in jail? We only pick them up so the police can record their details.'

'That is systematic persecution. You all are acting just like Giolitti's minions when they arrested everyone who voted against the government—just to take hold of them.'

'You don't know a thing about the South!' someone yells from one of the back benches.

'I *am* from the South!' Gramsci yells back.

His comrades applaud, the fascists make noise, a few deputies turn towards Mussolini. The Duce nods. He should not underestimate this one here, his antagonist could indeed become a danger.

'And now, you can prepare my funeral,' Matteotti had told his comrades after his last speech before Parliament. Gramsci cannot get this phrase out of his head. In the cafeteria, he orders a coffee and a water, his throat feels raw, as if he had yelled uninterrupted for an hour. Here he feels safe, nothing will happen to him in Parliament. 'Down with the Murderous Regime', Gramsci had written across the top of *L'Unità* after Matteotti's death. They will not forgive him that either. Everything began with Matteotti, he was their test run.

When Mussolini steps into the room, everyone turns around. Gramsci is standing at the bar, cup of coffee in hand. All of a sudden the loud voices turn into a whisper. Mussolini walks towards Gramsci with an outstretched hand.

'What an opening!'

Gramsci turns away, downs his coffee and walks out without looking at Mussolini.

Tania is waiting for him outside, sunk into the front pages of the newspapers which have been hung on the side of a kiosk. Over the last few weeks, they have met each other at a *trattoria* numerous times, and he has taken her on a walk down to the river and onto the other side of the Tiber past the Castel Sant'Angelo and the Palace of Justice.

He walks up to her, she turns towards him hesitatingly, almost like a kind of sleepwalker, her smile is shy, like one learnt in a girls' school, only when he embraces her does he feel her tension fall away.

'I thought they weren't going to let you go.'

'They would have preferred to make me minister straight away,' Gramsci answers and grabs her arm.

They walk through the old city, cross the Via del Corso, a tiny man is playing violin on a street corner. Gramsci closes his eyes for a moment, sees Parliament before him, Mussolini, his mask of a face. He would gladly turn around, challenge him again, make him look like a fool, he wants to see this great leader go weak in the knees on account of a tin voice one more time.

'Are you all right, Nino?' He hears Tania as if from a distance. He nods, presses her arm tighter against his body. They climb the Spanish Steps up to the Pincio, buy a few small bouquets from the flower girl, and make their way through the park grinning before winding their way back down to Piazza del Popolo. Next to Tania, the Parliament, Mussolini's clown face and the whole collapsing constitutional state slowly begin to fade.

'Look!' Tania calls out and points to a shop window with a pair of shoes. 'For Giulia.'

Gramsci looks at the extremely thin heels which would make Giulia strut around like a petit-bourgeois fairy.

'She would never wear something like that!'

Tania does not allow herself to be discouraged and drags him into the shop. She even finds a pair for Delio on one of the hind-most racks. And then another. Gramsci shakes his head. 'I will never understand this. Your mania to shoe the entire world.'

'But I've found a pattern for you,' she says, 'with a good sewing machine, your suit will be done in thirty minutes.'

'You are as manic as your sister. Giulia knows every specialist for nervous conditions in Moscow. She's even sent our son. I cannot imagine that this dreamy archivist of illness was particularly helpful in the development of his personality.'

'Well, in her own way, Giulia is concerned about Delio.'

'In her own way! Like a lioness which has to defend her young from some great animalistic pain. One should raise a young person to be able to fight whatever his surroundings throw at him with his own common sense.'

'So, how did you free him from the specialist?'

'Upon parting, we gave Doctor Vassilyev a drawing by Correggio.'

'Why Correggio exactly?' Tania asks.

'Because . . . ,' Gramsci hesitates. Does he have to have an explanation for everything? 'Because Correggio painted *putti*.'

'Naked children with wings.'

'At least they look healthy.'

'Middle class and frivolous.'

'But, imagine this: Giulia and I had just written our names beneath the picture, and as I went to push it across the desk, Eugenia bent over it and wrote her name next to Giulia's. And with it: the mothers. I really had no idea what I was supposed to say.'

'And what did Mr Vassilyev say?'

'He said . . . '

Gramsci holds Tania back by the hand and stares at the black paint of the Fiat which has just stopped in front of them. Once again he has to think of Matteotti. A few days after his speech, an automobile had parked outside his flat on the Lungotevere. When Matteotti had walked out his front door, the men had walked up to him, dragged him into the car and pushed him onto the backseat.

'Nino, what's wrong?' Tania asks. A door is pushed open. A woman with a brightly coloured summer hat steps out, bewilderedly nods at the two of them, then saunters down the street.

'So what did he say?'

'An *amor*,' Gramsci murmurs. 'And so naked.'

The leather of the backseat is glowing. A fist. The car rumbles over the uneven stones, sweat, leather, metal, another punch, the white sun flickering in the window, a blade is thrust between his ribs, blood soaks the shirt and drips onto the upholstery. The heat of the blade and then another and another and the sun in the window rushes in upon Matteotti.

'I need to eat something right away,' Gramsci whispers.

'Yes, you should,' Tania says and holds his arm until they arrive at a restaurant.

It is dark and cool inside the converted wine cellar that smells of fried fish. Tania steadfastly sticks with her half-portion while gnawing at a few zucchini flowers for a long time.

'And will they come to visit you now?' she asks.

'Us. Your sisters want to see you.'

'Want! Some things look a bit differently in our family. You don't understand that.'

'Be that as it may, I know one part of your family very well.'

Gramsci puts half a fish on her plate.

'Oh, you with your strength again,' Tania declines.

'Since Nadiana's death . . . '

'Since what?' For a moment Tania looks at him with hostility, as if he were responsible for what he has just said.

'I thought you knew . . . She did not come back from the Civil War.'

'I know little about my family,' Tania says drily and adds: 'We shall have to find a flat for Julca and Eugenia.'

'We shall.'

No sooner had his own plate been cleared away than Tania's is in front of him. She has not touched her fish, and smiles apologetically.

'Well, I know a thing or two about flats. I've moved around a lot here.'

As soon as they're outside, she's interested in shoes again, for her sister Eugenia, for her mother, they have to stop in front of every shop. What would the *squadristi* say if they had to search his flat and found nothing but shoes?

'And now you would also like to become a representative for women's fashion, Mr Deputy?'

XXIII. THE LOVE OF DESTRUCTION

'Perhaps it really will be better once you're gone,' Hedda had said the day before I left for Rome. I'd retreated to the bedroom in order to pack my suitcase which I'd been hoping to be able to do in peace, but, almost as soon as I heard her enter the flat, there she was, leaning in the doorway and staring at my fingers. She was in a fancy dress and her lips were done as if she were about to go out, but she'd just got home, which explained the dress but not her lips.

'It is not all that particularly pleasant to watch a relationship in the process of its demise,' she said.

'Then don't watch,' I answered. 'It's got something to do with discipline, Hedda.'

'Yes, of course, discipline,' she replied sharply. She didn't listen to me, she simply did not want to understand what I meant. She just acted like she had no will of her own, no power of decision in her life, she preferred to constantly be a victim. A victim of circumstances, a victim of other people (above all, me), a victim of a past relationship, the past in general, which really was just like it was because it was like she was and nothing could be changed. In any event, one could attempt to allow the present to be more enjoyable, Hedda however dived straight into unhappiness, and when it was almost over, she'd wave and cry out: Wait for me, I want to come with you!

'What relationship are you talking about, Hedda?' I asked and pulled a stack of shirts out of the wardrobe. 'We decided not to have any relationship any longer. You aren't sticking to the terms of our agreement and reproaching me at the same time.'

156

The shirts exploded in a burst of colour. Hedda knocked them over with the palm of her hand, and what had just been in order now lay in a heap on the floor.

'We decided?' she screamed. 'You decided! You decided everything. What I was to wear, how I was to have my hair cut, what city we were going to live in, the name of our son. You decided my whole life for me and never allowed me to say a single word. What I wanted, what I wanted for my life and perhaps for yours too and for Lasse's never interested you in the slightest. You took the decisions and then in the end spoke of a "we". That is no joint decision, Anton, that's just talking in *pluralis majestatis.*'

I bent down and picked up the shirts. They were fine, they could still be folded without having to be ironed again.

'*Of course* I was never interested in what you wanted.' I lay the shirts down on the bed and smoothed the arms flat. 'Weren't you the one who wanted to be with me?' I asked but did not look at her, for it would've been taken as a provocation. How much her daily blackmail bored me. 'Weren't you the one who wanted to move in together?' I asked. 'Weren't you the one who wanted to get married? Weren't you the one who wanted to have a kid? Up to the end everything I did was for you.'

'At most, you did whatever it was that *you* wanted for me,' Hedda said. 'In truth, of course, you were only ever interested in yourself.'

'I did whatever it was you wanted while you were busy thinking about your job at the gallery and your boss and the next spot of paint you could sell and, at most, Lasse. All that time I was simply unimportant.'

'Maybe you were too important for me, maybe that was my problem,' Hedda answered softly. I could tell by her voice that she was about to cry, which she always did whenever there was nowhere else to go with an argument.

'I did not get the professorship and you never asked, I lost my job at the university and you didn't care.'

'Because it was unimaginable. Because I simply didn't believe that something like that could even happen to you. Because you were never weak. Because you never made any mistakes. That was something other people did.'

'But it did happen to me, Hedda. It happened. You're not a kid any more.'

'You told me you were letting Kalkreuther take the lead. I didn't want to interfere. I didn't think I had the right.'

'How old are you, Hedda? Do you have to act like a fifteen-year-old?'

'You turned me into a fifteen-year-old.'

'Your accusations are becoming increasingly more bizarre.'

'I had respect for you, Anton. I did a few things wrong out of respect, or maybe even a lot of things . . . who knows? Maybe everything. But it wasn't because of indifference. I could never be indifferent towards you, even if I wanted to.'

'Are you even listening to yourself?'

'For far too long I've only listened to you,' she said, and now her voice skipped with stifled sobs. Fifteen? What was I thinking? More like five. 'That's what you wanted, Anton. You didn't want me to listen to anyone else.'

'You are slowly going insane, Hedda, do you know that?'

'You alienated me from my friends. You wanted to sleep with all the women. It was so bad I didn't risk running into them any more. Sofie, Carolin . . . and Magda least of all. And all of my guy friends were beneath you. You talked so badly about them for so long that I began to find them intolerable myself. And now I'm alone. I look at the walls of our flat which was never classy enough for you, I run my hand over the armoire you inherited from your mother, or was it your grandmother? Sorry, Anton, I can't remember all the details of your history any more. At some point it will become unimportant, but I believed in you, Anton ... did you ever notice, coming home, did you ever notice that I was more distraught than usual, that maybe I had red eyes, I don't know, I don't look in the mirror, but you never said a word.'

She sat down on the bed next to the shirts I'd just smoothed out and, with her head on her hands, stared into the open wardrobe.

'You never allowed me to get close to you,' I countered. 'Did you think I'd be able to stand being alone for ever?'

'I simply didn't know what to do any more. No matter what I did, it wasn't right.'

'I'm so sorry to have offended your vanity. It's nothing else. A narcissistic disorder. And you're sitting on my suit trousers.'

She raised her eyebrows, but too much, everything was always just a bit too much with her. She'd never understood how to use her charms at all, and so I'd given her instructions, it'd gone OK for a little while but then, after a few months, she'd let everything slide.

'It's not a disorder, it's quite simply sadness,' she said, 'but you wouldn't know a thing about something like that. You're the one who broke up, but you have no idea what breaking up means. You have no idea about your entire life any more.'

'I have always found your overconfidence ridiculous.'

'I always thought your character was so complex that I'd never figure it out,' she said meditatively. 'But maybe you just have a poor one.'

'Good, Hedda, now we've said it all. Now you have what you want. In the future, I won't decide anything for you.' I pulled down another two pairs of trousers, folded them once more then placed them on top of the shirts. 'You will no doubt find a man who will stay out of your life much better than I could.'

'He already does.'

'Sorry?'

'I've been fucking your boss for months and you haven't noticed.'

'Well, that's lovely, Hedda.' I shut the drawer and tossed my socks and underwear into the suitcase. 'Why do you always think you can make me jealous?'

'I can put you at ease, I don't give a shit about your jealousy.' She was standing in front of the bed, let her hand run over my suitcase, picked up a pair of socks, a pair of underwear, then a tie, which she unrolled and pulled between her fingers like a cord. 'The worst thing for you,' she said slowly, holding the tie against my jacket, 'is that, when I think about it, none of us ever loved you. I didn't and certainly none of your affairs did. We just wanted your infatuated eyes on us. That gleam you saw in us for a time. And we didn't want to admit that that gleam didn't exist.'

She turned away and clumsily wrapped the tie around her neck. 'And when you begin to deprive us of that gleam, we run after you even more. We beg, and you scold us. We try to do somersaults, it's never good enough for you.'

'You are awfully vain, Hedda, do you see that?' I asked and reorganized my socks and underwear.

'Anyhow, I've noticed something else. The longer one's with you, the emptier one feels. One becomes dependent on you because nothing else is left. Just you. Your demands. Your desires. But in truth it's your emptiness, your endless interior emptiness, Anton. That's why no one can love you. And you cannot love yourself either.'

'Are you done, Hedda? I'd like to take the tie with me. And the way you continue to circle around my love life is really manic.'

'Your love life means as little to me as your jealousy.' She threw the tie onto the bed and went to the door. 'But don't you dare criticize me for having played a role for me in the past!' she said and slammed the door behind her.

'You could have at least hooked up with someone of my calibre!' I yelled after her. 'Nordhoff is dumpy all the way down to his belt buckle.'

Her steps in the hallway grew quieter. I stood in front of my jackets trying to decide which ones I wanted to leave behind. I liked to change clothes twice a day, especially in a Roman summer when even a passer-by's sweat could make your shirt wet. Nordhoff, of course, would get by with just three jackets because, as far as style was concerned, he understood just about . . . ach, he didn't understand a thing about style, full stop.

XXIV. FAMILY LIFE   Tania and Gramsci are standing on Track 8 at Stazione Termini. Billowing steam, the train comes to a screeching halt. Gramsci looks up at its dirty metal skin as the first door is pushed open, then the second, hands heave luggage out, women with bobbing skirt seams and overly tired faces struggle to keep their balance coming down the metal steps before being met with bouquets of flowers from pale-faced men. A small child clatters over the mound of suitcases. Gramsci wants to stretch out his arms and hoist the boy into the air but a matron has already grabbed him and pulled him over the platform. He is so nervous that he is ready to take any child to be his own, and by now the train is almost empty.

'There,' Tania whispers. 'Compartment 4.'

Gramsci starts. It is all going so quickly now, he doesn't know what he will say. He isn't prepared (as if you could prepare for a reunion like you could for a speech in Parliament). And then, when the face comes into the light, he recognizes that it's only Eugenia. That little piece of wood with fiery eyes. She is holding a child on her arm. Soft, downy hair, bright brown, almost blonde. The second she sees him she begins walking over. Just like Reverend had taught her, of all things! Gramsci feels her thin neck on his chin, her wispy torso on his chest, the child's hair on his cheek. Delio's frightened face is immediately pressed into his aunt's shoulder; he has not seen his father even once.

The past winter, when he was in Moscow for two weeks, Gramsci saw his son for the first time. Before that he had only seen photos which reached him with a delay, tricked him as to the

162

boy's actual stage of development. Now it is like meeting him for the very first time. He doesn't know what he should say, what he should feel. At first he simply notices: the boy has grown, as Gramsci had expected. He is handsome, but is he as handsome as Gramsci had imagined or handsomer still? Gramsci tries to conjure up the boy from his imagination and notices that the categories (bigger, smaller, more handsome, uglier, more and less) become unimportant. His son here is real, and he is a stranger. Gramsci wants to hold him, look at him, touch his arms, his hair. But Eugenia does not hand him over. The boy looks fearfully at Gramsci. But what had he expected? Closeness cannot be ordered. He will have to win Delio's affection, and that will be tough, for the boy already has parents: Giulia and Eugenia.

And there she is. Giulia. Discreetly glowing she steps out of the train, looks at him briefly, looks at her sister, then the ground. Gramsci walks up to her, caresses her arm, feels the warmth of her body through the fabric of her blouse. He can touch her, pull her to himself, touch her skin with his fingers, carefully. No longer a figment of his imagination, but Giulia in flesh and blood.

'It's you again.'

'Yes, it is.'

'If you say so, it must be true.'

She looks around as if she did not recognize a thing any more, the longer she looks into the openness of the terminus the more confused she seems. She is even more fragile than her sister and too strong a breath will blow her away, as weightless as a cocoon. Gramsci attempts an awkward embrace. He sees Tania leant up against a pole, staring at him with empty eyes.

The flat she and Gramsci have found for the two sisters and Delio is clean and bright, not as spacious as the Schucht's in Moscow, but why should it be, Eugenia never leaves her sister's side. Two rooms, the bedroom with a double bed and a po-faced Madonna where the two can talk themselves to sleep like husband

and wife. The other room is the living room, with a chaise longue, a dining table, even a piano which Delio likes to touch. As the plane trees have grown up over the window, the kitchen is small and dark and the faces of the two women seem to be concealed by a breath of verdigris. Tania has remained out in the hall, she is keeping her distance from her sisters, even when Giulia reaches for her hand and softly tries to pull her to herself.

'Do you all like it?' Gramsci asks.

'It will do,' Eugenia answers.

They could begin a normal family life here, an almost normal one of aunt, mother and child. Gramsci will continue staying at the Passarges', he is careful, he does not want Giulia or Delio to be put in danger on his account. He will eat with them in the evenings, he will bathe his son and put him to bed, he will sleep with Giulia when Eugenia is off doing the shopping at the market or on a walk which her doctor has ordered her to complete because of her weak legs.

An almost normal family life, for he knows that a completely normal one will never be possible. He is under surveillance, two policemen follow his every move, sometimes more, sometimes less discreetly, but always enough for him to feel their presence. That's one thing. The other is Eugenia. At Silver Wood, once Giulia had travelled back to Ivanovo and she'd had him to herself, she was distant, or, rather, it was her body that was distant, her comportment, for what was she supposed to do with her useless legs? In retrospect, maybe they were what she held responsible for Gramsci choosing her sister instead. She was distant yet insistent somehow. She suggested he go for Giulia, she pushed him towards her, she almost acted like a match-maker, and yet he could feel that she was unhappy with his choice, that she believed she had a claim to him, that she saw Giulia as a kind of mediator through which he would be connected to her, Eugenia, in the end the real object. He is her conquest, back at the fence she'd scooped him up, she shared everything with her sister, but now she expects her sister to share everything with her.

Gramsci and Giulia steal out of the house with their son, carrying him off from the safekeeping of the sister-in-law. On the street, Giulia ties a thin cloth around his head, *against the sun*, she says, and pushes the pram forward, a white wicker contraption Gramsci had got from Sraffa, pushes it through a nearby park, sometimes Gramsci walks beside her, sometimes behind her, then all of a sudden overtakes her to bend over the basket and observe the head stick up out of the bundle of blanket and sleep and wake and begin to cry. Yes, that's him. This is what's become of the 3,600 grams Giulia wrote to him about and which he measured out with books to see how much 3,600 grams were: three books of Benedetto Croce's, Marx's *Das Kapital* and Dante's *Divine Comedy* on top. Giulia pushes the carriage back and forth until the child grows quieter and only gurgles. Gramsci crouches down, then looks to the sky to see what his son sees. He is startled by how large and savage the world seems from the basket of a children's carriage.

They circle the park a few times. Gramsci makes faces, turns his hands into rabbits and foxes and, seeing him, his son stops crying and cautiously begins to laugh. *We're slowly getting used to each other*, Gramsci thinks, reaching into the basket to stroke his son's hot little head. Delio bites him. Right in the middle of his index finger, and a toothless jaw can be very powerful indeed. Gramsci curses in Sardinian, a sound of distant and endlessly dry fields.

'He's nervous,' Giulia says. 'What did you think would happen, with *these* parents?'

'What parents do you mean, Eugenia or me?'

Guilia shrugs and pushes the carriage back in the direction of Via Nomentana.

'We found a new doctor for him in Moscow. A specialist for nervous disorders,' she says.

'You two?'

'Eugenia and I.'

'The parents!' Gramsci says sarcastically.

Giulia pushes the carriage away from him.

'Isn't it a bit early for specialists?' Gramsci asks. 'Where is he supposed to go when he can speak?'

'To kindergarten and then to school.'

'Here in Rome we're going to have done with all that nonsense.'

'It's good for him.'

'No doubt,' Gramsci replies and sucks his finger.

When they arrive home, Eugenia comes barrelling towards them and grabs Delio as if he had been kidnapped and now was safe again.

'You were gone too long, he can't take that much sun,' she scolds her sister before casting Gramsci a disapproving glance. Her face seems shut, the face of someone who rules through simple but unbending means. And once a woman like Eugenia has made up her mind, once she uses her intelligence to get what she wants, she will be successful, Gramsci knows that much, even if he doesn't know what it is she wants. She smiles at him, a bit of her right incisor is missing, or is it a gap due to the uneven growth of her teeth? But now it's gone again.

That evening in bed, Giulia cautiously reaches for Gramsci's hand, their fingers close around one another, on the nightstand an edition from Lenin, one of Eugenia's severely ironed dresses hangs by the wardrobe, her proxy to watch over them while she's out for a moment to walk with Delio down the street and now is probably already on her way back. It has to be quick, very quick. Gramsci kisses Giulia's eyes, her mouth, her hand runs over his arm and up to his shoulder, he moves closer, listens for steps out in the hall, lays on top of her, and as always the steps—the sister-in-law hanging by the wardrobe, standing outside the door, looking through the keyhole—can come at any moment. Giulia spreads her legs, he edges in-between, pushes in to her, sweat begins to collect between his stomach and hers, her hand grabs his neck, then moves down his misshapen back, he breathes more heavily, they hear the front door close, they move away from each other in fear.

It could be an almost normal family life. Giulia finds a job at the Soviet embassy, Eugenia reads Lenin every morning and takes care of Delio, Gramsci goes to Parliament and meets his comrades, Tania is irritable and leaves the room whenever Gramsci caresses her sister's cheeks. All of them are suffering from insomnia because it is so hot, Delio cries and cries and is then too exhausted, he lies awake and beats his hands about him. Two flies chase each other above his head. Giulia hears her sister waltzing back and forth at night, sees her damp forehead, and her own nightgown clings to her. Gramsci comes by in the mornings for breakfast, sometimes Tania too. They meet in the kitchen around nine o'clock and drink strong Italian coffee together. Tania hardly speaks. Lost in thought, she just stares at Giulia while Gramsci longs to take her by the arm, she seems so depressed. He misses their walks, how quickly she speaks when she wants to convince him of something.

'The kitchen is no place for meetings,' Eugenia decides, then gathers up the coffee cups and they follow her into the living room. Delio is lying on a blanket next to Giulia. He sleeps, starts awake for a moment then falls back asleep, he's such an undemanding child, but then the undemanding little beast starts back awake again. Giulia bends over him, tries to calm him down with a bit of cloth. Eugenia forces her way in-between, 'Giulia, please,' and Giulia's cheeks turn red, once again she's done something wrong, once again it did not escape her sister, just her, and she doesn't know where, Eugenia doesn't tell her either, she simply presses the child to her own flat chest. '*I would like to be loved by one, two, one hundred children, yes, there is something sick in my desire,*' Eugenia will write later, but right now she is cradling Delio to sleep while Giulia sits there like a stranger, looking at the child, and maybe thinking about how she would like the same one day, in a few years, but she knows that in this family Eugenia alone is responsible for the fulfilment of wishes, she's the one who will stamp or discard the requests, taste all the sweet refinements of bureaucracy.

Once Delio has calmed down, Eugenia hoists him onto the piano stool. He places his tiny fingers on the keys and just when Gramsci is sure they will break, a sound escapes the instrument's body. Delio has understood some of the notes with the help of animal sounds, left a bear, right a young chicken, and in-between an entire zoo. 'Listen, *dyadya!*' he cries.

'*Dyadya?* Who taught Delio to call his father uncle?' Tania asks.

Giulia lowers her eyes. Eugenia raises her head.

'It was easier that way. His father wasn't there,' Eugenia explains.

'His uncle wasn't there either,' Tania counters, walks up to the piano and lays her arm around him. She points to Gramsci and repeats the two words *papa* and *nana* while pressing down on the key to the left of the bear.

'Papa. Do you understand?'

Delio nods but it doesn't seem to interest him that much. He turns away, slides off the piano stool and runs after a celluloid ball Gramsci has brought for him. The ball is filled with water, swans sway back and forth inside it, a whole family with three grey swan children wobbles up and down the room. Piero Sraffa had given Gramsci the gift, perhaps he bought it in London, Gramsci has never seen something so peculiar in Italy. Delio seems to find the toy strange as well and keeps trying to open it.

'Do you see how clever he is already? He wants to understand how it's made,' Gramsci says.

'Please, he just wants to get at the swans,' Giulia says. 'Furthermore, he thinks you can repair everything that breaks.'

'Genia, have you taught him that I possess super powers?' Gramsci says and laughs.

Eugenia raises her head. There is a twitch near the corner of her mouth; she refuses to allow anything else. She knows that she will defeat Gramsci, and Giulia too, for in the end Delio is the one to choose. And Delio, Eugenia is certain, will choose her.

Gramsci bends down to his son. The child drapes his arms around his father's neck for such a long time and so intensely that Gramsci eventually has to free himself. His train is scheduled to leave in half an hour. Turin, Lazio, Naples. Gramsci has to travel across the entire country for the Party. Today it's Florence. That has disrupted their almost normal family life, to which Gramsci now says goodbye with an almost customary kiss of his wife's cheeks. He and Tania go down the stairs together, he rushes ahead to hold open the door for her and as she makes her way past he grabs her hand.

'I miss you, Tania, do you know that?'

'Let go, Nino.'

He caresses her arm, moves up to her shoulder. She shrugs away.

'You have to look after your family now. I have nothing to do with that.'

'We could walk together for a bit in the direction of the station.'

'Yes, we could,' she says and turns. 'When the three are back in Moscow.'

He watches her go and for a moment feels as if he has been abandoned by all three, by Tania, Giulia and the terrible rest of the world. Tomorrow, the day after tomorrow when he comes back from his trip, he will have Giulia once again, he thinks in order to calm down. But then he is once more plagued by the thought that things might not be so pleasurable the next time. Because it's all too much for him, because he cannot grasp it, bring it together, be in control. He is afraid she will only have been an illusion, a trick of his emotions, and once he is back and standing out in front the Schucht sisters' flat, an old man in a bathrobe opens the door.

XXV. MICHELANGELO　　Tatiana had stopped showing up at the Institute. After a few days, however, I saw the pony again. It had discarded its fur and was wearing a grey, washed-out T-shirt and acting important at the other end of the room with all kinds of papers a wafer-thin boy had brought it from the archive. I stared at it for a while, then stood up and walked over.

'When will Tatiana be back?'

'You again!' it said in a hushed voice.

'Is she on holiday?'

'How should I know?'

'But you know her.'

'Know!'

'You were talking with her.'

It waved its hand. 'Come on, talking, whatever.'

'Why don't you want to tell me? What kind of claims of ownership are these?'

'Sorry, but I think there's been a misunderstanding. On top of it, I've got work to do.' The pony bent back down over its papers.

'You can't keep a woman all to yourself,' I said so loudly that even the mummies turned around. Well, they finally had to learn that there were more things to life than coming to an end in the alphabet. I turned away and left the reading room.

I stopped at reception, the librarian peeped up.

'Could you tell me if Tatiana reserved any books this week?' I asked.

He inched his glasses down his nose and looked over the edge. 'Who?'

'Tatiana. Light brown curls. About this long,' I explained and held my hand flat against my earlobe. 'Delicate. And her mouth. You're familiar with Michelangelo's statue of David, right? Of course you are. That mouth. In reality, it's a woman's mouth, that's why it's so beautiful.'

'If you are looking for a book, you can easily submit a request,' the librarian said, pushing a grey cardboard box across the counter. 'Processing can take a while, as you know.'

I shook my head.

'Maybe it'll go a bit quicker today,' he said with a conciliatory tone. 'It seems'—he flicked his glasses up his nose—'to be somewhat urgent.'

'Thank you,' I said drily and turned away. I didn't want to read a book. Nothing that would bring me closer to Gramsci, to the Party congress in Livorno, the one in Lyon, to the schism among the socialists and their coming back together, I had absolutely no interest in making my way through all of those things any more, what was the point? Just stones and pebbles, footnotes and references.

For a while I stood out on the slanted stretch of asphalt in front of the Institute, looking at the old tyres, and couldn't say if anything had ever struck me as that empty. The earth was a cold stone falling through the universe. Research was absurd, life was absurd and life without Tatiana most certainly was. After Tatiana, I knew that much, it'd be over. Tatiana was perfect. No, worse, she outdid the perfect, she left it behind as a given and went beyond it. Her mouth was that of a David, that's what made it so refined. She was extraordinary in a way you could not invent but simply run into. And once you've experienced something that beautiful, everything you previously thought was beautiful just seems gruesome and dull.

On Fridays she had a violin lesson, I imagined, and Saturdays she'd leave the house late to meet friends at a pizzeria. Sundays she slept in. There was no way Tatiana was a fan of Sundays, that day of traditions and table manners, when, at three o'clock, you had to be on your way to your family with a package of sweets from the baker's or be consumed by a melancholic sense of dejection much greater than those few remaining hours of the weekend would lead you to believe. No doubt she liked Calvino and Ginzburg, she liked the silence of 4 a.m. when you awake unexpectedly, she liked oranges, *Saltimbocca* and the snow in Tuscany which clings to the slopes like an unreal mist and disappears as soon as you approach.

'And what did you find out today?' Brevi asked as I attempted to creep past his living room. He was sitting in front of a pile of manuscript pages, had pushed back his snow-white hair and looked like Pasolini's older brother.

'It's complicated,' I answered.

'I have no time for such statements,' Brevi replied. 'That philosophy is something difficult is simply a generally held prejudice, but you, Anton, cannot fall into that trap. Use your common sense.'

'The research material in the archive,' I defended myself. 'It was sorted out in private.'

'Perhaps the archive is not the right place for you.'

Ach, Brevi. *You don't get it.* You believe in archives and facts. You believe that you simply have to come to the right conclusion.

'I was at the Quisisana Clinic today,' Brevi announced. 'An old caretaker took me through the storage room. He nattered on a bit about the poor morals of the doctors and nurses. Everyone so busy trying to fill their own pockets that they pay no attention to everyone else trying to do the same. Nothing new really, it was already like that decades ago. You should have a look around Tania's building,' Brevi decided.

'Tatiana's building. Right, of course.'

'And Tonio, I want results.'

'Of course,' I repeated. 'It's just that it's a bit complicated,' I said, then added, 'very complicated' and with that retreated to my room in order to stare at the wall.

XXVI. VIA RICCOLI   Gramsci is scheduled to depart on the morning of 31 October 1926. After a change of trains in Milan, he is to continue on to Genoa where a driver will pick him up and take him to Val Polcevera. There, on the direction of the highest authority, he is to meet Comrade Humbert-Droz. Gramsci does not know him and is not sure what he wants. Is he to be spied on? Will they be giving him a lecture all the way from Moscow?

'We are very worried,' Gramsci wrote on 14 October in the name of the Politburo of the PCI to the larger sister party in Moscow. 'Comrades, in these last nine years of world history, you have been the organizing and propulsive element of the revolutionary force in all countries . . . But today you are destroying your work. You are degrading, and run the risk of annihilating, the leading function which the CPSU won through Lenin's contribution.' He had named those who had by now been discredited, Comrades Zinoviev, Trotsky and Kamenev, 'they have been among our masters'. At the end, he had even added a warning: 'We like to feel certain that the Central Committee of the USSR does not intend to win a crushing victory in the struggle, and is disposed to avoiding excessive measures.'

Gramsci is sitting up straight in his seat and watching the Umbrian landscape blur past, vast yellow fields, pines. A few days after his letter, Trotsky and Kamenev are expelled from the Politburo and Zinoviev is ousted by Bucharin as the chair of the Comintern. Gramsci had sent his letter to Palmiro Togliatti, but does not know if Palmiro kept it to himself or showed it to someone else. Bucharin perhaps? Togliatti had not allowed Gramsci's letter to be read before the plenary session of the Central

Committee, Stalin still knows nothing about it. But who had Togliatti showed it to? Bucharin? Someone else had to have read it, otherwise Gramsci would not be sitting in a train to nowhere to meet Humbert-Droz.

Nevertheless, Giulia is safe. 'Here it is winter already,' she'd written him shortly after arriving in Moscow. 'When I think of Rome, I become quite sad . . . In Rome today it is the 15th of September.' She's recovered from the birth well. Giuliano. They call him Julik. Gramsci tries to imagine him, he thinks of a smaller version of Delio, but he hadn't known Delio in the first months either, and in any event it was pointless for they would have their own personalities.

He opens the newspaper, sees photographs of pompous parades, the march on Rome had been celebrated for the fourth year in a row, the fascists continue to celebrate. Earlier that day, Mussolini had arrived in Bologna, waving to all the people on the streets, a military band played, fascists in sharply creased uniforms marching before him, behind him, in strict blocks, with arrogant faces. Gramsci sees a photograph of one of Mussolini's speeches, it will look exactly the same in Bologna, in Naples, in Turin, throughout the country it will constantly be staged in exactly the same way. He puts the newspaper down, reads in a book by Benedetto Croce, takes a few notes, thinks about Humbert-Droz again—whom he imagines with a very thin moustache and a tall top hat, even though he knows full well that no communist would appear at a secret meeting in a top hat—and then dozes off, sees Giulia for a moment, heavily pregnant and in a deck chair, she is on summer holiday in Trafoi, just a few kilometres from the Swiss border.

Gramsci wants to get off the train in Milan, elbows his way to the door with his luggage but is blocked by a police officer. Gramsci is brusque, he must catch his connection, he does not want to discuss a thing, he is a parliamentarian, they cannot simply do whatever they want with him. The officer places his hand on Gramsci's underarm and says quietly: 'Mr Deputy, I know who you are, and I suggest you travel back to Rome. It'd be the best!' The man's voice sounds confidential, even trustworthy, and Gramsci is tempted to believe him. But how can he trust him? What does he know about this officer? What does he know about why he's being warned? He only knows that he is in danger. The laws still apply to him, but what are they worth?

An attempt on Mussolini's life, Gramsci learns. Shots. Fired by a fifteen-year-old. Was he hit? Is he wounded? Is he dead? Through the window, Gramsci sees the police on the platform. They have mixed in with all the people departing and arriving and are controlling what's getting off the train, this mass, this crowd, and, with forbidding faces, stopping particular people. A small boy tears himself from his mother's hand and runs away. Nevertheless, Giulia is safe, as are Delio and Julik. Thanks to Eugenia's insistence, Giulia left on 7 August. Moving to Moscow any later than that would have been too difficult and they wouldn't have been safe for too much longer in Italy. When Gramsci came back to Italy two years ago, he knew that it could cost him his life. He came knowing as much, but today he is too exhausted to die. Today he is keeling over unconsciously, without a final thought, without a final word.

On Via Riccoli, near the Palazzo Re Enzo, the shots missed the Duce. The perpetrator, Anteo Zamboni, a child almost, is dead. An infantryman from Mussolini's bodyguards, Carlo Alberto Pasolini, detained him but by then it was too late: screams. Punches. Shots. Fascist lynch law in the open street.

'Please stay seated,' the policeman says. 'Do not get close to the window. It'd be the best for you. Travel back to Rome.'

Gramsci nods, and, when a few minutes later the train leaves again, sinks back, almost in relief.

The fascists take revenge. For days. They plunder, they set fires, they even destroy the flat of the great bourgeois intellectual Benedetto Croce in Naples. It is the moment they have been waiting for. At last, they can carry the terminally ill constitutional state along with the young Zamboni to the grave. At last, the course of violence agrees with them. On 5 November, passports are declared invalid. Whoever attempts to leave the country illegally will be shot. Anti-fascist newspapers and parties are banned and dissolved.

Gramsci is finally to go abroad, the Party decides, it has become too dangerous for him. The fascists will not miss the chance to bring all thought and expression under their control, to bring the whole country into line. Against his will, Gramsci's acquaintance, Esther, wants to bring him with her to Switzerland but he hesitates to leave the Passarges' flat.

'I can only leave when circumstances are clear,' he insists.

'But they are clear.'

'I do not want the workers to feel like they've been abandoned.'

'They won't think that. They can see what the fascists are doing. They did not stop before entering Croce's flat. And he's not even a communist.'

Gramsci himself doesn't believe in his immunity any longer, but he wants to speak out against Mussolini in Parliament on 9 November and attack the proposed legislation to reinstate the death penalty. He will not be able to stop it. Nonetheless, he wants to hold out. For optimism's sake. A few days more, then he will follow Giulia to Moscow. In mid-November perhaps. One week. Six days. On 10 November, he will flee.

On the evening of 8 November 1926, at ten-thirty, uniformed fascists break into the Passarges' home and, in violation of parliamentary immunity, arrest Deputy Antonio Gramsci. Exceptional measures, they say. Carla Passarge stands silently in the kitchen door; she is holding the porcelain funnel for the filter coffee in her hand as if she meant to delay Gramsci's detention by means of a few cups of brewed beans. The uniforms do not look at her. Gramsci spends the night in the jail of Regina Coeli, oh heavenly goddess, as if the holy mother of God actually cared about the few poor sinners sitting there.

The first thing Gramsci hears upon waking the next morning are the seagulls. He can see them through the narrow window of his cell. They seem somewhat unreal, sailing high above the jail with their yellow, sceptical eyes. Just a few metres away, the Tiber flows lazily and indifferently by. Up until noon, the men standing on its banks will be casting their hooks into the water and hoping for a good catch.

XXVII. SAGE   Above me, an old, grimy sign of the Partito Socialista hung out of the wall. Hammer, sickle and red carnation. The Party had been dead for twenty years thanks to bribe money and the collapse of the Second Republic, and when its general secretary Bettino Craxi took off for Tunisia, he left the sign behind like a tissue lost during flight.

It was four in the afternoon and, naturally, the door was closed. Softened by the rain, a few boxes next to the entrance were sagging into papier-mâché. On a note taped below the bell, I could read the opening hours, whatever they were for: Tuesdays, Wednesdays and Fridays from 10 to 1.

I took the call slip from the library out of my jacket pocket. Martinelli. I'd looked up her address in the phonebook, and although I immediately saw the name next to bell, #4, T. Martinelli, I read all the names above and below, I read them multiple times, as if there might be some kind of mistake, and then one more time for good measure. Bertoni, Franceschini, Inglese.

Tatiana Martinelli's flat, App. 4, was in the basement, a small, barred window looking onto the street. Hers. I was sure of it, like you sometimes—well, rarely, or almost never—do when the situation is vital yet impossible. The walls were being devoured by useless tubes and differed from the old ruins most of all because they weren't lit up at night. Looking skyward, I got lost in the confusion of cables but, behind the door, I could hear slow and scratchy, turtle-like steps.

An old woman wearing a sky-blue scarf slid open the door.

'What do you want?' she asked.

'*Ufficio*,' I mumbled, which could have meant agency or office or even just workroom and left unclear whether I thought the PSI still existed or was simply sharing a desk with a friend.

'I didn't wait for the right time,' I added.

'Not the right time,' she confirmed. Sparkling out of soft wrinkles, her eyes first sought me, then the street. 'It's been done and over with for years,' she said, straightening the knots of material beneath her chin. 'Since then, nothing's got any better. My leg hurts, and the cancer's now in my lungs, they're telling me four months or maybe four years, they don't want to commit to a thing, the cowards. And the way they build themselves up in front of me with their white coats and carry my life in the palm of their hands, I just want to tear out their throats. Have a nice day.'

She waddled past me, I pushed myself into the entrance before the door shut, and watched her hobble down the street, the left leg stiff, without a natural joint, a quack's prosthesis. Then I pushed open the door.

Something scurried along the shadow of the wall. A mouse, I thought. I was standing in the courtyard, or what Tatiana was allowed to see of the courtyard, which really was just the backside of the rubbish bins. Maybe it'd been a rat. Only when it walked by again and paused did I see it was an emaciated cat, like the dozens that lived at Largo Argentina. A sickly palm stood in the middle of the courtyard between sacks of concrete and bicycles and there too pigeons had made nests in-between the joints of the stem.

From where I was standing, I could see into Tatiana's kitchen: a gas stove, some worn wall cupboards, a table, a spice rack, on a board a bottle of vinegar and a large plastic bottle of olive oil. On the stove was a pan with pasta, glistening with butter and a few sage leaves. On the table a plate and a wine glass.

Two plates, two wine glasses. In front of each other.

I went closer to the window to see if maybe Tatiana had put them on the table to dry or just forgotten them there, leftovers

181

from two evenings she'd eaten here alone while looking out onto the rubbish bins. Two wine glasses. Two plates. Two clean napkins.

Was it really necessary for me to run after a woman, to stand between rubbish bins and half-emaciated cats? There were enough women who'd kept my number over the years. Ones that, once a year when they were overcome by memories, would call, let it ring ten, fifteen, twenty times to make sure that, yet again, I wouldn't pick up. And now, here I was, standing and imagining Tatiana's unremitting swinging movements as she let the butter melt in the pan. Carefully, almost delicately placing the food onto the plates . . . nothing special, a pasta with sage leaves, but it smelt better than anything I'd ever eaten in my life.

A ceiling lamp, probably left by the last or next-to-last tenant, came on and a deadly pale man tottered into the kitchen, he was so thin that you had no idea how old he was. Hunched over, he made his way to the table, yawned—there was not a single tooth left in his mouth—and let himself slowly sink onto one of the chairs. He checked his glasses in the light of the lamp, and then I recognized him. Gramsci. He didn't look up at me. He did not, as was so often the case, take any notice of me whatsoever, he just picked up a corner of the tablecloth and began to clean his glasses. He sat there, short, fragile, his hair foaming, boundlessly alone, and his solitude did not cause him to cast at me even a single glance.

A shadow crossed the room; a sky-blue scarf fluttered past the old man. Now the woman with the turtle-like walk was next to him, her white hair follicles exposed, in her face a stiff sadness practiced over decades. Her hair a miserable halo. I wanted to say hello, return some kind of polite and empty phrase, but her severe face told me that something intimate was going on. She kept her face turned towards mine, then walked up to the window and called over to me: 'Which office are you looking for?'

I stared at her silently. The pinched mouth, the pale, cold skin. When she realized that I wasn't going to answer, she pulled a curtain in front of the window and I found myself standing alone in the shadowy courtyard. I looked up the wall. The windows with their at-times open but mostly closed shutters were all the same in an oppressive way. That one over there was Tatiana's flat, I thought, or perhaps that window on the second floor? The one over there could just as easily be it, or did she live all the way up top, right under the roof where, from my perspective, the windows grew together into small strips? I turned and saw even more shutters, most of them closed, a few slightly ajar, only two open, and on all of them the paint peeling from the wood.

There it was again, the pigeons' deep, soft, almost painful display of courtship. I turned towards the tree but wasn't sure if it was coming from there, from the window above me or maybe even the one to my left. I thought I could dimly make out a woman in the darkened room and hear her heavy breath before it turned into a moan. I took a step forward, and another, my chest almost touching the sill. In front of the window, a thin, gauze-like curtain had been drawn through which I could make out an antique wardrobe, a nightstand, an engraving of Savonarola on the wall and on the bed the woman, her naked pelvis pushing upwards. Her body twisted the sheet and her hands grabbed after the blanket, more to hold onto than to cover herself, and the man—I couldn't see the man, but he had to be there, I could see his thrusts in the woman's movement. Her mouth opened, she laid her head back onto the pillow. Her lips were too full, something I'd never liked on women. It was vulgar. He continued to drive into her body with a quick rhythm, she tore open her eyes in surprise or shock, her stomach shook, the man sank on top of her. I still couldn't see him, and I stared at the woman and wondered if she looked like Tatiana. But all of a sudden I didn't know what Tatiana looked like any more.

I didn't dare to move. I just looked at the rotten shutters, open, partially ajar, closed, more and more shutters wherever I looked, and they were all alike, and they were all falling apart. I felt a light pressure against my leg, an insistent caress. I looked down. The scrawny cat was rubbing itself against my trousers, whining, with torn fur. With a kick I frightened her off and rushed back to the street.

Leaving the decade-old sign behind me, I passed the flat-blocks with their rusty flower boxes, satellite dishes and sooty clinker brick up to a pale, modern church. A kiosk owner was retracting his awning. A heap of used cardboard boxes was being pushed out of a supermarket. At that point I wanted nothing but the normality of bread prices and shopping carts and so I slid in behind a group of schoolchildren and walked into the store.

In front of the refrigerated section full of yoghurt and milk, I calmed down. The cool air was like a soft anaesthesia. Then I saw a woman with the same curly hair as Tatiana. Her hair was cut high on her neck, which made the curls even livelier. I stopped in front of the bread counter, inched closer to her in my by-now-cooled clothes, took a number and hoped her own wouldn't be called for a long time. Perhaps I was looking at her neck too intensely for she turned around and ran into the little basket with all the used numbers, they flew into the air and sailed down over the floor like numbered pollen. Her face was severe and at least a hundred years old.

XXVIII. ISLANDS　From now on, these walls are his everyday life. Four square metres, if you're feeling generous. Here a desk. There a bed. A wardrobe for clothes and for moths. A window. Or, rather, an attempt at a window. But whether the light comes from a cellar or an aquarium, Gramsci cannot say. It is flat, as if it had been extinguished years ago.

On the prison island of Ustica, his first stop, he had seen incomparable sunsets and one-of-a-kind rainbows. Nature there was mild and remote, a small sliver of Sicily washed into the sea, a smidgeon of volcanic rock. The trip had been postponed three times on account of rough seas. They had to wait in the jail of Palermo. Their nerves were frayed. During the night, Molinelli fell unconscious three times, wracked by convulsions. On 7 December, they finally arrived, and would stay twenty-four days, feeling like Robinson. Robinsons and Fridays founding a communistic island state, peeling potatoes, cleaning lettuce and free to do whatever they wanted during the day. Gramsci shares a hut with Bordiga, Ventura, Sbaraglini, Conca and a friend from Abruzzo. His roommate, Ventura, often wakes in the middle of the night, screaming and thrashing. The other one, Conca, stays up, propped on his pillow, smoking cigars and sighing. In the mornings, Gramsci drags himself through the hallway, the gait of a man who has not had any coffee yet, in Bordiga's opinion. It was only after coffee that life began, that or whatever they'd been assigned in its place.

All in all, however, it isn't so bad: they cook for one another every day at noon. In the afternoons, they sit outside in the still-warm November sun, play cards on the heated stump of a tree and turn brown while in Moscow it is already deep winter, the streets frozen, people's eyelashes white with frost. Once a week, the postal ship arrives.

'I feel like I am going to break apart at any moment,' Gramsci writes to Giulia while being transferred to Milan. On 20 January, they'd torn him away from his island idyll. Locked in an automobile, he's being driven through the winter cold of northern Italy. He is shivering as if with fever, his teeth are rattling so loud that it keeps him awake. He is certain he will not live through the trip, that his heart will freeze on account of the cold. He is sleeping in transit, the darkest hole between two holes, a cell for travelling prisoners. The unlucky are kept there for up to a week. Gramsci lies on the straw sack with his legs tucked underneath him, he can hear bugs inside it, he rubs his wrists, blue because of the cold and the heavy handcuffs. When he is out in the courtyard during the day, he meets a lifelong inmate quoting Nietzsche. He laughs and is in a good mood although he has been imprisoned for twenty-two years, and Gramsci hopes that he can hang on to that over the course of his first days, weeks, months in that prison which is now his new home. The lifelong inmate triumphs exuberantly over the rules of the jail. That's how you have to do it, Gramsci thinks and hugs his legs, hugs them tight, real tight, so that nothing of his will touch the ground if he falls asleep.

A few days later, Gramsci arrives in Ancona. He avoids looking at himself in the, oftentimes missing, glass or shard of mirror. It will be grey, with red eyes, surrounded by dark blue shadows. In the prison-registration office in Ancona, there is a short-tempered young man in uniform who has something to say about everything. 'Speak more clearly!'—'Can't you stand up any straighter?'—'Stop carrying on like that, this isn't any *casino*, here you have to act decently.'—'What are you grinning for? This isn't a brothel, but an office!'—'Look at me kindly when I speak to you!' The man in front of Gramsci turns around, and their eyes meet. His face is closed, his gaze probing yet lifeless. Then Nino recognizes him: the lifelong inmate. He now looks like a bone that has been completely leached. A few days in transit have managed to break even him. Gramsci's naturally tanned skin colour will not return; that is the first thing to which he bids farewell when he comes out of transit into his new home, the cell which shall only allow him cold light, and not much at that. You cannot regret things, you have to let go of the unnecessary while keeping the necessary alive against the whole atmosphere of the prison with its values, routines, hardships and imperatives, the tiniest tings which mechanically follow one after the other for days, months, years, grains of sand in an immense hourglass. Every molecule within him resists, and yet he knows that he too can break, that imprisonment can break a prisoner to such a degree that he is no longer capable of any moral resistance. Sometimes that little heap of shivers even turns back to the very prison van which brought him to Milan.

Only he who learns how to breathe underwater will survive in the aquarium. You have to get used to the fact that everything drifts past, every impression is muddled and blurred. But, having taken the plunge, at long last you risk opening your eyes, and you understand that it's really not all that lonely down there. A fly flies busily back and forth above the bed. A snail secretes its slime, leaving behind a silver trace on the wall. Ants have founded colonies close to the door. As long as you don't become an ant, watching them make their way about, observing how they follow invisible lines carrying the tiniest yet too-big grains, is an interesting way to kill time, and Gramsci has to think of how, when he was eleven, he would carry the registers—heavier than himself— in the land- registry office of Ghilarza, for eight, nine hours a day and on Sunday mornings too for nine lire a month, which was next to nothing but necessary, for ever since his father had been arrested they had no income and his mother didn't dare ask for help, she didn't want to be a beggar or admit to the shame, not in front of others and certainly not to herself. Nine lire a month, that was two pounds of bread a day. His mother Peppina would sew their worn-out socks late into the night, and the children did not dare desire a thing, for any desire would destroy the strictly established balance of *we can manage*.

His brother Mario steals the neighbour's cat and has the baker cook it. Peppina stuffs him into his sisters' clothes so he won't run out of their one-storey house that is smack in the middle of Ghilarza, its pink lava-stone walls seemingly ashamed for the family too. And Gramsci thinks about how he escaped in order to watch rabbits dance in the moonlight, about how he pointlessly tried to chase off a fox with some stones but which only disappeared in an orange flash once a shot was fired off in the distance. About sitting on the outcroppings and looking over the fields, endless fields that, once considered, do not fit into these cells. About catching frogs and hedgehogs, about hiding in the bushes with a friend, waiting for a whole family of hedgehogs to come into the moonlight, mother, father and three little babies, their backs skewered with so many apples as to be almost unrecognizable. Then he and his friend jump up and put them wiggling and squeaking into a sack. They bring them back to Gramsci's house where, for a few months, they stay in the courtyard. They catch roaches and beetles and let Gramsci feed them lettuce. He examines their stomachs and snouts and now, lying on his jailbed, he attempts to call to mind every one of their quills. He can't, and has to think of the day he walked into the courtyard and they were gone, how he looked in every corner, tried to entice them with more salad greens, whistled, stamped his feet, even raised the sandy dust with a stick as if they'd buried themselves without a trace.

'Somebody must've taken them,' his sister says. 'And eaten them.'

Perhaps Mario brought them to the baker, and they can't hold it against him, they too were often dizzy with hunger. Gramsci thinks of his sister's smile that hides the sadness in her face, he thinks of his brother Mario, how his mother would paint his feet black with shoe cream when the girls' clothing no longer kept him from running off. He thinks of the smell of the saltworks. He thinks of Giulia's thin neck, the small birthmark on her left shoulder blade. He thinks of her sitting in front of him, and he kisses her back which bends slightly forward and is so skinny you can see her spine, the ribs . . . she weighs 50 kilos, she should gain 10 at least, he wants to admonish her, and yet he simply caresses the range of her spine. Her hair stands up, everything is alive. He edges closer, embraces her, his fingers pull at her breasts, she leans back her head, suppresses her heavy breaths while Eugenia walks back and forth outside the door and he sees every single one of Giulia's eyelashes as her lids start to flutter. He sees them and counts them and sees the pale blue in-between, reads it all as if a philological issue he was bringing closer through his analysis.

'I imagine you smiling,' he writes to Giulia, 'and that makes me happy.' Every second Monday he is allowed half an hour to write a letter, never more than two, and primarily to relatives, which prevents him from writing to Piero Sraffa and his comrades in the Party. But he can write to Giulia, and he writes her first of all. Even on days when he is feeling cheerless and apathetic, he writes her. Not a single day is allowed to pass, not a single one of these precious thirty minutes. Often he doesn't even have enough time to correct what he's written. Half an hour. Every two weeks.

Otherwise nothing has any meaning. Every day he reads six newspapers—apparently Trotsky has been expelled from the Party, Stalin has become the absolute ruler in Russia—but he doesn't know which to trust, much less what information they have kept from him, as if he were an incompetent child. And what good are the headlines to him, now, when he can no longer be involved in politics? He does not write a single line about politics in his letters, it could harm him and, worse, the addressees, Giulia and Tania. He is haunted by the idea of doing something to last 'for ever', he writes his sister-in-law. That is the only possible response to the censor.

In addition to the papers, he receives one or two journals and once a month makes a random and crude selection of around thirty books from the prison library or from Tania: from Wilhelm Busch's *Max and Moritz* to a chivalric romance novel where Sicily was located at the pole. He studies Russian and German, translates Grimm's fairytales and learns Pushkin's 'The Squire's Daughter' by heart. But, contrary to what he had thought, it is difficult to study in prison. He is too tired, every night the warders jolt him from sleep. He doesn't know whether it's intentional or not, whether they enjoy torturing him or not, and which would be worse? He is angry, he wants to get up, but feels too weak. He closes his eyes. Giulia. Over and over again. Giulia. The thread which keeps him to the world. Even though he can now only remember her laugh with great difficulty.

'You are my Japan,' he writes to her. A place he cannot imagine. And if he fails to envision such an important and distant island, if he cannot manage to grasp it through his senses, then he no longer knows a thing. Nothing at all. And his own life is lost to him as well. It is November in the window now, a cut of November.

Giulia's letters rarely reach him, and he wonders whether a few don't get lost along the way, what with the double censor or, considering Eugenia, maybe even a triple one. The Soviet authorities, then the Italians . . . it's a wonder anything arrives at all.

One morning, Gramsci is called to the prison director's office. 'A bit more quickly,' the warden says to him when he arrives, a brief escape from the ghostly monotony, but the further they make their way down the corridor, the more uneasy Gramsci begins to feel. He doesn't know how far they will go with their interrogation. He only knows that he will not say a thing. That he has to be certain he will not say a thing.

'What does Kitai mean?' the director asks, his explosive mass teetering dangerously forward in his chair.

China, Gramsci thinks, but stays silent. That was so easy, he could have looked it up in a dictionary.

'And what does it have to do with Austria?' he adds, squinting.

Gramsci hesitates. He can only guess, no, he cannot guess at all, how this letter connects Austria and China and what he is allowed to say and what he is not. He is playing a game of blind man's buff against this man, about whom he knows nothing, and as to the content of the letter he only knows the words the man slams towards him, not the connections.

'And who are the people having their sleds dragged by dogs?' the director snaps.

Gramsci is fighting three opponents alone: the director, a cloze text and a censor. He knows that there is no way he can win. It's time to retreat and give the letter up as lost, but to allow a piece of Giulia to be lost is even more impossible. He must at least see the few words, the one hundred or two hundred words, or read them if he cannot take them with him. He must concentrate, he doesn't know the connections but he knows what she usually writes to him about. About her illnesses which have nothing to do with China or Austria, well, perhaps a little to do with Austria but definitely nothing to do with dogs and sleds. About her work, which could perhaps have something to do with sleds but which certainly would not mention either of the two countries. About the family which in its elegant city flat also has nothing to do with sleds. Without any doubt, however, she would tell him about their sons.

'Do you even have a wife?' Gramsci asks. 'You do not seem to understand how a mother writes when she wants to tell the father about their child.'

All at once the director seems self-conscious; these 90 kilograms of superiority cannot win. He doesn't have any children, but he does have a wife, and, well, at one point they had wanted children but no, it's true, he doesn't know the way a mother writes, though he would like to be able to imagine it, and the fact that he could misinterpret a child's game for encryption, that he himself had such a difficult time differentiating between reality and deception, concerns him. He doesn't know how to respond, he simply hands Gramsci the letter. And even if it is some kind of trap, he no longer cares to extend this moment any longer than necessary.

Gramsci smiles politely and leaves the office with a boyish bow. Out in the hallway, he has to keep himself from breaking into a run or even a skip. In the end, though the censor is always right, at least this one time he won. Back in his cell, he is finally able to read about Delio lying on his bed, to his right Austria, to his left China, Crimea by his legs, and by his head the people having their sleds pulled by dogs. Sled dogs. The first lesson in geography.

XXIX. PIGEONS   'Oh, Tonio, how lovely to see you!'

I stared at the ghost with its raisin-like skin and plush slippers. Brevi's housekeeper was standing in front of me, she'd spruced up her evening dress with a few sequins which flitted about her chest and made me feel slightly dizzy. Her hair was hidden beneath a blue plastic bonnet and behind her left ear, where it had slipped a little, I could see a curler with a strand of hair, as thin as a spider's web.

'Wouldn't you like to each lunch with us?'

I tried to find a way out but then her wrinkly, fleshless hand grabbed mine and pulled me down the hall.

'Tonio will be eating with us today,' Gabriella said, pushing me into the dining room. The windows looked out on the garden side of the building which, until now, I'd only guessed might exist behind the grey outer wall. Now, however, I could see into the park-like space. A whole group of white figures emerged, a sandstone nobility: women with pinned hair, monarchs in antiquated dress, between them a water basin, everything battered, weathered and grey. Three steps led up to the piano nobile.

'Everything is going down the drain,' Brevi said and smiled tiredly. 'But, please, have a seat, please,' he urged while Gabriella spooned lentils out of a pot onto my already overflowing plate. A rainbow of pills surrounded Brevi's glass.

'Heart,' he said, counting. 'Liver. Kidneys. And this one here, what's it for?'

'Cholesterol.'

'Where is that?'

'In your arteries, Pippo.'

'The important thing is that they find their way there. How's Gramsci coming along, Tonio?'

'Are you still busy with him?' Gabriella exclaimed. 'We'll never get rid of the communists here,' she complained. 'Even in Russia they've gone, but here, until yesterday, they were still sitting in the office of the president. Do you know, Tonio, sometimes I think that this country has been run by so many crazies, the people have just grown used to it.'

'Napolitano is not crazy, *cara*,' Pippo said, 'and he's no longer a communist.'

'Come on,' she snarled. 'One thousand disabled deputies and this president rules the country alone. Since when has that been democratic?'

'Democratic!' Pippo cried out, teetering on his chair. 'A great way of making all those who do not care about politics one bit forty euros richer every four years. They get as much for donating blood as they do for voting. But you have to consider how much longer the body needs to recover afterwards. After going to vote, I've always slept like an infant.'

'You drink too much out of anger with the results, that's why you go to sleep.'

'That's not true at all!' Pippo countered.

Gabriella's chest rose and fell, the sequins blazed. When she shook her head, her hair appeared from under her bonnet like whitecaps.

'But do have some more, have some more, Anton,' she said and with that was rushing back in to the kitchen in order to get the roast out of the oven. Brevi leant forward and whispered: 'You mustn't misunderstand me. I think as little of electoral fraud as I do of these pills I must take every day. What am I saying? Every hour.' He let the colourful capsules roll across the tablecloth, then caught them in his palm. 'What am I supposed to do? I don't believe in them at all, and yet, without them I would have been dead a long time ago.'

He placed a pill in his mouth and took a sip of water. 'Oh, and do not think "scruples" is an empty word for me. You can win a democratic election by various means, and if you ask me, none of them are honest any more. Perhaps we did not understand that from the very beginning.' He put a second pill between his lips, rocked his head and took another sip from his glass. For a while he observed the iridescent bands the crystal cast onto the tablecloth and attempted to shift them with his fingers. 'It was such a beautiful idea, a democratic Europe,' he said. 'But ideas freeze the moment we turn them in to reality. At that point, they simply continue to stand there, cars swerve around them and pigeon droppings fall from their shoulders.'

He nodded and looked out the window, lost in thought. For a while we sat next to each other in silence, observed the martyred sandstone heads out in the garden and I almost dozed off it was so still.

'Did you adjust the temperature in the oven, Pippo?' Gabriella called from the kitchen.

'Why should I have?' he murmured and finally looked back at me. 'Did you have a look through Tania's flat?'

'I was—' I began and broke off. A thin cat scurried through the back courtyard, pigeons cooed in the palm tree.

'I was close by.'

'Close by? What do you mean by that?'

I poked at my lentils; Gabriella made noises in the kitchen.

'Have you ever been to Moscow, Anton?' Brevi asked, letting the pills roll back and forth across his plate.

'No,' I admitted. 'But I wanted to.'

'You wanted to!'

'My proposal was rejected by the funding body.'

'How do you intend to understand Gramsci when you have never been in Moscow?'

'But today's Moscow doesn't have anything to do with his.'

'Today's Moscow may have little to do with Gramsci's Moscow, but every other city has even less to do with it. We must be content with what we are given. Have you ever been to Sardinia? Have you been through the streets of Sorgono or attended Mass in Ghilarza?'

'I've been to Cagliari. It rained for four days. Then I took the ferry back.'

'And Sorgono?'

'I wanted to.'

'You wanted to!'

'I waited for two hours in front of the closed bus, but the driver never showed up.'

'You let yourself be discouraged by a tardy bus driver? If it had been fifty, or a hundred or a general strike of the Sardinian bus service, maybe. But a single driver, Anton! Just one!'

The Roman light—glaring, glittering, unbearably clear—was too much for me. I'd gone down into the old city and was wandering through the tiny streets. Everywhere, saints stuck into the facades for centuries looked down on me, the heat was relentless and I felt a dull rage against all the relics that this city kept within itself. One church stood on top of another, when you stepped in to the sacristy you found the remains of another, more distant age, there had never been a clean break anywhere, not in the first or twelfth or even twentieth century. You would never be able to rid yourself of anything because everything was charged with meaning, because this was Rome, the city of all cities, not Bottrop, Brandenburg or Lazio.

At the edge of a piazza, the tables of the tourist traps were protected by parasols and awnings, waiters with open menus were attempting to charm people as they rushed past, laughing off the inflated prices while behind the glass barriers families ate overcooked pasta in loveless cream sauce and a young boy about Lasse's age was whining about his Cola not being cold enough. His mother rolled her eyes, his father turned away and I wasn't sure if I felt sorry for them or if, at that moment at least, I was envious.

Without knowing where I wanted to go I turned into another little street. On a corner a misshapen little man was playing violin, in front of a bakery a young couple was arguing. I passed by the old synagogue and stumbled up onto the Lungotevere. In front of me, Tiber Island squatted in the water like a prehistoric amphibian, that island where the contagiously ill had once been locked away along with the mad and the sad so that they wouldn't infect the whole city.

I followed the river with its glimmering green water, the plane trees along its banks whose trembling shade gnarled the pavement. Two nuns were waiting at a bus stop, a homeless man was asleep on a bench, and I too just wanted to go to sleep, back in my bed in Göttingen with its adjustable frame and new mattress, I wanted to sleep until everything around me was ordered again, had reverted to the predictable uniformity of our first years together back when there was just Hedda and me and the promise of a future professorship, when the irritations—sometimes named Teresa, sometimes Laura, sometimes Verena—did not rip open any gulfs and Hedda still forgave me my mistakes.

I saw Tatiana's courtyard in my mind again, the face of the old woman at the window and behind her back the deathly pale man with his piled-up hair and round glasses. I shook my head. It must have just been the glasses that reminded me of Gramsci, but it was no wonder I was having such strange ideas in this city. Nothing moved forward because everything was blocked by the ancient shards shooting up from the ground beneath my feet. They'd been trying to build a third underground line for fifty years and every few days construction would stop when, yet again, the digging machines unearthed some remains or other which were supposed to explain something about our past but which really wasn't our past at all but the past of people who had lived hundreds of years ago. It was simply impossible for the city to join the present. It was impossible to end anything, much less let anything come to an end, and there was nowhere I could escape. I'd have to flee to the far ends of the city, to Ponte Mammolo or Anagnina, just to reach some high-rises from the '60s, or, if I was lucky, an eyesore from just a few years ago, dusty white bowls which, had the contractors not run out of money, would have been turned into blocks of flats. And that's what the new seemed like too, made up as it was out of the outlines of rooms that had never seen a roof, everything just an outline, like the ancient excavations at Largo Argentina.

A heavy summer rain broke without warning. People ran down the Lungotevere, from out of nowhere umbrella sellers appeared, tourists waved them off, you just never knew about these street vendors. If Lasse had been with me, he would have put his head under my arm. I began to walk more quickly and sought shelter beneath the monomaniacal columns of a church. Buses snorted past, their windscreen wipers wagging. The vendors yelled after the people streaming past, shouting in to their mobiles, cars honked, and I just wanted to be back in the quiet of a little city in central Germany, among the taciturn and beneath a sun which in August was already pale.

XXX. 20 YEARS   On 10 February 1928, three letters addressed to inmates of the prison of San Vittore in Italy are stamped in Moscow: to Terracini, Scoccimarro and Gramsci. Ruggero Grieco, a leader of the PCI, reassures each of the three prisoners that the Party has always been there for them, even when they did not have reason to think so, and promises to get help from Moscow.

Perhaps, Gramsci thinks, they have heard something new from the Berliner Nuntius Pacelli. Perhaps he has been successful in arranging the prisoner swap the Party tried to achieve last year. If the negotiator Pacelli is successful in convincing Mussolini, they will free a few Italian priests from Russian imprisonment in exchange for Gramsci and some other communists. So, his destiny now hung in the hands of a Catholic priest, of all things. Gramsci would be able to laugh if he ever received something from Moscow other than a telegram with the message: 'No news.'

'Deputy Gramsci, you have friends that would like to see you behind bars for a long time,' the examining magistrate, Enrico Macis, greets him and lays one of Grieco's letters down on the table.

'This will have repercussions for you,' Macis says and eyes Gramsci with a blank face. 'For the trial in May. If you had got your hopes up for a release, you can forget it. If the Party is indeed behind you to the degree we can read here, you will never be able to talk your way out of here.'

'I know what you can accuse me of. You do not have to threaten me with any monsters.'

'We simply arrested you, Gramsci, but your comrades are doing their best to make sure you stay here. With this letter, the prosecution has everything it needs to keep you out of service for many years.'

When the trial begins three months later, it is early summer and the most beautiful time of the year in Rome. The heat is not yet oppressive, the blooms have not yet been overwhelmed by the sun and fallen over, and the streams of pilgrims have lessened since Pentecost and will only pick back up towards Ascension Day. The seagulls are back too, Gramsci's distant companions in solitary at Regina Coeli. It's been one and a half years, and now they are sailing above the Palace of Justice. How old does a seagull grow? he wonders. How far do they move in one and a half years? Could they still be the same ones?

In front of Gramsci sit six sweaty judges in a row behind a lot of virtuous wood, as if waiting to be fed. They are wearing military uniforms instead of robes and the president of the Special Tribunal in Defence of the State—in existence since November 1926, the same month Italy definitively became a dictatorship—General Alessandro Saporiti is staring relentlessly at the accused. Twenty-two communists have been brought before the court; though not in handcuffs, they are being guarded by militiamen. A reporter from the *Manchester Guardian* is there, as well as one from *Petit Parisien* and the *TASS*.

The official charges are: instigation of civil war, conspiratorial activity, incitement to military insubordination, armed conflict, class hatred, looting. A few of Gramsci's comrades are excused from taking part in the trial, one on account of illness, one on account of corruption, one for being mad.

'The state has already been infiltrated by the communists,' Professor Li Causi says, enjoying the lie that causes the six judges to experience a brief moment of terror.

'Mr Ferrari, you have a previous conviction on record. A strike in Modena in 1913,' General Saporiti says and attempts a serious look in his guinea-fowl eyes.

'The fact is, Mr President,' Ferrari answers calmly, 'that the said event brought me the highest praise from the then-director of *Avanti!*, Mr Benito Mussolini.'

Stifled laughs in the room. One of the five associate judges undoes a button of his coat to allow a bit of fresh air to reach his smouldering body.

'You stand accused of conspiratorial activities,' the general explains to Gramsci. 'Incitement to civil war and class hatred. What do you have to say in your defence?'

'I refer to the explanation I gave the police. As to the fact of being a communist, I take full responsibility.'

'In the confiscated writings, there is talk of war and the seizure of power on the part of the proletariat. What do these writings mean?'

'I believe, General, that sooner or later, all military dictatorships become involved in war.'

'Objection, your honour,' the state prosecutor interrupts.

'You will lead Italy to ruin,' Gramsci calls out excitedly, 'and it will be up to us communists to save her.'

Closing remarks for the accused come from Terracini. 'When in the future someone reads what monstrous sentences were imposed upon us,' he calls out, running a hand through his thinning hair, 'he will come to the conclusion that this trial and the sentences themselves are part of a civil war and a violent act of incitement and class hatred.'

The state prosecutor stands up indignantly, the president tries to interrupt Terracini but Terracini leans forward and continues to speak in an even louder voice.

'But one is not allowed to say so, no? Mr President, this hearing was the most dignified and appropriate way you could have ever used to honour the eightieth anniversary of the Constitution, which you celebrated in the streets of Rome yesterday with cannons.'

'Mr Accused, I hereby forbid you to speak!'

When the court withdraws for its deliberations, it is quiet among the defendants, they only exchange glances. All their hope is gone. That which is to come will without a doubt be catastrophic. As the sentence is being read out, Gramsci feels the room grow steadily colder. He looks at the black-helmeted soldiers with their bayonets. 'We must stop this brain from functioning for twenty years,' prosecutor Michele Isgrò states. He hears Terracini sentenced to twenty-two years, nine months and five days, and then he hears his own: Antonio Gramsci receives twenty years, four months and five days. Everyone in the room knows that he will not survive his sentence.

XXXI. HUMANS AND ANGELS   The fact that I had not worn a wedding ring in two years was more of a circumstance than a decision. I hadn't planned it with any great gesture or anything, it was just chance. At some point I'd simply forgotten it, like you forget an umbrella (though I had to admit I lost umbrellas more often than wedding rings, even if the latter happened too). It just happened.

I forgot the ring one night when washing my hands, or maybe it was after a party where I'd dropped it in.to my jacket pocket because of the pale woman at the next table. Or maybe I left it on a hotel nightstand because I didn't want to get another woman off with my wedding ring on my hand, something that didn't make any sense because I generally used my other hand, the right one, to get women off, and, apart from that, now that I thought about it, the whole hotel episode didn't happen to me at all but a colleague from Barcelona who told me about it at a conference, laughing heartily the whole time. I didn't laugh, and certainly not heartily.

It just didn't work any more. Hedda was irritating, she was there too much yet not enough. From day to day she retreated more and more, leaving me completely alone in that city where I had nothing left to seek or to hope for. We'd reached a point where we could only say hurtful things to each other. And even if we managed to say something nice, something conciliatory, it came out like a clumsy attempt to hurt. Weeks, maybe even months, had gone by where we looked at each other in contempt or looked away, as if the other wasn't there. And then silence. We no longer fought, we'd given it up, and Hedda slipped away from me as if she were dead. We thought we'd understood that there was nothing left to lose, nothing left to gain. I did not refuse to leave Hedda because it would be the easiest thing to do, but, possibly, because it would be the most difficult.

We'd made an effort around each other, we'd been making an effort for years. We had tried to establish a middle-class existence when we moved to Göttingen. We looked at a flat with herringbone parquet and a living room for our piano, right in front of the winter garden so Hedda could practice, but we didn't end up taking it because it was on the fourth floor and there wasn't an elevator and we were sure we'd soon have a child, that things would run the way they're supposed to and getting up to a flat on the fourth floor would just be too much with a baby basket. And even if the child—the reason why we didn't take the flat—came later, it really was the right choice because it matched our idea of what life was supposed to look like: Hedda in soft wool socks at the piano, me on the sofa or in my study. And even if it would be a few years before she became pregnant, not taking the flat was the right choice because it was a concession that we wanted to try to do it all together and to make our life as a unit.

I continued to see Hedda every morning. I'd see her before I even had a piece of bread in my stomach or a coffee. I had to look at her now and again because there really wasn't too much else to look at and because we still had a few things to settle. And once those things were settled, of course, there was Lasse, for whom we were both responsible, and the further away from each other we got the more that responsibility seemed to grow. When it could not be avoided, or once she or I had put Lasse to bed, and we'd find ourselves sitting across from each other at the kitchen table— Hedda with her Bordeaux, me with a bowl of peanuts—to discuss something urgent, I could feel how she was taking Lasse further and further away from me. I thought about how he'd look at me sometimes with distant eyes or even scoot away from me, how an aversion carried over to my son, one that he did not understand

and that had nothing to do with him or with me and yet still affected him and which he picked up, a child who had adopted a way of speaking for which he was still far too young.

In the meantime, Hedda made more money than I did, she'd take over the flat, I'd have to move out, and she carried it around triumphantly, but it was only a result of the circumstances, circumstances she could do nothing about, circumstances I could do nothing about. All in all, things could have gone quite differently. Kalkreuther had never been a good researcher, and, if he hadn't been around in the first place, then he wouldn't have been able to steal the professorship from under my nose and I would have been able to pay for the flat and Hedda would have had to be the one to move out, she would have had to be the one to press Lasse to her chest and leave with theatrical gestures, she would have been the one that had to leave. As it was, however, I was the one, me, who was abandoning them, or rather, *had* to abandon the two of them. First, I forgot my wedding ring, and then I forgot where I'd forgotten it. I had never imagined what the end of a marriage looked like, and once it was there, it seemed depressingly unspectacular. It just happened. Because it was hard to bring oneself to make the grand gesture. Because, in the end, I was unsure.

To be honest, I hadn't begun our marriage with the grandest of gestures either. Two weeks after ending the thing with Teresa, I'd made Hedda a proposal, or, rather, she'd asked if maybe it wasn't time . . . if the two of us shouldn't think about . . . how did we envision the coming years . . . Three months later, Hedda and I got married, quickly, as if something could come between us if we waited too long.

The weekend before our wedding, Teresa had moved away from Göttingen, as I found out from my colleague Joachim Wendtland who had fought for a professorship at the university in court and who since then had felt he not only knew everything there was to know but that he also had to share that wisdom. I hadn't asked. I hadn't wanted to hear about it. I hadn't wanted to hear a single thing about Teresa.

Hedda and I wanted an uneventful wedding, a wedding without any faux pas, I'd even invited Wendtland in order to ward off any offence. Ilsa, of course, was a faux pas in and of herself, but that was unavoidable. The morning of the wedding, she welcomed me to her hotel room in a flurry of far-too-colourful fabric. She'd already had a bit to drink—*Sekt* I hoped, schnapps I assumed—but in the end it didn't matter, she simply couldn't watch the failure of her marriage happen one more time, that marriage which had ended before they'd even applied for an appointment at the registry office. She had not allowed someone else to outright commit themselves to her or she to someone else, for, in truth, she was afraid that if she had, there wouldn't have been anyone there, she was afraid that there was no one who would have wanted her completely and not just as a passing ornament, a short-lived moment of excitement. No one who would have wanted to share an entire life with her, who would have taken responsibility for her and expected her to do the same in return. Who would have demanded that—and this is where she would have failed—he not be left on his own.

'And a church wedding too!' Ilsa groaned. She was not a fan of the Catholic church and even less so of the fact that Hedda had converted for my sake. 'As if she hasn't already converted her whole life for you,' she observed.

There was a knock on the door. She didn't move.

'Your father, your business,' was all she said.

Bernd walked in with a drab bouquet of flowers which he stuck in to my hand, mumbling something about vases and Hedda, something that was only tangentially related. He was wearing a corduroy jacket, as if he'd just come from a teacher's conference. The woman with him smiled at me. She was probably around my age and looked as proper as a tax return, and, as Bernd informed us, was the editor of a magazine for modern and contemporary history in Hamburg.

'Ah,' Ilsa observed with scathing terseness. I refrained from any commentary.

'What do you have to do with the Catholics?' Bernd, who in his Calvinistic pusillanimity held any religion whose stronghold was below the mouth of the Weser River to be a bunch of lax hocus-pocus, enquired. 'Is it so some spiritless authority figure can forgive all the crap you get up to, is that it?'

'On the contrary,' Ilsa said, immediately knowing better. 'He wants the prohibitions because they transform every mistake into something respectable. Only through sinning do you develop an eye for salvation.'

So, now she was reading Kierkegaard's *Either/Or* and thought she had finally seen through me.

'It's the incense, I'm addicted to incense,' I called from the bathroom and splashed my face with water. By the time I came back, Ilsa's partner Jürgen had appeared. He was a mouse-grey, bald man who had once been the head of the German Communist Party in Bremen and worn a hammer and sickle on his lapel up till the fortieth anniversary of the GDR, not till the end of the German Democratic Republic, something he never tired of repeating.

'My son conducts research on Antonio Gramsci, by the way,' Bernd explained to his history editor.

'Civil society,' she said cleverly right away. 'Cultural hegemony. The integral state.'

'They never go together in life,' Hedda hissed to her grey mouse and then loudly: 'And Hedda has just finished a rather excellent piece on the spouses of leading socialists.'

'On the spouses?' Bernd asked. 'Why not on the socialists in general?'

'Marriage,' Ilsa said softly, 'was the dilemma of their lives. The basis for their crises. Almost all of them spent time in mental hospitals. Just imagine. Because it was their only way out. Crises, one after the other!'

'Nothing is more difficult than being the wife of an important man,' the editor quoted Emma Adler.

'At best, the wife of a man who *thinks* he's important,' Ilsa added, looking at me sharply.

'Actually, the quote is: the wife of a famous man,' I corrected them.

'And how was it with Gramsci's women?' Bernd asked, his tone giving away how much he wanted to be back taking history classes.

'Three,' Ilsa answered for me. 'Three sisters. And all of them had breakdowns.'

'You should write something about that,' Bernd said.

'Each of them in their own way revolved around him,' Ilsa added.

'You can't quite put it that way,' I replied.

'You sure can put it that way. He wouldn't have allowed it any other way.'

'He would gladly have avoided Eugenia's way,' I countered. 'She denounced him, she talked badly about him in front of the whole family, in front of his own son too.'

'Are you suggesting she did not have any reason to? He led Tania around by the nose, he dominated Giulia and hurt her, and, presumably, in the end, Eugenia was the only one who saw him clearly.'

'An entirely new perspective on your Gramsci,' Bernd said. 'I always thought he was a sort of idol for you.'

'You haven't known me for thirty years,' Ilsa replied. 'Furthermore, you have to be able to differentiate between the work and the life. Anything else smacks of dilettantism.'

208

I'd already spotted my colleague Wendtland from a distance. Ilsa and Bernd and their respective partners were still dragging themselves out of their taxis. I was walking past the display board with our banns, and he was standing in front of the door to the church talking to a red-haired woman who'd tied her trench coat too perfectly, or too perfectly for Wendtland in any event, around her waist. Naturally, she was bored. Wendtland had been boring me for six years, and soon he'd be telling me about his oh-so-important work in university admin, about the waves of students coming to his office, about those unending meetings where people, or, rather, Wendtland, had personally reinvented the state of research, about his secretary that he was unable to get rid of thanks to all the protections for public employees that allowed such confused birds to remain tied to their chairs.

'Be happy you're only non-professorial teaching staff, Anton, there's just too much crap to deal with,' he'd whine, something he'd have considered on the drive over in his Saab 900. Or did he have a Saab 9000 in the meantime?

I smiled at the red-haired woman in the trench coat. Ilsa poked me in the side and hissed, 'Do you have to make eyes at women you don't know even at your wedding?'

'It would be better for us both if we stayed out of each other's lives as much as possible,' I said and stared at the worn red handbag she dangled in front of me. That she had not thought about how to act at my wedding, her indifference to the world and its people, her libertinism overall, provoked me. I had never been able to handle her chaos which she attempted to balance out with too tidy a head, and that head could barely do anything else but make fun of others any more.

'You have never paid any attention to the rules which apply to everyone else, Anton,' she, of all people, said.

'The lover exists beyond the law,' I explained and grabbed her handbag so that I wouldn't have to look at her any longer.

'You don't love, Toni, you only want to dominate people.'

She smiled at me and ran a hand across her childishly colourful dress. Naturally, she knew better, having loved my father, me and all the other men who'd come through our shared life like people on a flat hunt in such an exceptional way. She pocketed all the commission but never gave anyone approval. If Ilsa loved anyone, it was those figures who had already retreated into the distant, tiny space that makes the alphabet available to us. Everyone else—at times, three a year—was unhappy with her but did their best, all the way up through self-abandonment.

I loved Hedda and had for years. I loved the little mark on her shoulder, her soft, throaty voice when she woke me up early in the morning. I loved her fingers and her toes and even the footnotes in her master's thesis, where, right before she handed it in, I'd pencilled in how much I loved it when she was in my arms, that she was the only authority in my life and that I wanted her alone and wished her so much of everything. But how, if you please, was I supposed to have given that to her if, in all those months lying next to me with her swollen stomach, I'd repressed all my appetites? How patiently I rubbed her feet which were more tired than usual because she had more of herself to carry around. All those weeks of morning sickness I made her decaffeinated coffee and cooled her forehead. I never would have made it if I'd completely given up on my needs, I would have become one of those grumpy, unsympathetic husbands who were as plentiful as sand on the beach and who, during their wives' pregnancies, went to the office or meeting rooms almost obsessively, that, or they ended up having a breakdown together with their spouses.

'I'd like to have my handbag back now,' Ilsa said, reaching out her hand. 'Furthermore, things are about to start. Your bride has even arrived.'

I turned. Hedda was standing between her father, who was wearing a strict confirmation-style suit, and the announcement board which, I hadn't looked closely, was asking the congregation to donate to some organ tube or other or a well in Africa somewhere. Hedda was wearing a dress that, under the circumstances, was too tight. I hadn't helped her choose it, that job had been taken over by a girlfriend who she ended up giggling with more than paying attention to any questions of taste.

Hedda had barely made her way through the door of the church when her pregnant appearance, her distended belly, became the centre of attention. My two aunts in their bundles of tulle turned to see her, and my colleagues from the university—the woman in the trench coat and even Wendtland—looked too. It was the first time I had presented Hedda in her new guise. I'd expected to feel proud, to finally show Ilsa what she'd been incapable of achieving her whole life, namely, a bourgeois existence.

Hedda hung listlessly on her father's arm, and, breathing heavily, walked up to me. She'd forgotten to put on perfume or perhaps too little, and her body was busy producing sombre mother hormones which caused everything to smell on her slightly female sweat that, to me, already had the sweet scent of mother's milk and baby skin. I would have happily stepped to the side but the priest had come up to greet us and a six-year-old girl in a bad mood from Hedda's extended family was walking behind her in order to throw flowers.

We entered the church. The organ played. The congregation sang 'Unser Leben sei ein Fest'. Hedda's mother pressed a tissue to her eyes. Bernd nestled into his corduroy, his companion looked on sceptically. Ilsa stood in the first row with a creased mouth, refusing to sing or to understand how good I was for Hedda and that freedom could only be won by freedom. *Read your Bakunin, Ilsa!* Freedom and constraint must be in balance, and if Hedda didn't know what she wanted then I had to tell her.

'If I speak in the tongues of men or of angels, but do not have love, I am only a resounding gong or a clanging cymbal,' the priest said, not seeming too full himself at the moment but a bit on the shrill side. I looked sideways at Hedda as she proudly lifted her chin. She was neither gong nor cymbal, this had to do with *her* love, the one she was consummating successfully, for all this had been written to be presented *right now*, and I asked myself whether it had anything to do with me or whether, uniquely and exclusively, it had more to do with her and with being loved.

'If I have the gift of prophecy,' the priest pointed out, 'and can fathom all mysteries and all knowledge, and if I have a faith that can move mountains, but do not have love, I am nothing.'

I thought of Teresa in her yellow lingerie. I'd walked away from her to end up precisely in this place because I wanted my life to gain a sense of order, because I wanted an ordered life, I wanted to be a married man among married men, serious, responsible, ready to take up a professorship, and I looked at Hedda, how much I'd wanted her, how much longer and more seriously I'd wanted her than any other woman, and right then she pushed out her stomach a little further.

'Love is patient, love is kind. It does not envy, it does not boast, it is not proud. It does not dishonor others, it is not self-seeking, it is not easily angered, it keeps no record of wrongs. Love does not delight in evil but rejoices with the truth.'

Hedda could have pushed her shoulder blades together. I'd seen an acquaintance of mine do that once, it optically reduced the look of being pregnant by a month, but Hedda had wanted to bear her pregnancy like a monstrance before which no one had prayed. She continued to breathe heavily, almost panting by now. There were women who were pregnant and women who performed being pregnant. I stifled a comment; after all, I knew how you were supposed to act. There was biology of course, but there was also care and the perfume I had brought her after a trip two weeks earlier. If her hormones were working harder than usual, then she had to work a bit harder on herself, shower twice a day, change her clothes more often. But Hedda didn't think about any of that, she was only concerned with herself and what was growing inside of her, I was merely an accessory, if anything, and my wishes no longer had any voting power.

'Now I know in part,' the priest maintained, 'then I shall know fully, even as I am fully known. And now these three remain: faith, hope and love. But the greatest of these is love.'

Suddenly I was gripped by the thought that she was not marrying me but the father of the child in her stomach, a man with whom she'd already forged a much stronger alliance than this thin priest, this Calvinist in disguise, this complainer who viewed the world of the senses so sceptically would ever be able to provide. At that moment, I was disgusted with her; or with who she had become because of the changes going on inside of her. She was the shell of an organism working on completing another. She'd pushed me to the edge of her awareness because all that remained was ultrasound, breathing and the maternity ward. I could run around in front of her and she'd barely notice me. There was only her and the child, and for her I'd left Teresa, I'd given up my habits and now I saw the best man coming with our rings, they were small, simple rings we had chosen together, Hedda had wanted wider ones of brushed gold, but I'd explained to her that, as far as rings were concerned, any kind of exaggeration would be out of place because in twenty, thirty years' time they'd just look passé.

The priest fiddled with his sleeves, blessed the rings and the organ started again. Everything around me hummed. Hedda looked like she was about to go into labour at any moment. The red-haired woman smiled in my direction, the only point of comfort in that whole church sticky with marriage euphoria. I winked. Wendtland's hand waved through the air then landed intimately on her shoulder, and I felt unbearably tired when it dawned on me that the woman was his wife. Hedda gave me her hand. I slid the ring onto her finger, then gave her mine and looked down onto what was now a marred hand. I had never worn jewellery. I didn't like the look of it on men's hands, above all on my own, I'd have preferred taking it back off immediately but I controlled myself, I'd always been able to do that. I put my arm around her, caressed her shoulder and felt the soft, even beat of her body. I kissed her because that's how things were supposed to go.

XXXII. WELTANSCHAUUNG *Good wishes, see you soon,* Tania telegraphs to Turi, that special prison for the ill, a new station on Gramsci's odyssey, as if the fascists intended to have him get to know every jail of their, of *his*, country. Here in Turi he is allowed to write in his cell, an effective means against the unassailable power of time which in prison has no beginning and no end. To the degree that he can, he divides his day with calisthenics and grammar exercises, the books he reads and, above all, the notebooks he fills, the one place he can put his thoughts in order instead of letting them dissipate in the air, the one place he can speak—as he has been kept from taking action—and that his doctor sees as proof of his insanity.

It is shortly before Christmas. Gramsci is sitting in front of the small shaft of the window, a pallid light trickles in, for days it has not really been light and the temperature has gone down significantly. 'The passage from utopia to science,' he writes, and pulls his sweater up to his chin, 'and from science to action (remember Karl Radek's pamphlet on this subject)' when a guard brings him the notice. Now the small message is lying on the pages of his notebook. Five words. 'Good wishes, see you soon.' Beneath them his handwriting again: 'The foundation of a directive class (i.e. a state) is equivalent to the creation of a *Weltanschauung*.' He does not understand what is so urgent about Tania's message that she had to telegraph him. Just yesterday he received a Christmas card from her, why did she have to add this? He scratches his throat which begins to itch beneath the wool, and thinks about the odd message. Why was she sending him good wishes? Why *see you soon*? Does she want to say that she will only write him again in

215

the new year? In late January perhaps? Is she ill again? Is she in a clinic? Is she sending the good wishes to herself? It doesn't make any sense, and he doesn't know if she means something else, if it's really a secret message he simply does not understand which therefore means it is not Tania's fault. She is not thinking from the universe of a prisoner for whom a 'see you soon' is too much of a promise, a person who clings to words in the absence of the people behind them. Gramsci lies awake until late, his stomach cramps over and over, around one in the morning he has to vomit. It is pitch black, and the acrid stench fills the room. He rinses his mouth with water, drags himself back to his bed; the vomit stinks in his bedpan. Nevertheless, he is exhausted and dozes off, then wakes back up, then dozes back off.

The next morning, the weak prisoner is ordered out of his cell and made to wait under a roof in the courtyard, but without knowing why. Giulia walks in. Gramsci can see her so clearly, just like on those bright, early summer mornings in Rome when the light washes all the colours clean. Then he hesitates. Only when she's standing in front of him does he realize that it is Tania.

'Pure Italian,' the director instructs her. 'Otherwise I'll have to end your conversation.'

'How are you, my dear?'

'Why the telegram?'

'Because I was on my way to you—'

'I didn't know that, it could have meant anything.'

'I thought you knew—'

'How so?'

'The stamp on the postcard. Bari. I was almost here.'

'You can't just make me so anxious,' he says. 'Here everything weighs three times as much as it does with all of you outside. There's a different force of gravity, a difference like that between the earth and the moon. You should know that by now.'

Tania turns away, silently observes the bored prison guard who is slouching lazily next to them.

'You look pale,' Tania whispers at last.

'No, no, don't worry about my health, I'm well, it's just that, last night, no, I'm well, Tania, tell me, how was your trip? How are Giulia and the kids?'

Tania tells him about the Meccano construction kit Delio received and with her hands shows Gramsci the movements of the stuffed goose Giuliano has been playing with, its long, wobbly neck. He likes the rustling of newspapers, and Delio can differentiate between living and non-living things, the born and the unborn.

'I had a rose for you,' Tania says, 'and socks and some chicory, but they took them away at the gate. I am only allowed to bring you the most necessary items. What do they even understand about what's necessary here? They don't understand a thing,' she says.

The guard yawns and Tania adds: 'They don't understand a thing, just pure Italian.'

'I was afraid,' Gramsci says.

'I know.'

'No, you don't,' he counters strongly, and it is as if something has broken. As if a vent has let out everything which has been pent up and that he did not even know was there. 'You cannot imagine what life here is like. What it's like to be forgotten.'

'I . . .' Tania attempts.

'You simply have no imagination. You imagine everything to be soft, lyrical somehow. Yes, indeed, all the world a Romantic poem, right?'

'Of course, Toni, you're right,' Tania says. 'You are always right. I was worried about you, that was all. I couldn't do any better. I simply cannot live for myself, I always just live someone else's life.'

'But we're not in an animal-welfare organization!' Gramsci cries.

The guard bleats into his moustache, stifling a laugh.

'Do you think I always need to be loved and looked after? And the socks,' he adds, 'have to be white, otherwise they will not be allowed.'

Tania anxiously runs a hand across her forehead. Gramsci stops speaking and stands there silently, grimly, before at last adding the absolution: 'I'm happy you're here. With you here, Giulia is here a bit as well.'

He moves to take Tania's hand, she shrinks; perhaps it isn't even allowed. Once again, the guard snorts in laughter thinking that Gramsci has confused two distinct people. But it's not as simple as this walrus thinks, there is no key to lock up anything it cannot understand. If he were to read Pirandello just once, he'd recognize what was going on, and if he would only think a bit for himself, he'd also understand that Gramsci is never simply speaking with Tania but with his family and Giulia and the Party. Tania is his mouthpiece to Moscow, and, even if he were not interested, Tania would be unable to stop it; beyond the thoughts of books and Giulia's letters, she is the only thing that continues to reach him from a world that grows ever-more abstract as he can no longer enrich it with experiences, as it must remain what it is: a landscape of letters, a desert of speech, an abstract deafness.

In closing, he hands her a ball of papier-mâché he has made for Delio, a small, miserable thing that is hardly round at all.

'That is not allowed,' the walrus declares.

Tania and Gramsci look at each other.

'You may not accept anything from the prisoner.'

'It's only paper.'

'And certainly not take it with you.' With disturbing speed, the walrus jumps up and removes the ball from Tania's hand.

'I have to give this to the head warden.'

'A toy?'

'This is no toy, this is an attempt to smuggle, Mr Gramsci.'

'I am waiting for letters from you,' Giulia writes him, 'I do not cease waiting,' and the papier-mâché ball is presented to the administrator of prisoner's belongings, Giuliano gets his second tooth, the ball is handed on to the board of Cell Block A, Eugenia has to go to a sanatorium, the ball is passed from the board to the lawyer Ligursi, Giulia is almost paralysed by depression, the ball is presented by Professor Ligursi to the one responsible for visits, Delio has to go to his grandmother, the suitcases are packed, he will soon be picked up. When the door rings, he sits up and asks: 'Perhaps it's Papa?' Giulia runs a hand through his hair, does not answer. His second mother sends a postcard from the sanatorium, and the daylight, as always, is too bright when Gramsci steps out of the eternal leaden gloom of the prison's insides. His comrades are walking in a circle. Children's photographs have been hung in the courtyard. The guards call it an exhibition, or were the prisoners the first to call it that? During their compulsory walks, they make their way past the series of children's heads, their own and those of their fellow prisoners, Delio is there too, and with every round, he looks a bit different to Gramsci, almost as if he would grow into the wall. Gramsci must pull himself together in order to not stay still. He wants to walk up to the wall as if he could simply take his son down and lead him by the hand through the courtyard, feel Delio's hand in his and show him this world which was not beautiful but all the same was his. He doesn't stop, makes the next round. Some of the photographs have become unrecognizable, a thumb has run over them so many times, they have been stuffed into a pocket and pulled back out. Others look new, as if they'd just been taken, perhaps they were adoringly kept behind a piece of glass in a frame. What will the

219

prisoners do, Gramsci wonders, when, going to sleep later tonight, they realize that everything they still have is out in the courtyard and they feel even lonelier than the hundreds of days they have already felt so lonely here?

XXXIII. UGO   The first time I travelled to Rome was with Ilsa. It was during the spring holidays in 1978 and she was in an irascible and nervous state. A few days before their official start, she excused me from school and we boarded a train for Munich. Inside, she checked when and where we had to change trains I don't know how many times (Munich Hauptbahnhof, 22.31) and, once we got there, ordered a local comrade to take me by the hand and wait with us for the night train to Rome in a bar, between clouds of smoke and blurry faces.

We arrived at Stazione Termini the next morning on Track 8. Ilsa, ever the lady, walked across the platform, shoved a pair of sunglasses over her eyes, strolled through the hot, dry air and forgot she had a son with gusto. I trailed behind her, dragging my suitcase. At the taxi stand, she finally remembered my existence and sent the driver to grab me. He came over with dejected steps, took the suitcase out of my hand. I could smell his heavy, tangy aftershave and beamed up at him, feeling that at any moment he would burst into hearty laughter.

We drove down Via Nazionale, past the so-called Typewriter or Wedding Cake which had been erected in honour of Vittorio Emanuele II and which had more nicknames than the seagulls drifting in circles above it. We were staying with friends of Ilsa's in a dilapidated, two-storey building near Trastevere Station. Out in the hall, an emaciated dog that would have fallen down dead if we looked at it long enough padded up to us. A tube had broken in a wall of the kitchen and caused the wallpaper to have large swathes of dark patches as well as the water bill to go up every year. The whole house seemed to be held up by a single beam which could break at any moment.

The rooms all led into one another and there were countless occupants, serious-looking men all somewhat younger than Ilsa who continuously spoke in soft voices about Toni Negri and Mario Tronti, about *Potere Operaio* and *Lotta Continua* and here and there wove in a quote of Gramsci's. There were two wives and then a third woman who was involved with one of the men or maybe the other, or all of them or, in the end, maybe none of them at all. And there was Ugo.

Elegant from his clothes up to the wrinkles around his mouth, the people in the flat called him the Player, referring to his effortlessly successful way with women as much as the luxurious ease with which he made his way through life. He had an uncle who'd made his way up to being a cardinal and, so they said, resided in a series of impressive marble chambers, which in turn impressed me, and so I tried to find out something about this uncle, but Ugo didn't talk about it much, maybe because he didn't like to refer to his proximity to the Vatican, maybe because it was thanks to this uncle that he had everything, Rome and the women and even his melancholic air. 'Loneliness is a son-of-a-bitch,' being one of his sayings whenever the people around him got a bit too joyful.

It was the middle of March and Aldo Moro was putting together a government of Christian Democrats and communists, the so-called *compromesso storico*, the historical compromise. Right in the middle of the Cold War, an unthinkable coalition was being formed: a slap in the face of Western European belief that communism was incapable of governing in a democracy and a monstrosity for the Soviet government which was now being threatened with losing its absolute authority over a smaller party. Could Moro be allowed to have that much power? Wouldn't the compromise break down internally? And what would be left? An aristocratically smiling Berlinguer who, at most, would reveal himself to simply be a social democrat who'd been labelled incorrectly? Soon the hushed voices grew louder and I was sent to bed.

I'd obtained a room on the second floor from where I could see the river, the green slime passing below me which broke up in little eddies around the height of the Ponte Testaccio. Everything had been dimmed somehow, the light, the volume, the chaotic beauty, as if I'd got stuck somewhere north of the Alps.

The following day, I took my first steps ever in a university, the Sapienza, the campus a fascist-looking little city near the train station. Mixed with the architecture of cheap car parks, it was a bastard that couldn't have sprung from anything but the head of a mad architect. And you could imagine just about anything at all being taught there, save how to find the right room. Wandering through the corridors of the Department of Law, we saw students hanging around the halls, and, when Ilsa disappeared into an office with a deadly-serious-looking university worker to discuss various conspiratorial affairs for a few minutes, Ugo pointed out the female students to me. We watched them saunter past, young, silky, chatty, with wavy hair or wild curls, with swinging skirts or slim trousers, and I stood there, holding Ugo's hand, and thought that it would definitely be a good thing to go and study later on.

When Ilsa returned, Ugo smiled at her with his noble charm and ran a hand through her hair. 'I'm happy we're saving the Republic, Ilsa, but at the moment I really need an aperitif.'

A little while later we were sitting in a bar on Via Veneto, among teetering shoe tips, skirt hems and bronze-coloured cleavage and I understood that the university had only been a preparatory study. Here the women drank Campari and laughed so effortlessly, it was like life was a silken scarf flapping around their necks as they cruised by in a convertible. And if that shawl happened to get lost, at least it still had style. The world was generous with them. They took whatever they wanted, and never asked who could pay the bill. Ugo always paid a good amount of it. I followed

the women with my eyes whenever one of them went to the bathroom, 'to powder her nose,' as her companion explained. My
whole body was tense; imagining the brush at first timidly then
vehemently passing over the bridge of her nose it tingled as if
being pumped with a powerful current.

One Thursday—though only spring, the weather was already
summer-like—I went with Ilsa and Ugo on a trip outside of the
city. We'd set out early in a rush, I hadn't understood why and neither Ilsa nor Ugo had bothered to explain. They looked half-asleep,
and Ilsa poured coffee out of a Thermos into plastic cups. Ugo
drove a rickety Fiat which was difficult to reconcile with his usual
elegance, but took the curves daringly if rather clumsily when
he decided, most of the time too late, to brake. I was happy that I
didn't feel accountable to anyone if I didn't survive our holidays.
Bernd had transferred his salvation to Cuxhaven where I imagined he'd be sitting in a roofed wicker beach chair after work with
a female colleague, eating meat patties out of a red-and-white
striped cooler. Here, Christian Democratic Prime Minister Moro
was leaving his apartment building to drive to Parliament where
there was to be a vote of confidence on the fourth Andreotti government to make the historical compromise a reality, and Ugo
was slowing down for a three-wheeled Ape with two sheep on its
rear bed.

Compromises, I came to understand much later, were half
measures. They were made between two or more parties that had
imagined something else, something they would prefer to have
stayed with. Coming to a compromise was often accompanied by
cynical observations, long faces and a lack of sleep. This one here
had other dimensions. Moscow was appalled. The largest communist party outside Russia had lost its revolutionary perspective
and was threatening to break away from the dictates of the
Soviets. Washington was close to having a heart attack: were the
door to be opened to the Reds, they'd fall upon the luscious grass-
lands of the capitalistic world like a herd of rabbits, and, with a

great appetite and five-year plans, destroy what had just begun to bloom. The little country of Italy was leading the great powers by the nose, creating a world conflict as if simply arguing about getting the sunniest place on the beach at Ostia. The Iron Curtain was trembling, and, up in the sky where it had been fixed to its heavy eyelets, you could hear a groaning as if at any moment the cumbersome material would come crashing down.

We drove through a heavy cast-iron gate and slowly up a long driveway to a mansion. Balconies stuck out into damp, green palm groves. Lights flickered in the windows, and, on the top floor, a few silhouettes stood out against the coloured glass. Wrapped in white material, a woman stepped out to meet us. Ugo allowed his lips to glide across her cheeks while Ilsa looked angrily on and the woman giggled drily before waving at us to follow her across an endless stretch of grass. The air was heavy. A palm damaged in the last storm creaked above me.

'Please excuse the mess. I'm just addicted to parties, I'm such a bad girl!' Her hands fluttered up and down in front of Ugo. In accordance with the times, they were terribly thin, as was the rest of the woman who could have been twenty-five or forty-five, her face had something stony about it and overall she was too haughty to commit to any particular age. With a tired movement, Ugo took hold of her fingers.

'Don't worry, Carla, the Pope will forgive you, your father's deep enough in to the Vatican's banking affairs.'

'Well, you know, nothing's sure any more. Did you know our prime minister was just kidnapped?' Carla asked. 'This morning.'

I don't remember how Ugo responded. I couldn't say if we'd already learnt of Aldo Moro's kidnapping in the car or if there was even a radio, and if there was, whether it had been on during the drive or whether it was there in that reality-defying yard that we first learnt that the Republic, the one surrounding us, had tumbled into a further circle of chaos.

A squad of Red Brigades had stopped Moro's Fiat on Via Fani, Carla said, killed his bodyguards and taken the prime minister captive.

'Dearest, worrying doesn't suit you at all,' Ugo said, running a hand across her forehead.

'You're terrible!' Carla cried and dropped her shoulders. 'I'm so happy you exist.' Ilsa stepped on the hem of her white dress and excused herself with a vicious smile not even I would have thought her capable of.

A hundred-year-old or so butler and his young companion opened the doors of the villa and greeted us in a displaced Venetian accent. Through the open entrance we could see into the foyer, a floor in red and white marble where just now a group of elegantly dressed people appeared. Without deigning to turn towards us, three men and a smattering of women walked past. A girl, just one or two years older than I, walked ahead of them with a candelabra.

'How much I love these days,' one of the women chirped.

Giggling and with fans aflutter, the group moved on through a massive oak doorway. From the cellar came the sound of pop music. With a great show of emotion, Carla stepped through the door and into a side corridor. The light was dusty, the marble looked like it had been gnawed by insects. From behind a door came the rattle of a washing machine in the spin cycle, from behind another the buzzing of the news. Carla walked on and Ugo followed gravely, Ilsa had too determined a step and I slithered behind them all.

'Now this country will go under for good,' Carla said and chuckled hoarsely. 'But it had to come to this. The agreement was a mistake. Piedmont ate us alive, that's what happened.'

'It's always such a pleasure to hear you talk about things as if you'd been there, Carla,' Ugo said. In his voice was something that at the time I couldn't grasp; today I think it betrayed a hesitant, almost aggressive attraction. Ilsa stepped behind them a bit. My being with them was a good thing. Or maybe it wasn't. In any event, I helped to prevent further invasions of improper terrain and they began to talk about the Red Brigades, the pinched PCI and communism which, in Ugo's opinion, continued to gallop across Europe like a drunken charger, forgetting the right way over and over again.

Over the following weeks, 6.5 million people would be checked and 38,000 houses would be searched, but not the one at Via Montalcini 8 where former prime minister Aldo Moro was being held in a tiny space behind a bookshelf, writing letters to Giulio Andreotti, to the pope and to his wife, ninety-seven letters in total. In one of the last ones, he wrote: 'My dearest Noretta, everything is futile if one does not care to open the door. The pope has done little, perhaps he has scruples.'

The room we entered had no end, no beginning either. There was the sound of light jazz and new chairs, people and glasses popped up everywhere we went. Ugo grabbed one, then handed a drink to Carla and another to Ilsa. Carla giggled and disappeared shortly thereafter, like a shadow when the light reaches too much space. Ugo didn't seem to care and just continued to squint in every direction. Ilsa, however, took a noticeable breath. His fingers nibbled at her bottom, but then a red-haired woman with countless freckles on her shoulders draped herself across his neck. He kissed her forehead but another was already there and he was turning towards a third.

I disappeared into a corner, leant against the oak-wood wall and took sips from a chalice-like glass. Bowls poked out of the wood and with my finger I made the tassels that hung off of them swing back and forth, producing a pleasant feeling of dizziness.

'You have to know one thing,' Ugo, all of a sudden standing next to me again, explained as he went into a crouch. This, however, did not affect his noble bearing at all and he peaceably let his glass ring against mine. 'Communism is standing on the shoulders of midgets.' He took a sip from his champagne glass and let me try a bit. The sweetness was terribly mixed with the tart, and the little bubbles were too small; in mineral water, at least, they were of a respectable size. 'Lenin was five-foot-five-inches tall when the Revolution claimed victory in Russia, Stalin fought his way into power at five-foot-six. Gagarin was shot into space in 1961 and was only one fifty-seven, short enough to make him the first man to circle the earth. And when Gramsci died, there was, at best, maybe less than five feet of him.'

The champagne enfolded my mind like a light drug, and Ugo shrank and grew in front of my eyes as if he'd had a bit of Alice's Wonderland drink.

'Your mother is an astonishing woman, as you no doubt know. I've always felt close to her, but she just does not understand me. Not completely. She understands Italian communism just as little. She saw someone in Berlinguer who wasn't there. It's pointless to try any further, I'm sorry. I'm sorry most of all for you.'

I smiled at him even though I did not have the slightest idea what he was talking about. His head wavered before me; fatigue was dragging me to the floor. Shoes scraped across the stone tiles.

Wouldn't that have been the right moment to free myself from my reluctant growth? To no longer direct all my strength to lazing about in the last row of the classroom or being bothered during break but to getting enough (and more than enough) to eat, to stretching and performing exercises to strengthen my willpower, to escape communism and with it our secretly romanticized bookshelf, the piles of books to the left and right of the Biedermeier sofa, all the earth-twisting kitchen discussions with Gerd, Jürgen and Werdner? Did I really want to march in a row with the likes of those men? Lenin with his cap was never scary to me, it always just seemed to be hiding something (in the end, the fact of his being bald) and I'd liked Stalin for a while because of his massive moustache but was forced to change my mind on the day Gertraud, a motherly friend of Ilsa's, threw up in the middle of the Persian rug at his sudden appearance on the TV. It must've been some anniversary or other, and after calming whispers and Ilsa's question as to why she'd had to vomit, she answered: 'Because I believed in him once.'

After that, I never really cared for Stalin too much. And today I know better. I know about the show trials, the purges, the murders without trial, the Gulag, the Terror, the totalitarian depopulation of a country and that Stalin's rage could have gone on for decades, right up through the domination of the whole world, the definitive removal of all people from the planet.

It must have also had to do with the cosmonaut, the one whose constant smile unnerved but bewitched me, the one who couldn't do anything but look happy in all the photos, which really made loneliness in orbit nothing and I imagined as making him holy, or maybe it was the feeling that you could be immortal without killing a single human being. Well, whatever the reason, Gagarin was the only one who remained as an explanation.

But I was tired and Aldo Moro had been kidnapped and I didn't get all the connections that spun and glowed or were simply the pearls of the champagne. I saw the snow-white shimmer around my uncle as he fell victim to yet another woman, and then the young girl who'd been carrying the candelabra walked into the room. She was delicate, but that had more to do with her age than her body type or shape. She could have been thirteen or fourteen, right in the middle of the greatest hormonal metamorphosis which to me was just a remote mystery. She seemed lost, but blissfully suspended somehow. She tiptoed up to this man, then that one, let them pat her hair, cheeks and even her waist and giggled just like Gina Nazionale. I don't know how long I had been staring at her by the time she noticed me. It must have been an eternity, one of those eternities you preserve and keep in-between heavy books like flowers. She hesitantly turned on her socks, then cast a second glance in my direction, let a man brush the hair out of her face and then suddenly and almost defiantly stalked over to me.

Her legs were covered in mosquito bites and the lazy scabs of childhood, but they had grown too long to completely hide anything. Her face was already busy practicing expressions whose meaning she did not yet understand, and her breasts were growing frighteningly, touchingly and unmistakably beneath her blouse. She crouched next to me and in place of a greeting blew in my face. Then she said something in Italian, and when she noticed that I did not understand, rolled her eyes, showing me in no uncertain terms that she thought I was pretty dumb. Nevertheless, she continued to sit next to me and here and there cast a provocative glance at one of the men dancing past.

As if she had forgotten her previously unsuccessful attempt, she spoke to me again. I listened to her for a while, her lips opened and closed and at one point I was convinced she was asking me how old I was, presumably because I felt exhausted and believed she too would have to be reasonable and recognize the all-too-large difference between us. With my fingers I showed her the number eleven, but she just leant forward, bent over my index finger as it lingered over the two blank palms, grabbed it with her hand, sank her head and enveloped it with her lips. I was so surprised that for a moment I bounced onto my behind, then just remained sitting. She pressed my shoulders to the floor, held my hand in hers, my finger caught between her lips, I felt her teeth graze over the wrinkles of skin on the joint, then the milky tip of her tongue. Shoes scraped across the stone tiles. I briefly opened my eyes and saw the shadowy form of dangling key tassels above me.

XXXIV. TANIA   In the morning it's 36.2°, at eleven o'clock 36.9°, at two o'clock 37.2°, two hours later still only 36.9°, at six o'clock 36.8° or 36.7°.

This is Antonio Gramsci at the beginning of the '30s. He subsists on milk, yoghurt bacteria, grapes, three capsules of Sedobrol at seven-thirty in the evening and the tenth Canto of Dante's *Inferno*. In Ivanovo, Giulia is celebrating her thirty-fourth birthday and going out with her father and the children to collect mushrooms. Gramsci is suffering from the *scirocco* and the summer heat, and, when he tries to eat some bread, his temperature immediately rises, and, as his digestion troubles wear him out more than his malnourishment, he tries to postpone eating for as long as possible. He writes to his brother Carlo: 'My general impression is that I am definitely getting better.' He has headaches and arguments with his sister-in-law Tania who he thinks views prison as a kind of boarding school for girls. Standing at a tobacco shop she writes him a postcard, in pen, because the feather isn't worth a thing, while Gramsci has pain in his respiratory organs, which he combats with turpentine inhalations. He still has two teeth in his mouth and a useless sweater in his prison wardrobe, infested by moths with their quiet, lead-like existence until he sticks his hand into its darkness and tries to swat them. They flutter upwards and escape.

A new prison ordinance in Turi allows him to receive letters once a week. He lives in a single cell which makes working easier as well as the concentrated reading of those books Piero Sraffa has sent him with the plea: 'Tell me what you think, write me a review,' in order to keep the ailing prisoner thinking and alive and to press page after page out of him. Gramsci will not survive his imprisonment. He suspects as much, and he knows that the others know it too, nevertheless he hesitates to beg for an adjustment of his penalty or even a reprieve, as, in his eyes, it would amount to political and moral suicide. He would have to kneel before Mussolini personally, for the latter has made Gramsci's case personal so that he can control, if not his thoughts, than at least his life.

During the day, Gramsci paces back and forth, it is as if he no longer only thinks with his body but with his movement. As soon as he has fixed a thought in a sentence he hurries to the table, leans his knee against the stool and, as if the sentence might escape again like a butterfly caught in his hand, stabs into the paper. He writes about the practical origins of every seemingly absolute truth, he writes about the cheap polemicists who make money off of them, he writes about the dramas of conscience they incite among the working class and he warns that Marxism itself 'tends to become ideology in the negative sense, that is, to a dogmatic system of absolute and eternal truth.'

Despite the little amount of available surface his body offers, the sweats continue; water, and with it salt, drains out of every pore. He must eat more but he can't, his stomach refuses to work. He relates the story of a shipwreck where a few people have made it onto a lifeboat and are then subjected to the sea, the heat, and, once the last rations have been finished, hunger. 'Before the shipwreck, as is quite natural, not one of the future victims thought he would become the victim of a shipwreck,' he writes, 'even less so cannibalistic. But are they in reality the same people? Only from the point of view of the law can one say that they are the same people.'

Gramsci's cell is on the first floor, and day and night guards, doctors and men of unclear authority, perhaps members of OVRA, the fascist secret police, stomp up and down the hall in heavy boots. A bed is rolled by, his room is on the way to the infirmary, in reality, his room is on the way to every other ward, no spot in the building is loved as much as this one and Gramsci wanders back and forth in his cell like a fly that doesn't know where to die. Its memory evaporated.

On 3 August 1931, in spite of the heat and the noise, he falls asleep around midnight but wakes up an hour later and feels a gurgling when he breathes. Like with a bit of catarrh, he thinks. He sits up and coughs, once, twice nothing heavy or strong but as if he had something in his throat, three times, four, a cough without any climax. He tastes something metallically sweet on his tongue. He spits and sees blood in his handkerchief. His whole mouth is full of blood. Another cough. And another. As nothing else is available, he spits into his bedpan, spits and coughs and sweats and feels like all of his remaining strength is leaving him.

By four in the morning, he has expelled more than half a pound of blood. It feels like someone has squeezed his head like a sponge. He continues to wheeze but only manages to spit out a bit of blood-stained sputum.

'A bronchial infection,' the doctor says and orders him calcium chloride with a thousandth of adrenaline.

'Likely tuberculosis,' Tania writes and sends Gramsci more Sedobrol. Five capsules over the course of the day, she says, three in the evening are too many, you hear! She suggests Forgenia, two shots at a time, and that he thicken his milk with a piece of bread, produce some yoghurt, bacteria for his intestinal flora, just like Metchnikov has recommended. After all, he won the Nobel Prize in Physiology.

'That is simply female-empiricism and not science,' Gramsci accuses her. They argue evermore frequently but she is the only one he still can reach. She comes to visit him, she lives her life along the route of his prisons, and perhaps that is what makes him so angry: even the last person fails to understand him any longer. When Tania was with him, he had tried again to explain that she could only send him what he asked for. The prison authorities do not allow more. She needs to once and for all stop thinking according to the logic of everyday life. She had stood before him without moving at all, looked at him and all of a sudden begun to tremble.

'What is it, Tanicka?'

'Nothing. It's nothing.'

She is standing in front of him, her body is older than Giulia's but it resembles hers. Tania's hands are too soft for all that he has got to know here in prison. Her breath streams across his cheeks when she crouches to bend over him in his bed. He faintly feels the desire to come back to life. But he knows that his life counts for nothing now.

'You should go to Moscow. One of us sitting here is more than enough,' he says.

'I refuse to leave Italy as long as you're here.'

'You must rest, Tania.'

'I will never leave you on your own. And do not force me to.'

She runs a finger over his hand. Up his arm. He smells her skin. It's like Giulia's, only a bit more pale. Schrader comes to his mind again, the joyless ghost Tania had lived with in Rome. How little he knows about Tania's love life. She caresses his face, his cheeks, his forehead, she places her head very close to his, he can feel her breath on his lips.

'What happens between Giulia and I will not happen with anyone else,' he whispers.

'I hope that you two see each other again.'

'We both know that that is not very likely. You'd better go now, Tania.'

It is one of the first days of November. Hardly any light reaches his cell. As usual, Gramsci is sitting at his table and spooning up some broth which was already just about cold when they brought it. In the meanwhile he has lost his last two teeth, they got lost in March, two pieces of dirty white spit in to the palm of his hand. He was familiar with the feeling of shock when a piece of his body broke off, and even though it was the thirty-second time, it still caused him to catch his breath. His last two teeth. Now his mouth is naked. Now and forever more there shall only be milk, broth and fresh juice which he usually cannot tolerate.

A key turns in the lock of his cell. They have never cleared away his food this early before. He tries to eat more quickly but his stomach turns against the food once again.

'It's an early Christmas!'

Gramsci, who had put his hand defensively around his bowl, looks at the guard uncomprehendingly.

'A telegram. From your brother,' he explains, lays a piece of paper on the table and stomps back off with his heavy steps. Only once the door has slammed shut and Gramsci hears the turn of the keys again does he bend over his message.

'Have learnt of decree on pardon,' his brother writes, 'I'm with you please telegraph necessity of my presence or otherwise.'

Pardon? Could that be possible? Could everything he'd prepared for internally—now when he hardly allows anything that once triggered his emotions to penetrate his defences—just stop all of a sudden? The table, the stool, the paper with its message: all that is real. He feels his heart beating, his organs beginning to work again as if salvation were right there, then his mind yields and then his emotions. Well, why not? Perhaps what he has just read is true. It's possible. It could indeed be possible. That in spite of everything, they managed to do something. But who? The Party leaders in Moscow? The Comintern? The Red Aid? The Soviet diplomats Keržencev and Makar? Tania? His friend Sraffa who works so closely with the Party that any of his acts become the acts of the Party? Giulia?

No, Giulia was not strong enough. Well, whoever it was—and perhaps they had all had a hand in it, perhaps Stalin himself had got involved—they hadn't forgotten him, as he'd believed. Someone had been able to convince them that he was not a Trotskyist, as he'd been accused, that they wanted to bring him back, that they needed him in the Party. What he had not counted on, what seems to go against his own power of logic, is that his story would have a happy ending.

Just take a deep breath, gather up strength. He can already smell the air beneath the cherry trees on Via Carlo Fea, his body will be able to move again, will finally be allowed to collapse, and someone, wanting the best for him, will bring him over to the bed which is covered with a white blanket and crackling with starch. Someone will bring him hot soup. Someone will hold his hand. His nerves will again grow strong in that body which seems to have grown necrotic in prison. His teeth will not grow back, but that is not important.

In the afternoon he is handed the decree that Carlo had celebrated, but his hope fades within the bureaucratic language. He hardly recognizes a thing yet also so much: there will be no release. Perhaps they will ease the conditions of his imprisonment, but he knows that his body does not have much strength left. Easing the conditions will not be enough. Every day can be one too many. He may indeed come to freedom a bit earlier, but dead.

For one whole day he wants to push everything away, he wants to curse his brother who, by promising such false excitement, demanded the energy he no longer possesses, his last reserves of peace and strength. His nerves are on edge and he already has enough to fight in order not to be overwhelmed by the weight of his reality. Everything must be cast off. Even what is closest, what is the most, what is the only: Giulia.

He has heard of husbands sitting in prison with long sentences allowing themselves to be separated from their wives in order to allow them the chance to establish new lives. He has heard of these women, has imagined how they, strong, emotional, split apart the moral bonds and forgot, or pretended to forget, their men. And isn't there something reasonable about it? Gramsci wonders. Why should a living creature be tied to another who is dead or as good as dead? 'The pain cannot be avoided, but it can be limited,' he writes to his sister-in-law Tania and begs her to suggest it to Giulia.

By now he is suffering from what he calls 'prison illness'—a deadening of feeling, a loss of sensibility—and one year from now he will possibly only be vegetating in a kind of animalistic egocentrism. He will endure, he will grow used to Giulia leaving him. He promises his sister-in-law. To retreat into his Sardinian shell and become more emotionless every day, that is what he imagines.

'Impressive in its abstruseness!' Sraffa, who has been forwarded the letter from Tania, finds. She has no idea how in the world she is to respond to such an offer. 'This is not a truly serious plea, Tania. This is not even a proper letter. This, if you would like to know, is only the testimonial of a sick man. We are losing Gramsci to the prison. But that was foreseeable, sooner or later it had to happen.'

Sometimes Tania is frightened by how Sraffa tidies up other people's emotional turmoil until it is lying before him as clearly as the gross domestic product of their soul.

'You should send it to Giulia,' Sraffa says. 'Perhaps she will then understand how sick he is. Perhaps she will finally come to Italy. If she continues to stay so far away, she will cut the last thread holding him to life. And then he will die,' Sraffa adds, and Tania asks herself whether in the end it might not be better for Gramsci not to have to endure a lover who is only a hastily scrawled signature on a censored piece of paper, whether Giulia

237

could get well if she were free of the gloom of the prison. And Tania has little idea of whether Sraffa truly wants the best for his friend or whether he just wants to goad Gramsci's genius on, page after page, before that irreplaceable mind ceases working completely.

Giulia is unsettled by what her sister writes her, and once more Italy is too far away to really grasp what is happening, but to leave Moscow, no, that she cannot do, not now, maybe later, once she has recovered from her crisis. 'You will never recover from your crisis so long as you stay where you are,' Tania writes her sister, but, instead of sending the letter, tears it apart. Gramsci in the meantime has again fallen into hope and is no longer thinking of being separated. He knows the decree by heart, without really understanding it, like a child singing a song in a foreign language.

Art. 79, 135 (repealed) with reference to Art. 118, Nr. 3 and 120 of the penal code (repealed)

Art. 79, 247 of the penal code (a) with reference to Art. 1, Law of 19.VII.1894, Nr. 135.

Art. 79 of the penal code (a) and 2 from the Law of 19.VII.1894, Nr. 135

Art. 251 of the penal code (a)

A.9, paragraph. Law from 25 December 1925, Nr. 2263

Art. 252 of the penal code (a)

Art. 134 Nr. 2 with reference to Art. 120 and 118 Nr. 3 and 78 of the penal code (a)

Over and over he recalculates what he does not understand, as if feverish. He has to be careful with his hope, for any disappointment could spell death. Of the six charges with which he was given six sentences, Gramsci thinks, four should be amnestied, and he calculates the gaps in the years that still lie ahead: fifteen years prison, ten years jail, minus five years for clemency, three years for clemency, one year for the preceding clemency. Twenty years, four months, five days plus a fine. The dates run together, the years remain merciless and the paragraphs too.

'These are the charges,' Tania answers in response to his plea for her to explain it all. 'And I think,' she adds, 'not a single one has been dropped. Tomorrow, I will send you socks.'

'If there were only fewer doctors and fewer diagnoses in the world,' Giulia writes to her sister. It is January 1933. In Germany, Adolf Hitler has succeeded in coming to power. Of all places, Germany, the land of Marx, will be brought to heel by the National Socialists. Yet another revolution from the wrong side. 'And yet I can be of only little help to myself,' Gramsci writes Giulia on 30 January. 'The more I realize that I'm going through bad moments, that I'm weak, that I see the difficulties become greater, the more I'm determined to stiffen all of my willpower. Your letter to Tania struck me as too melancholy and grim.'

In February, the Reichstag in Berlin burns. The communists are held responsible and now in Germany too they are hunted by the state. By March, Gramsci is close to dying. The prison authorities decide to put a fellow prisoner in his cell to keep an eye on him. A few political prisoners organize eight-hour shifts among themselves. They crouch next to Gramsci's bed, who is too weak to lift himself up, they come in and out of his cell and do not know what to do about his decline. Getting a glimpse of Gramsci is depressing, he is so emaciated it is like having a elderly child before one's eyes.

It is two in the morning when Gustavo Trombetti arrives. Gramsci appears to be sleeping, but his chest is still. Gustavo comes closer, attempts to check Gramsci's breath by placing the back of his hand beneath his nose when all of a sudden his empty, watery eyes flash open and he looks at him without recognizing him. Then, as if all his strength had returned, all of a sudden he is determined, he reaches out his hand, he wants to hold Gustavo or to be held, but his voice is weak when he whispers: 'You see what these scoundrels have managed to do to me?' His head sags to the side and he dozes back off.

'A severe case of kyphoscoliosis,' the prison's medical officer at last declares after Gramsci has been shuttled from one doctor to another, doctors bound more to fascism than Hippocrates. Pott's Disease, tubercular lesions causing two discharges of blood, fainting spells, memory loss, early senility, arteriosclerosis with hypertension (190/100 mm Hg.). Over the last few months he has lost 7 kilos. 'In closing, I believe that Gramsci, on the basis of these symptoms, will not survive long under the present conditions. In good faith. Umberto Arcangeli.'

In May, the medical report is published in the Party magazine *Humanité*. Gramsci is furious, despite how weak he is. As if he were an animal for slaughter, they just want to show him off, what do they think they will achieve with such indiscretion? His release? A bit of pity from people who do not know him and that he will never see? In the end, the publication only succeeds in causing everything that would be so necessary—his transfer to a hospital or at least to the infirmary of another prison—to be delayed. 'Yet another bit of misfortune,' Sraffa, who is no less angry than his friend, complains. His attempts to have Gramsci released are more destined to fail than ever.

Gramsci receives a pale photo of his wife and children. Giulia beams weakly. Day by day, his feelings grow weaker while the dulling of his senses grows stronger. He can barely smell, he tastes nothing, he feels only the failure of his organs. When awake he can think and even manage to write a little, but soon collapses again. He sees Giulia in the faded picture and it is as if she is pulling away from him, even on the paper. Like everything else. Like the world. Like all he loved within it. And it's OK. In his current state, loving is too great a chore. He has no more strength to feel a thing. He still registers the dizziness and daze in his head, but does not venture anything else. The photograph did not turn out so well, he writes to his sister-in-law. That is all he wishes to share with Giulia.

XXXV. HEDDA   'Anton, is that you?'

Hedda's voice sounded so familiar, it was as if the last few weeks hadn't really happened. Brevi had handed me the receiver and retreated into the living room. I cleared my throat. Hedda went silent. I could hear her breathing on the line, more familiar than her voice, and had no idea what I might have expected at such a moment, what, if you will, I would have wanted, but when she finally said something, she sounded prepared.

'Lasse is ill.'

'Listen, we're here in Rome in the middle of our work and—'

'Anton, Lasse is ill. For days he's had a high fever, I was at the doctor's with him, but he's not getting any better. He wants his father here.'

I walked through the hall. Brevi was hunched over his desk, lost in his papers, unaware of joy, and unsuspecting and uninterested to boot.

'I understood that, Hedda,' I said as quietly as I could.

'You haven't understood a thing, Anton. You didn't even listen.'

Naturally, there they were again, her accusations, and beneath every layer was another, and the deeper you dug, the more corrosive they became. Why couldn't she be mild with me, just once? This was the first phone call in weeks, why didn't she ask how I was? How my work was going? In the end, she could care about me for a change and not just Lasse and Ilsa and herself.

'Why didn't you anticipate all of this?' she said flatly.

'What, if you please, should I have anticipated, Hedda? Don't be puerile.'

I heard her push something back into place on the table, she was probably standing in front of the window in my study. Earlier that had been her favourite place to make calls, earlier, that meant a few weeks ago. Maybe it was a glass of water, or a paperweight, something completely banal, in any event, and I slowly breathed in and out: it could all turn out all right, it could all turn out to be a minor issue.

'Why didn't you stop this from happening?'

'Hedda, please.'

'No!' she screamed through the telephone. 'No "Hedda, please". Lasse barely speaks any more. He wakes up every night. He walks into my room, completely hysterical. When he cries, at least I know what I need to do. I take him in my arms and wipe away the tears with the sheet and at some point he is so exhausted that he falls asleep. But most of the time he doesn't cry. He just sits there, on the edge of the bed, and doesn't want to talk and doesn't want to sleep, and when I try to get him to come under the blanket he kicks and says he will only go to sleep when I let you come back. And that, goddamn it, you will do immediately. If you're not here in three days, Anton, then it really is over. You will not see your son again.'

'Are you threatening me?'

'Do you have any idea what you've done? You do realize that you've let him down—that's clear to you, right?'

'I haven't let him down, Hedda. It's just that, professionally, at the moment . . .'

'Professionally you don't have the slightest thing to do in Rome. What are your romantic whims really worth?'

'Hedda, I think it'd be better if we ended this conversation.'

'Fine, Toni. Forget everything I've said. Forget me. But come for Lasse's sake. I don't know what to do with him any more. Ilsa's bought you a ticket, she's already sent it. The flight is in three days. And please, Toni.'

'What?'

'Don't disappoint him.'

When I hung up, Brevi was standing in the living-room door. He must have heard the conversation, or at least parts of it, even though his face, as so often, showed no sign whatsoever. I had no idea if Brevi was interested in love or its end. I didn't know if he understood anything outside his research or whether he experienced everything in a mediated form, whether he only knew the feelings of Tania and Giulia through Gramsci's analysis, his emotions ordered into a kind of text, comforted by grammar, distant from that which overwhelms us, what causes us to take the wrong approach over and over again because we can't do anything else, because, in the end, the order of the text doesn't comfort us.

'Brevi,' I said quietly.

He remained silent. Through the open living-room window I could hear the noise of the traffic, a backdrop of exhaust and worn-out aluminium, and softly, almost soothingly, the flapping of a fan.

'Yes, I understand you,' Brevi finally said. His voice sounded dry, as if he had held his tongue for too long.

'What do you understand?' I asked.

'I understand you all too well. Consider our research now, believe in it, believe in the fact that we are getting closer to Gramsci than anyone has ever before. Not even Giulia Schucht got this close, you see. It was a romantic relationship, nothing more, nothing less, the two of them never permeated each other, not completely, their emotions got in the way, the fight for oneself, then for the other, then for oneself again.'

'He had kids with Giulia, and we can't even get our hands on his goddamn notebook. We don't have a thing of his.' I walked into the living roomwhich was surprisingly cold. A heavy whirr hung in the air. And then I saw how Brevi had a number of fans going at once, and the pile of papers on the floor had been secured against the draughts of air with ashtrays and crystal bowls.

'They have two children, well,' Brevi replied, 'these things happen, but that does not demonstrate anything, that is an invalid exaggeration, a child does not express anything, it is simply there. Outright there. Don't be afraid, Anton. That is no competition for us.'

'I don't really know if we're talking about the same thing, Brevi.'

'Giulia and Gramsci were too consumed by longing, and that is precisely what made them blind. We are the ones who shall finally see what eluded them. With clear minds and clear senses,' Brevi said. He walked along his bookshelves before stopping in the historical corner, Russia up to 1917, where he stood framed by a number of mud-grey grant publications and a few pompous editions of various classics. 'What we need is "a pessimism of the intellect" and an "optimism of the will", as Gramsci wrote, echoing Romain Rolland. In our feelings too, Anton, and that is not for lovers. They lose themselves in fears and hurts.'

Brevi was glowing. His head was a wreath of chaotic hair and, illuminated by a floor lamp, looked as if it were aflame.

'If we really want to understand, feelings stand in our way,' he said. 'And when we understand, we can no longer honestly believe in feelings, in this exaggeration, this unease in our stomach and chest, in these Baroque lunges that go far beyond our mutual understanding.'

'You don't understand a thing,' I said, slamming my fist against the doorframe. 'You think that everything is a secure as an index. Were you ever married, Brevi? Can you even imagine what it's like when something like that ends?'

Brevi did not look up, but continued to leaf through a manuscript that had been typed on an old typewriter; the letters had gone through the paper.

'Of course I was married,' he answered so calmly that it sounded cynical. 'But do you really believe in weddings, Anton? I got married because my family had expected it, too early perhaps, the wrong woman or the right one ... can one still say such a thing with so much distance? Up close, definitely not.' He thoughtlessly let the manuscript fall to the floor. 'A beautiful wedding at an estate in Umbria,' he began, 'and a Mamma Roma, driving in a pig, was there as well. My mother slapped me, perhaps my bride should have too, but she remained quiet, she took everything, including what was to come, with such a docile ease that at some point I was brought to my knees. I escaped to Turin, she remained in Rome, where she had her affairs, conducted with the same ease with which she had suffered the one with me for eight years. Perhaps after our separation she remained alone, who knows, I never asked.'

'Did you love her?'

'Love? Well, perhaps I loved myself. To tell the truth, Anton, I do not know. We all understand something different by that term.' He ran his hand across the books of his colleagues who had ventured into more popular territory than Gramsci and ended up even being popular, with bound volumes which yielded a few royalties and invitations to Harvard, Yale and the École normale supérieure.

'Do you have children?'

'Sophia. She was four at the time it fell apart. After that there was Gramsci. Before that there was Gramsci. The only constant I rely on. Romantic feelings are fleeting. Strictly speaking, they are not even there. For a brief moment we believe we see something, out of the corners of our eyes, but when we look more closely, there is nothing there. A spoilt kiss, an empty glance into which we futilely read something. Nothing, Anton, be clear about that: nothing.'

'You simply do not believe in the person standing across from you.'

246

'I believe in research. That is the gist of seventy-five years. Not a bad one, actually. Do not disavow our Gramsci.'

'But you disavow him when you don't believe in his being in love!' I said harshly. '"The intellectual's error consists in believing that one can know without understanding and even more without feeling and being impassioned." Gramsci wrote that. Have you even read him?'

'You call that feeling? Back there in Silver Wood he was confused, stretched too thin, he was in a clinic for psychologically damaged people. That was a burn-out. A moment of lunacy. But what was it that ruined him? His body? Fascism? Or this toxic relationship with a tall blonde from Ivanovo who was unable to differentiate between laughing and crying and confused everyone around her?'

Tatiana's steps in the hall. Her fingers leafing through old pages.

'Are you lonely, Brevi?'

'Loneliness is a son-of-a-bitch,' he answered and broke into hearty laughter. His hair had been tousled by the fans and suddenly, feeling the cold in my face, I stumbled backwards. For a moment I stood there without moving, staring at the chaos of fluttering manuscript pages, then I turned and fled back to my room.

Leant up against the violet wallpaper flowers, I tried to feel the peace which had to be passing from the shafts of light into the shutters, but they just remained bright strips of light on splintering wood, and I thought about going to the phone and calling back and waiting for Hedda to answer 'Stöver?' and telling her what I'd forgotten, what I, for whatever reason, hadn't said and at the moment hadn't thought. Things weren't like they had sounded. In any event, they hadn't always been that way and could have gone differently, the chances weren't all that great because they are never all that great in the long run, at some point stumbling's a lot more likely than never having stumbled at all. But we'd cared about each other once. We'd tried to establish a middle-class life, four rooms and a garden, a piano in front of the winter garden, we'd moved to Göttingen because everything led us to believe we would manage to work out the life we'd imagined together, with its herringbone parquet, a piano, a kid and you in an elegant, but sporty, pinstripe suit, and even if it all looks a little different now, it was the right thing, *don't you think, Hedda?*

XXXVI. MOSCOW   'Be quiet! Quiet! Quiet right now!'

Giulia is standing on the stairs yelling at her sister. Delio is walking away, Julik is hiding behind a door, Genia is looking up at her punitively.

When Giulia is exhausted, when her thoughts are spinning through her head, when she is dizzy from accusations she would not be able to refute in one lifetime, and Delio wants something they don't have, that doesn't exist at all, she screams down the house.

All afternoon long he has been begging her sister for a wooden puppet that comes to life, over and over again, and Genia just pets his head and promises him the accursed thing which does not exist, not even in the best of all societies: the Soviet.

'Tomorrow, we'll bring you a piece of wood from the shed,' Genia says, and Giulia screams: 'Stop this nonsense!' And to Delio: 'Forget about the puppet! Wood is wood and doesn't come to life!'

'But in Kolja's book—'

'I don't want to hear any more! Be quiet! Right now! All of you, just be quiet!'

But she is the only one yelling. The others look at her in silence. For months now, Giulia has been suffering from headaches, from screaming children and ever-more often from how inactive she is, how she is a superfluous piece of society that cannot contribute to growth, to construction, to the blossoming of the country, and even travelling to the countryside for a rest tomorrow will not change a thing, she knows that much, nothing will change, and she can barely endure it. She cannot do anything for anyone, not for her sons and not for her husband, and as soon as she goes to give Genia a hand, Genia admonishes her: 'No, leave it alone, go and rest, you'll just make a mess of things for me here.' Sends her away if only to be close to her again later. Giulia and Genia—the mother pair, the duo, the informant and the censor—are always close to each other. Genia barely lets her out of her sight, as if she could run away like a naughty child, and now too, when Giulia finally takes a breath of air up there on the stairs, sits down, weakened by her outburst, Genia keeps a steady eye on her. Giulia's mother, Grandma Schucht, simply stands there, shaking her head and murmuring: 'Papa in prison and Mama making a fool of herself.'

As if Giulia didn't know about his situation! She knows far too much: that he eats and sleeps far too little, that his health is poor even when he writes that he is doing better, by all means better, that he lies when it has to do with him though he always demands the truth and nothing but the truth from her and everyone else. She knows too much about everything but too little about how he is really doing. And then this silence that says more than she wants to hear, that says how right the newspapers are which have written that he is dying, that he may already be dead. She cannot think about it.

Of course Giulia is worried about Nino, but she cannot think about him all the time, it would drive her mad. And what can she do from here anyway? Nothing, she can only cause him more worry because, in addition to all the strain, she too is sick. For years she has been visiting psychoanalysts and doctors, the diagnoses could be strung together in a line and yet change very little. Crises, they say, psychophysical exhaustion.

In the mornings, sometimes, she thinks about Nino, the images of him are weak, she appears quite distant and hidden to herself and can only remember him through the photographs which have been exhibited in his honour in Gorky Park in

Moscow, she needs these pictures as memory aids, she stands in front of them for a long time, looks at his face, oversized and intimidating, and then, heavy as nausea, memory rises up and she sees his face again at last, as only she had seen it, how it truly was outside of the photographs, nights in Silver Wood when he'd stick out his tongue at her, and in the flat in Rome when they'd bathe Delio and Nino would whisper: 'We really have a handsome son.'

But what good are these thoughts of Nino? No good at all. She does not want to present the children with a weak man in chains, they should be proud of their father, they should see the way he looks down from a canvas in Gorky Park and the people admire him with his stormy hair and mild, but determined look, the small, round glasses, the thin wire across his nose, the slender lips . . . no one knows what he looks like now. 'For years I have not looked in a mirror,' Nino had written to her.

Giulia is so weak that yelling has made her more tired. She takes books from their library but leaves them on the table, unread. Soon she will not be able to stand up, she is nothing, nothing, nothing, there was only one time when she was something and that was when Nino was by her side, that great intellect which rubbed off on her a bit as well, which let her grow in its shadow.

She could endure twelve, fourteen hours at the typewriter when she sat in the office, and she held out because she thought that if she could not bring any important qualities into that new life, to the new country, then at least quantity might counter-balance it all. She was impractical, she was scattered, but she had always kept trying, over and over again . . . while Eugenia took away her Delio. And as listless and ineffective as she was, she had never been able to give her son anything either, nothing warm, nothing spontaneous. She could simply look on whenever Genia hoisted him up and he laughingly blew out air, and how bright his face grew when he saw her! But whenever Giulia holds him, his eyes seem a little sad. His skin is pale, and a few days ago he brought a letter home from school in which his teacher begged her to make sure there was more of a balance in Delio's free time. 'Whenever he writes something in class, he immediately tears it up and is nervous afterwards. He disturbs the other students.'

Giulia opens one of the books but notices how irritable she is, the lines seem abstruse and hostile, she tosses the book back onto the table and stands up. She slowly walks down the hall, up the stairs, remains standing out in front of the door to the children's room. Delio is softly rocking Julik in his arms, they are playing father and son, as they often do.

'Are we going tomorrow? We're going to the countryside tomorrow, no?' Delio asks. She nods but wants to cry, even though she doesn't know why. She watches Delio run his hand across his brother's head and how Julik snuggles up against him.

'That's good,' Delio says. 'I've promised Julik.'

Giulia wants to go to her room, to leave the children alone, but she is afraid for the young one. She'd once caught Delio biting his arm. With his back to her, without noticing she was standing behind him, he bit into his flesh over and over as if he'd gone wild. It yielded too little and only showed a reddish trace of teeth, no blood, and so again and again he bit himself as if punishing himself for something violent. He had bitten Giulia too, driven his small, dull milk teeth, lightning quick and hard, into her shoulder as she carried him, and she is afraid he could have one of these attacks when he's with Julik.

Against Nino's wishes, she had brought him to a specialist in Rome for nervous children. 'Neuropathic,' he had explained. 'You must allow the child to run around, or he will not know what to do with all his energy.' In Moscow, she took Delio to a psychiatrist who asked about his habits and peculiarities before having a look at his head, tapping his knee, his elbows, checking the speed of his eye movement, and finally giving him a series of brainteasers which, although he did not always answer correctly, he answered cleverly. 'Bright,' the psychiatrist said, 'intelligent. It is incredible that parents like you could produce such a child,' he observed, then scribbled something onto a piece of paper and turned back to Delio.

'How many friends do you have?'

'Three,' Delio answered.

'And what are their names?'

'Sascha, Kolja and Oleg.'

'And how many enemies do you have?'

'Oh! A thousand!'

The doctor briefly looked at Giulia, who kept her head lowered. What was she supposed to say? She would have liked to apologize, but for what?

Finally, after a five-hour trip in which Delio grew steadily more restless and drummed his fists against the seat, they get out in front of the datscha. Here in the countryside, far from the city and its noise and the nervous masses of people, Delio is more relaxed. He runs off into the fields where, just like last year, he wants to catch frogs; and while Genia and Giulia are busy unpacking the suitcases, making tea and straightening up the terrace, Julik chases the cats and dogs around the front of the house. He keeps falling over, but always gets back up with a laugh and sings when he wanders after the chickens which flutter about in fright. They are not yet Young Pioneer songs, just syllables and sounds, but he too has grown taller. The son of an acquaintance is now using his baby bath, a newborn is sleeping in the old crib, the brother of one of Delio's friends is in the perambulator and Julik always wants to play with one of the youngest children.

'And I want a sister!' he says to Giulia once he's back from his forays.

'Yes,' she says. 'Later.'

He sits on one of the small children's stools and whistles dreamily. Giulia likes to hear him, perhaps one day he will study at the conservatory, or become a carriage driver, for he likes horses and gets excited whenever they trot past the terrace pulling a light wagon full of people. They all look happy, certainly happier than the people in this house.

Genia brings out some tea, sits next to her sister and looks at her, just like she has for years.

'Giulia, you don't eat enough. You could stand to gain 10 kilos, and, if you don't manage during the summer out here in the country, you certainly won't in the city.'

Giulia nods. She will not be able to manage this either. She needs so many doctors, so many diagnoses. Earlier, she didn't want to get healthy at all. She went for cures in order to break them off. After all, the doctors had long considered her an epileptic; only recently did a female doctor certify her as hysterical. In Sevastopol, a doctor found her hysterical-epileptic. 'How is it that all the other doctors until now have failed to give me this diagnosis?' she had asked. 'Well, doctors do not like to give out a diagnosis like this too much,' he had answered casually. 'Because the illness does not really exist. But Gogol and Dostoevsky both suffered from it. You are in great company.'

So, with hysteria too she has top-ranking comrades-in-suffering. In the Gospels, there were cases, her new doctor had explained, which were very similar to hers, and Napoleon was hysterical too. 'Big names, Ms Schucht.'

'Well, my own name is enough for me.'

Delio walks up to her, completely soaked. He used his shoes to go fishing, he says, but was unable to catch anything except a couple of small, fidgety things. He hands Genia his shoe, then Giulia is allowed to have a look at what is swimming around in the leather pool: a few tadpoles.

'You must not go into the water with all your clothes,' Genia admonishes him and runs a hand through his wet hair.

'But, Mama, that doesn't matter, I won't let the current wash away my shoes.'

'But have a look at the leather. We'll put the water in a jug and stick the shoes out in the sun. Do you think they're a good net?'

'Djadja said that in Sardinia they catch fish with hollowed-out stones. Shoes are much more practical, they've already been hollowed out and they're lighter too.'

Genia sends the boy into the house, she will dry him off with a towel once he's in his bedroom, and put him in to dry clothes. Genia follows him without compliant and Giulia hears her ask: 'And what fish do you want me to catch you tomorrow?'

'Since when has he been so interested in fish?' Giulia asks her sister once she is back out on the veranda.

'You're surprised? When Antonio writes such crazy stuff? I don't think reading Antonio's letters out loud to him is a good idea.'

'But he is their father.'

'What a father! Does he make any effort to help? He goads you on, he reprimands you, everything revolves around him. And he is incapable of loving. Where do all your crises come from? As if you didn't know yourself. Do you want things to go the same way for Delio?'

Giulia could scream into her sister's face that the way she raises her children—as well as her relationship with Nino—is none of her business. 'Be aggressive when necessary,' her female doctor had told her. 'Be unfair. That is essential for your recovery.' But though Giulia's throat may throb with rage, in the end Eugenia will be proven right.

'I did not want to tell him that the letters come from prison,' Giulia answers flatly.

'That is not the point. Antonio has never understood how to be a loving father. He is a cold man. He lives in his thoughts. He is not good for the children.'

Giulia knows that it's not like that. Or she thought she did. For a while she was certain that Nino wanted to be close to the children, for he wrote her so. He wanted to know how they were developing, how tall they were, whether they got enough to eat and were gaining weight. But could Genia be right? His letters are terribly pedantic, he reproaches Julik for writing so fleetingly and criticizes Delio for not thinking rigorously enough. But they are just kids.

Once they are back in the city, she will look for all the old articles and photographs of Nino that she's collected. She will read Delio what others have written about Nino as opposed to what's been said in this family, where everyone's personal opinion is the only one and any other is censored.

Delio should get to see his father as he was, an active fighter for the Revolution, for communism, who was now in prison, but not for having done anything wrong; on the contrary, for having too many good things, because he had hesitated to leave Italy, because he had only wanted to leave when it was clear and unmistakable to every worker that the situation in the country was forcing him to go. He did not want to leave them in the lurch, he did not want them to feel as if he was leaving them in the lurch, and Delio should know this so that he does not have the need to hide from reality, like she did.

Delio comes back out, his cheeks seem redder than normal, perhaps his spell in the creek had really been good for him.

'Were you alive when Pushkin was alive?' he asks, and finally cuddles up to his Mama-Giulia.

She laughs, puts an arm around him. 'No, I wasn't even a thought back then.'

'Was Grandmother alive? And what about when the Montgolfiers were alive?'

'No, she wasn't either.'

'But how can that be? Who was?'

'A lot of things happened before the oldest person that you know was even born. But you're lucky, they were not good times. Back then, the few told the many not to want anything and not to think anything and simply to serve. And the many had no idea that they could fight back, that it was, that it is, possible to change society. You are lucky to have been born in a very good time indeed.'

'How much time will it be before a child is born for whom I will be as old as Djadja is now? Before I,' he calculates and opens his eyes wide in shock, 'before I am a *forty-year-old?*'

'Not that long, dear. Not long enough for everything to change again. In any event, that won't happen any longer, there's no reason to be afraid,' Giulia says and strokes his cheek. It feels like a puppet. Something completely foreign. Delio pushes away from her: 'Leave me alone, leave me alone!' he cries and kicks the table. Giulia jumps up in order to catch the tableware, and Delio is already hanging on to her arm. And biting into her. And biting again as if his very life depended on it.

XXXVII. CYPRESSES 'I really am sorry about our project,' I said again to Brevi as I was getting ready to leave.

'Well, that's the way it is,' he answered. We were out in front of the building, and he was leant up against the garden gate, his shoulders slumped. When I moved to give him my hand, he pulled me in and embraced me for a long time.

'All the best, Anton. Look after your son.'

I climbed into the taxi and looked back at Brevi. He limply raised his hand, waved, and for the first time looked like an old man. The driver turned the engine.

At Porta Pia, we dove into the underpass. I stared at the orange lights beyond the windscreen, a motorcycle overtook us, a bus turned its headlights on and off. The taxi sped up and we came back out into the daylight. The buildings blew past, dirty windowsills, cables, tubes. To my right, plane trees lining the pavement. Behind them the Tiber.

'This is where Matteotti was kidnapped,' I said.

'Who?'

'A socialist.'

'Was that in the paper today?'

'No, that was ninety years ago.'

'Well, there you go.' The driver flicked the rosary hanging off the rear-view mirror and turned up the radio. To my left, the narrow side-streets. A rusty sign with a red carnation. I leant forward and tapped the driver on the shoulder.

'Excuse me, are you sure this is the right way?'

'You want to go to Fiumicino, right?'

'No, I think . . . '

'Do you have to go to Ciampino?'

'I don't think so.'

'Ciampino's got the cheap flights and the pope. All the others are at Fiumicino.' The driver cast me a quick glance over his shoulder. 'And you're definitely not the pope.'

'Sorry. I mixed up the days.'

'Why don't you have a look at your ticket?'

'My flight's tomorrow,' I said testily.

'Should I drive you back?'

'No, no. Here's fine,' I replied. 'Here's fine.'

'Whatever.'

He stopped in the car lot in front of the old slaughterhouse, heaved my luggage out of the boot and smiled at me quizzically.

A group of tourists was standing in front of the entrance to what had, in the meantime, become a museum for modern art. Red faces, shirts soaked with sweat, guidebooks at their chests. A small girl pulled at her mother's hand, her cheeks were so red she looked like she was feverish and I asked myself if Lasse was really as sick as Hedda claimed or whether it was just another one of her exaggerations. Behind the gate, a bamboo sculpture like a wooden flame towered 10 metres up into the air. A massively delicate cone leaning to the left, as if bent by the wind.

'And you would be happy to know that the new slaughterhouse was opened on Via Togliatti in 1975,' a tour guide said, with her yellow umbrella she looked like a giant pole. A man with a camera strapped to his neck raised his arm and, without anyone having called on him, began to share his painstakingly superficial knowledge: he'd read that, in the past, the nobility's horse troughs had been filled with clean water while the horses of the middle class had no choice but to drink the dishwater from the kitchen. What did she have to say about that?

'Well, first of all, the animals were not brought here to drink,' Miss Pole said in her defence. The next gust of wind would blow her away together with her umbrella, the goddamn know-it-all. That's when I saw Tatiana in front of the wall to Monte Testaccio. She was just turning into the road that lead to the *cimitero acattolico*, to the Protestant Cemetery, as it had often and erroneously been called. I turned away from Miss Pole and hurried after Tatiana.

'Please donate three euros, we need it urgently,' I read on a sign next to a Perspex box with a few coins and some bills from who-knows-where. Leaving the pyramid of Cestius off to my left, I passed Lenore Kipp-Cotten who'd been immortalized with an oblong memorial stone from her husband and, like every time I came here, tried to find the right way. An Englishman in colonial garb was hanging around Keats. A woman was watering a grave. No one was looking at the architect Muller or the memorial to Lenore Kipp-Cotten.

I looked around for Tatiana, but didn't see her anywhere. Two thin women dressed in black were standing in front of a bush like widowed guardians and didn't even look up when I walked past. In one of the rows, a few columns had fallen over each other; in another, a mourner was missing their stone head. Between Hermann Immer, who'd disappeared from Bern one hundred and fifty years ago, and a certain Herr Wendriner whose grave was in the process of being exhumed, there were recent birth and death dates which made me feel caught somehow, as if I'd overlooked my own demise out of simple carelessness.

I followed a bald German man with his wife. Distraught by the Roman summer, the couple made their way through the rows of graves without looking up at the cypresses towering into the sky at all, which, in my opinion, were well worth seeing. A little later a stocky, dark-haired man ended up behind us. He had rolled up the arms of his shirt and had a red guidebook, the *Giro d'Italia*, a book which had not been in print since the '60s.

The atmosphere was oppressive. The traffic which had stupefied me on those few steps to the cemetery entrance, the streets tangling into one another with all their pedestrians—*HolyMaryMotherofGod, let me cross over to the other side in health*—fell away like a feverish dream. Just one more step and then everything went silent, as if I were stepping out onto the open, wind-still sea. One of Gramsci's stories came to mind, the one about the shipwreck survivors in their lifeboat who turned into cannibals.

I shook myself. What an awful idea. I looked for Tatiana among the rows again. I knew that she had to be close by, that she would soon show up, nothing else was possible. But my eyes weren't made for this kind of sun, they were too lazy and my body too porous. Your pupils had to be elastic, like a cat's, or covered by a particularly thick cornea. The heat spilt through my mind and I thought I was beginning to hallucinate. I saw an old, tall man strolling through the lanes. In and of itself that was nothing. But the fact that he looked like Piero Sraffa unnerved me. He came closer, stood in front of the headless statue and looked at the grave. Then he looked up and we found ourselves staring at each other. His eyebrows were like swings. His ears and nose were so large it was as if they had grown together with his intellect. His few remaining white hairs billowed about his head. In short, there was no doubt that this man was the ancient Italian economist and partner of Gramsci's, Piero Sraffa. He turned away and looked into the distance, as if waiting for someone.

From the upper rows where Shelley and Goethe's son were buried, a woman rushed past. She must have still been young, or moved that way at least, despite wearing an old-fashioned skirt of bright fabric that rocked stiffly about her ankles. Her face was transparent. Her shoulder-length hair was dark blonde. I knew that I knew her, but could not remember from where.

The branches crackled, a hissing arose at every step. The noises sounded as if they were coming from an old radio. Sraffa went to meet the woman. She held a hand to her chest as if she'd been running and now had to catch her breath. They spoke to so softly I could barely make out syllables. I thought I heard the word 'cannibals'. And again: 'cannibals'. That was the only word that made its way over to me.

And then I knew who the woman was. All at once, the correlations seemed to grow clear; that, or the ambiguity lost its strength. If the man before her was Sraffa, then she was no other than Gramsci's sister-in-law. Tania Schucht. She held Sraffa by the arm of his shirt, he bent to her, her lips close to his ear, she spoke quickly, he nodded, his expression composed but with an almost unbearable melancholy. A melancholy I knew only from Brevi.

And then everything went black. Switched off. I felt a shock. That was it. Maybe I fell over. Maybe I was lying down. Maybe I was still sitting in a taxi on my way to the airport.

'You said something,' someone said.

I shook my head without knowing if it was me they meant. There was my fatigue, the heat, not to mention all the coffee I'd had since waking up, without once having a glass of water. A red dot floated before my eyes.

'You called out to someone.'

The red dot began to take shape. I could read the gold lettering: *Giro d'Italia*. Under my back, I could feel the scratch of stones; I'd fallen down right onto the middle of the path. Someone helped me up—the bald man, his wife, the man with the book—and before me I saw a withered carnation the wind had blown off a grave.

'If you'll allow me,' the man with the guidebook said shyly. Standing there in a daze, he took hold of my arm. The couple nodded to us encouragingly, and we took off along the path like two old lovers—past the Orthodox crosses, past Muller and Kipp-Cotten—for the exit. Quickly looking back to the headless mourner I saw Brevi and Tatiana, my Tatiana, abruptly split apart.

XXXVIII. ROBINSON   At six in the morning, the guards take Gramsci out of his cell. It is an extremely rushed trip to Formia; they had told Gramsci they would be leaving in a few days. For months, Tania and Sraffa had fought to have Gramsci moved to the prison infirmary and the answer had been delayed time and again, but now every minute seems to count. 'Come on, come on, we have other things to do,' the guards bark.

With trembling steps, Gramsci leaves his cell, held up by his comrade Gustavo Trombetto. The wagon is waiting out on the street in front of the prison, like a giant insect in the darkness. Everything is pitch black, there is not even a strip of light at the horizon. Feeling the cobblestones beneath his feet, for a moment Gramsci sinks. You walk so differently outside the prison, and how long has it been since he has been on this side of the walls, out in the free where the sky does not have corners like the prison yard? He had already begun to believe that this side no longer existed.

Gustavo places the suitcase next to the automobile, they embrace their goodbyes, then Gramsci gets in. He feels the wagon take off, stares out the window then onto the black nothing where nothing moves. He thinks of Sardinia. That's where he wants to return when he's free. He will find a small house in Ghilarza. He will have a goat and maybe a few sheep. Perhaps Giulia will be with him. It will be a quiet life, a life that belongs to him.

By the time they reach the train station, dawn has begun to break, the first outlines are to be seen, shadows suggest that there is indeed something beyond the darkness. In the train compartment, Gramsci is watched by two officers; outside the window, the landscape grows lighter and he cannot understand it. He does not want to understand it. The meadows, forests, people, the groups of children, trees and gardens are still there. For six long years he has seen the same rooftops and walls and faces, but life outside has carried on.

At his first stop, the prison infirmary in Civitavecchia, he is sent down a dark corridor and has to wait out in front of a closed office door. He looks around in the half-dark, looks at a window that looks onto another corridor—an ancient man looks back. He is so old it is hard to guess how old he is. He has no lips, his cheeks have caved in and his skin is as grey as cheap paper. It could be the face of someone seriously ill, or dead. Then Gramsci understands that it is his own. He is seeing it for the first time since being imprisoned.

'You must write to me what you think,' Piero Sraffa asks his friend when he visits him in Formia and lays a stack of books on the table. But Gramsci just shakes his head.

'What is that supposed to mean?' Sraffa counters. 'I refuse to accept that.'

'I can't any longer, Piero, I don't have the strength.'

'Write!' he growls. 'Write! You must write, that is the best instrument against madness. And it is the only one we can deliver to you while you're in prison.'

Like Tania, Sraffa had hoped that Gramsci would do better in Formia but Gramsci just continues to withdraw, he hardly speaks any more and he no longer cares to write to Giulia or the children but lives, instead, within a cocoon of memories. He has become a regressive, feverish little mound of a human being that is tired, deadly tired, and neither Sraffa nor Tania can rouse him.

In the autumn of 1934, that which none of the three had any longer expected happens: the motion for release is given. Tania's voice is a croak when she receives Sraffa's late-night call.

'What does that mean?' she asks.

'I don't know. It can mean everything and nothing.'

'They will not allow it. They think anti-fascists from New York have arranged for his escape.'

'They don't believe it, they are spreading the rumour in order to have a reason to keep him confined.'

In the end, almost nothing changes: the bars in front of Gramsci's window disappear, the guards leave his room for the garden. For a moment Gramsci sat up, but then sank back into himself. One of many useless hopes. Tania sits at the desk in his cell in order to write a letter to his doctor, the only one who might still be able to get something done.

'Write him that I am going mad,' Gramsci says.

'What?' Tania asks, sitting up. 'What do you mean?'

'Oh nothing, I just said it.' He shuts his eyes briefly. For days he has been trying to think of Giulia, but she barely exists for him any more. She grows paler and paler, an unreal memory. Something whose loss no longer even hurts. 'One only wants to live that much more when one knows it is no longer possible,' he says.

'You have to hold on.'

'But there is no point any longer. My connections to the outer world are dissolving, one after the other.'

'You must write to Giulia. You haven't written a letter to her in months.'

'Why should I write to a person for whom my letters are inconsequential?'

'That's not true.'

'She is no longer happy to receive my letters, otherwise she'd answer.'

'I will not allow you to give up. Even if you only hold on for her. Even if only to prove that Mussolini did not break you.'

Tania walks around his bed, stands there motionless, as if made of wax.

'I simply do not know who she is any longer,' Gramsci says.

'She was once the most important thing in the world to you.' Tania turns her face from Gramsci and stares at the wall. 'And she still is,' she adds.

'What do you know about it?'

'You know that I understand,' she says softly. 'You know that I have feelings. Even if I cannot express myself. I simply cannot do it. I am reserved, maybe even cruel, yes, without a doubt I am horrible.' She runs her fingers across her forehead, then her dark eyes again rest on Gramsci. 'Forgive me, Nino. I do not have anything to say to you or to anyone else. I am empty.'

She touches her hairline, makes sure not a single strand is out of place. Like her sister, Gramsci thinks, but this time he doesn't mean Giulia. She is like Eugenia.

'Why do you want me to write her letters?' he asks. 'Who do these letters go to? To Giulia or the Party? You all want to spy on me. But I cannot go on any longer. I do not want to. Palmiro has taken over my former course, you have all overtaken me. Giulia never existed. She was only there so that you all could hear what I think. So that you could see into my mind. You are just like the fascists, you want to control my thoughts, you simply tried through other means. And your means turned out to be the more effective ones.'

'Be quiet, Nino,' Tania says and grabs his wrist. 'What are you talking yourself into believing?' she asks and runs a reassuring hand over his paper-like skin.

'You all are lying to me, just like everyone always has. My parents told me that a nanny let me fall to the ground. They did not want to tell me that I was sick, that my skeleton is deformed by Pott's Disease. Nor did they tell me that my father was in jail. Always this sense of shame. Always these lies. Be brave enough to tell me the truth. Now, in any event, it is too late. Tell me that Giulia was only brought into my life to spy on me. She was nothing else for me! Nothing else!'

How bizarre his weakened voice sounds when he tries to yell and only manages to emit a thin whistling. Tania has walked up to his bed and wipes his damp forehead with a tissue; he wants to push her away but lets his hand fall back onto the blanket as soon as he's lifted it.

There is a knock at the door, they both look up and then back down.

'My biggest weakness was not finding the mettle to remain alone,' he adds more quietly, 'without any connections, attachments, relationships at all. That is the source of all the misery.'

A guard walks in and nods to Tania.

'I can no longer answer you, Nino,' Tania says. 'Even if I would like to. You wouldn't listen.' She removes the papers from the table and follows the guard out into the corridor.

Gramsci continues to listen to her steps, or are they those of others? How similar they all sound as they pass in front of his door. He looks up at the ceiling and tries to think of something that will calm him down, but his thoughts get away from him, even his closest memories fall away, and soon he no longer knows what just transpired between the two of them. Only distant memories appear in his head, clear and quiet and so much more real than reality.

He is hanging from the beam in his parents' home and looking down at the stocky figures, he sees his puppy trying to plod up a stair, it is not a beautiful animal, in fact it's quite ugly, very ugly, when he really thinks about it. As a child, he could recite sailors' language even in his sleep, at seven he'd read *Robinson Crusoe*. Back then, in Ghilarza, he would only leave the house if he had grains of wheat and matches wrapped up in wax cloth in case he was carried out of his Sardinian life and washed onto a desert island. Of course, he was already on a kind of desert island, Sardinia, and he loved it in spite of the malaria and the hunger, it had been forgotten by the mainland, Sardinia had, and in the end he wasn't the one who'd been washed away but his father, taken away by two policemen, he can still see them walking away, no one wants to tell him what is happening and since then he has been afraid that they will come back and take him too. Back then, he loved to build proud, two-decker ships, and a tremor shoots through his body when he realizes he would like nothing more than to have just such a ship, now, but in the meantime paper has become too precious and sacrificing any is out of the question. Or maybe not.

Giulia will not send him any more letters that require a response, of that he is convinced. She is no longer his Japan, as she was at the beginning of his imprisonment, that distant point still promising him something of the world. That is gone. She has disappeared for him, like everything else. It no longer hurts, as it did some months ago, and he is no longer furious, like he was for eight weeks although he hardly had the strength. It doesn't matter. And that is the worst feeling of all for someone who, outside himself, has nothing. Japan is no longer in the League of Nations, what's the point, perhaps it is no longer even an island in the Pacific, Japan no longer exists for him nor does the prison island of Ustica with its rainbows nor Bordiga's way of making coffee. Gramsci is neither Robinson nor Friday, he is not stranded, he has not been washed into a lonely bay but is going down with all the others. He hears it growing quieter, and quieter still. As if sinking into the deepest depths of the sea, down into the stillness where even the great currents no longer move. Still. Be still now. Still at last.

XXXIX. *IN BOCCA AL LUPO* The mound of sugar in my cup steadily grew taller as I waited on Via Marmorata for Tatiana to arrive. Sooner or later, she'd have to come by, I knew that for a fact. Blonde and brown-haired women walked past, women with white and black and strangely dyed orange hairdos, and I thought about Tatiana, dimly imagined I saw her curls against the sunlight and thought about how Giulia Schucht could barely have been any more real to Gramsci, that female comrade sitting off in distant Russia, his wife who existed only in letters.

I nibbled a mignon pastry and drank my cappuccino while looking onto Piazza dell'Emporio where Tatiana would soon appear. Above me, on a flickering TV screen, two football teams faced off, behind the counter an old man was busy polishing glasses and the girl at the register leant her large but supple body against the clients while constantly ringing up more than was right. The team in the red jerseys won, the girl lasciviously and lazily busied herself around the till and, serving me a second cappuccino, the old man told me about his dying cat that he'd have to get rid of with a blow of a spade to the head, something he just could not bear to do. He sat in the chair next to mine and talked about all the weeks his cat had already been sick but never quite given up, all those weeks in which she'd got tangled up in life with her artistic power of resistance, though it wasn't the best place for a body riddled with abscesses. Was I waiting for someone? 'Of course you're waiting for someone!' he cried.

The slight reddish tinge to my cheeks must have had to do with the blazing afternoon sun. The old man winked at me with his wrinkled lids.

'*In bocca al lupo,*' he said, as if he understood something, and there was nothing for me to say in return but to wish his cat the best of luck as well.

When I walked outside, the street was still empty. Which meant that it was unquestionably filled with people running here and there or standing still, but so what, in reality this street simply existed so that Tatiana would be on her way to me. But she didn't come, and all these people, these accessories, lost their point.

Giulia Schucht, I had to admit, had always replied to Gramsci, they'd written each other intimate letters which, despite the incomprehensible ways of the Italian postal service and the revolutionary course of Russian postal planes, had managed to make their way, they had promised each other that they were thinking of each other, that they would see each other again, a reunion which, thanks to a general strike, a secret meeting, yet another fascist blow, ended up being postponed again and again and again, and how dumb I was, I thought, standing there on Via Marmorata waiting, just like I always had, at all the important moments of my life I'd always been standing somewhere, wasting time, how naive I was to imagine that somewhere there was a Tatiana for me, just like Giulia Schucht had been there for Gramsci.

It was shortly before seven, my departure gate had closed an hour ago. Couples were walking down the street, arm in arm, students were huddling together in groups, passers-by greeted one another and then kept on going. The sun had just left my field of vision and was hanging behind the plane trees when I started to walk down the street towards Ostiense Station. I stopped at the traffic light by the old city gate while cars clattered past the pyramid which had taken up its position on the square, and behind it lay the cemetery with all its illustrious denizens, intellectuals, travellers, partisans and others who, hardly back from their wars and travels, had slowly killed their wives with their monosyllables.

I walked on through the streets, past Ostiense, beneath a railway line, behind which the buildings turned into shabby little boxes, then back to the old workers' buildings, across a square full of young people leaning against their Vespas and drinking Campari out of little glass bottles. In front of an ice-cream stand, a young server swayed alone to the crackling of music from a radio. I stopped, looked at her and smiled.

'Do you know what I just had to think about?'

'Do you know that that doesn't interest me whatsoever?' she answered and disappeared into the shop.

Through the glass, I could see her cleaning the tubs of ice-cream with a rag. She had caramel-coloured skin, and, when she stretched her arm out to clean the furthest corner of the display case, a tendon stuck out on her thin neck. She briefly looked up and made a sign to me. I winked and she came back out.

'Are you OK?' she asked. 'You seem, sorry for saying so, a bit confused.'

'I'm fine,' I said and laughed. 'You have no idea how well I'm doing. I am always happy.'

'You don't look like it. Where do you need to go?' She pointed to my bag. 'Are you looking for a hotel?'

'You coming with me?'

'No way. But I can give you directions.'

Suddenly, I felt the whole day's exhaustion come crashing down inside me, or maybe it was the combined exhaustion of my Roman holiday, or maybe even all the months I'd lain more than slept on the sofa in our living room.

'You have to promise me you'll follow.'

'Don't worry,' she said and with fluttering gestures explained to me how to get to a nearby hotel.

The corner building seemed abandoned, an envelope stood upright on top of the letterboxes, and yet walking past the door I heard a key turn in the lock. But no, I must have been mistaken, for the noise died out without the door moving. I was already about a hundred metres away when I turned and saw the metal door open inward and a man step onto the street. He looked to the right and to the left, his hand felt along the wall until it took hold of the letter. Then an ugly and muscular dog with two heads sprang out the door.

Bursting with strength, it surged forward on trembling legs. And although it seemed it would be impossible for him to restrain it, the man pulled at the lead and then pulled at the lead once more. To my surprise, the monster split into two: an English pit bull, and some kind of mixed breed whose parents must have been a mastiff and a boxer. The man shoved the letter under his arm and continued on his way so leisurely it was as if he was leading two trained dachshunds.

A threadbare carpet led to a reception counter behind which an old woman was asleep. The ceiling light flickered. Empty pistachio husks lay in a crystal bowl. Once I was standing directly in front of the woman, she was startled awake and looked at me from tiny, feverish eyes.

'What can I do for you?'

'Are there still any rooms free this evening?'

She turned around and looked at a board where a few keys were dangling.

'Just one. You're in luck. It's ninety for the night.'

She fished for the uppermost key ring and scraped together the money on the countertop; her fingers seemed as shabby as the place that had surrounded her for who knows how many years.

'Follow me,' she said and walked up a small staircase, which was more like an old servants' entrance, and opened the door to a broom closet furnished with a bed and a stool.

'Here you are!'

I pushed my suitcase into the cubbyhole and struggled to find room for myself. The old woman wobbled back down the stairs. I looked around, although there was hardly anything to look at. Outside the window, it had begun to rain.

Sitting on the bed I opened my suitcase and pulled out the notebook Brevi had given me as I was leaving. In the upper right-hand corner, someone had written *Incompleto XXXIV* in what seemed like a woman's handwriting. I unfastened the cardboard covers and began to leaf through the empty pages.

XL. THE NOTEBOOK

§1 *On the State*

At one time I wondered how it was possible to love a mass
of people when one has never loved a single person oneself. This question is fundamental to a classless society,
for, in order for it not to disintegrate into groups of leaders and subalterns, it must recognize the masses at its
very heart. The answer is simple: for such a person, it is
impossible. The unconditional love of a single person
always precedes social love. Here, however, we encounter
the essential problem, which shall be examined in more
depth later. For what exactly is this love? An aberration
threatened by loss. It seems to me that there is no way to
maintain a State based upon this kind of love. And yet,
any other kind of State would be impossible to bear.

'Gramsci's ashes have been placed inside a zinc container within
a wooden box and have been buried where they can remain for up
to ten years without payment,' Tania informs Piero Sraffa in a letter dated 12 May 1937. Two months later, she tells him that, by
now, she has rid herself of all the notebooks. 'All of them,' she
writes. 'As for me, at present, without any further instructions
from you, I can only stay silent. Please see to what needs to be
done, I do not recommend any thing in particular, and must
admit that I do not feel up to taking such a responsibility. Please
write. Cordially, T.'

Translator's Notes

Though at times adapted or even invented by the author for the purposes of the novel, a great number of the quotations attributed to Gramsci in the text can be found in the following works:

David Forgacs (ed.), *The Gramsci Reader. Selected Writings 1916–1935*. New York: New York University Press, 2000.

Quintin Hoare and Geoffrey Nowell Smith (trans and eds), *Selections from the Prison Notebooks of Antonio Gramsci*. New York: International Publishers, 1971.

Raymond Rosenthal (trans.), Frank Rosengarten (ed.), *Letters from Prison*. New York: Cambridge University Press, 1994.

A translation of Lenin's address to the Second Communist International can be found here: https://www.marxists.org/archive/lenin/works/1919/-nov/22.htm [last accessed 17 July 2018]

More on the circumstances of Gramsci's burial at the Non-Catholic Cemetery of Rome is available here: http://cemeteryrome.it/press/web-newsletter-eng/no10-2010.pdf [last accessed 17 July 2018]